CHIEF PIAPOT
"I WILL STOP THE TRAIN"

VINCENT MCKAY

Copyright © 2009 by Vincent McKay

Printed and bound in Canada.

ISBN 978-0-9865096-0-5

To contact the author:
Telephone: 1-888-949-1877

About the author:
The author was born in 1939 on the Saskatchewan plains somewhere between a lake and a sand hill.

Sources:
Royal Canadian Mounted Police Heritage Centre
Saskatchewan Archives Board
Office of the Provincial Secretary - Protocol Office
Regina Central Library – Reference Desk
First Nations University of Canada – Rob Nestor
Maria Anne McKay -the author's grandmother who was niece by marriage to Chief Piapot

ArtBookbindery.com

How to purchase this book – www.ChiefPiapot.net

This novel is based on certain sourced facts.

Dedication:

A special dedication to my Assiniboine Grandmother who was born near Wood Mountain and was a niece to Chief Piapot by marriage. I could not visit her house without hearing a story about the exploits of Chief Piapot.

Notes

Contents

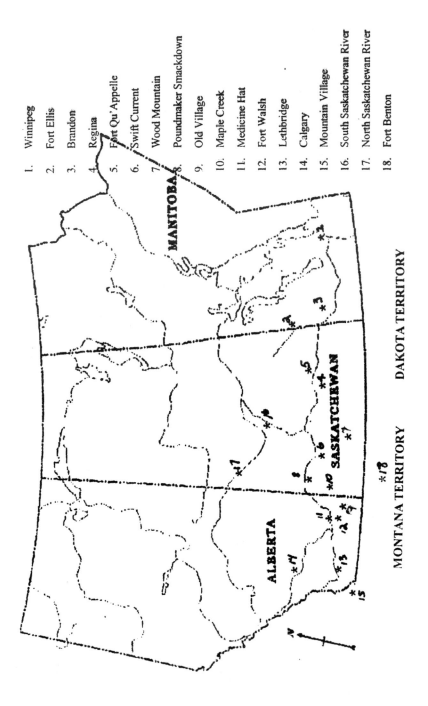

1. Winnipeg
2. Fort Ellis
3. Brandon
4. Regina
5. Fort Qu'Appelle
6. Swift Current
7. Wood Mountain
8. Poundmaker Smackdown
9. Old Village
10. Maple Creek
11. Medicine Hat
12. Fort Walsh
13. Lethbridge
14. Calgary
15. Mountain Village
16. South Saskatchewan River
17. North Saskatchewan River
18. Fort Benton

MANITOBA

SASKATCHEWAN

ALBERTA

MONTANA TERRITORY   DAKOTA TERRITORY

Chapter One

Kisikawasan

"I am Strong Eagle and I fear no man!"

The small hunting party watched a slumped over white trader approach from the horizon down to the small stream. He led two pack horses, roped to his saddle, loaded with goods for trade. A short distance from the stream, the horse stopped and the white trader slowly dismounted. They watched him untie the rawhide from a rolled up blanket which he wrapped himself in as he fell to the ground.

The hunting party spread out a short distance apart and with weapons to the ready as they cautiously approached the white trader. The four Assiniboine hunters slid from their horses and stood before the white man. The leader took his spear and motioned to the trader with a back and forth movement to open his blanket. As though in a trance, the shivering white trader did exactly as commanded. He was unarmed with only the musket he had tied down to the saddle on his horse.

The hunting party spoke to one another deciding what to do with the white man for they knew he was sick. They spoke of killing him and returning to the camp with the three horses and the goods. At this moment, the white trader slowly looked up at the young leader and said to him in Cree, "Do not kill me, I am sick. I have come only to trade".

The four Assiniboines understood Cree and they were impressed.

The young leader said to the three, "Tie him to his horse! We will let the elders decide his fate"

One of the young hunters rode ahead so by the time the white trader arrived at the camp, his fate had been decided. Out of the group a shaman came forward and gave an order.

"Take him to my lodge! I will give him medicine. He has traded his life for his goods! Take them!"

It was the summer of 1821. There was order and freedom on the plains.

Born in a Snowdrift was not in the crowd for she had taken her grandson Kisikawasan of three winters down to the river as she did each afternoon. Kisikawasan, which meant "Flash in the Sky", was born of a Cree mother and an Assiniboine father. The name was an omen of greatness which would prove to be true even though the name would change. The Cree and the Assiniboine hunting grounds were shared where the territories met. The Assiniboine nation was a mixture of both nations.

On return to her lodge, the grandmother learned of the sick trader and she would not allow her grandson to leave her lodge. The grandmother was wise for she remembered the sickness to the east that killed thousands of her people. It was a sickness of sores that medicine could not heal. It meant almost certain death for anyone infected. The grandmother knew that not all of the white man diseases were fatal but would not take chances with her grandson who she loved as her own.

It was late in the afternoon when the grandmother stopped a young hunter who rode near her lodge.

She said to him, "Tell my son and Red Flower that Kisikawasan will remain in my lodge until the white trader leaves".

The young hunter left immediately to deliver the message.

It was early afternoon of the second day since the sick trader arrived. Many of the camp elders and wives were gathered outside the shaman's tent as they did each day. The shaman said to one of his elder wives. "The white trader has not moved and still shivers. I do not think he will live. Go into the lodge and give him water. Do not touch him with your hands for there is shivering and sickness among the camp."

The woman entered the lodge and poured water into the white man's cup. The trader was lying on his side underneath a blanket in a dark corner of the lodge. Using a piece of buckskin, she rolled the trader over and saw the horror. The trader's face was covered with large pussy sores mixed with blood. She knew it was the sores that killed and screamed as she ran from the lodge. She kept running past the elders into the camp. Just screaming and not speaking.

The shaman quickly entered the lodge and returned immediately with both arms raised and spoke with a mighty voice, "The trader has the sores that will not heal! You must take what you can carry and leave this place with great speed".

The camp began to run for their lives with the young carrying the younger. Some were on foot and some on horse back. The elders ran towards the level plain away from the camp and the banks of the small river. Falling down, getting up, running and then crawling.

"Do not stop for us" they shouted to the young hunters and the warriors. "Ride away from here!"

Kisikawasan's young Assiniboine father leaped on his horse and rode to find Red Flower. People and horses were running towards him as he made his way towards the lodge. Red Flower, who knew that her young husband would come, ran to meet him and jumped up behind him. They rode away from camp in a different direction towards the river riding downstream in search of Kisikawasan and his grandmother. They were never seen again.

The shaman, standing alone outside his lodge, watched as his people fled in all directions across the open plain and some to the river. It was still early in the afternoon when the shaman, with only a blanket over his shivering shoulders, walked slowly towards the river. He knew where Kisikawasan and his grandmother picked berries. The shaman walked upstream along the bank for he knew that the grandmother was wise and she brought back only upstream water. The shaman continued a short distance, tiring as he went, until he came upon the grandmother and Kisikawasan. He stood on the bank watching the boy play in the water as the grandmother sat on a flat rock.

The shaman spoke in loud voice, "Born in a Snowdrift, the white trader brought the sores that do not heal. The camp has fled in different directions. Your son and Red Flower have travelled downstream to say goodbye but they are sick. You must return to camp and gather pemmican and robes. You must pass on my right side and make great speed while the wind blows toward the camp. Tie Kisikawasan to that small tree and I will talk to him while you are gone."

The grandmother ran across the shallow bed of the small river and up the bank to the camp to her lodge which was very close to the bank. She took only one large buffalo blanket so that she could also carry a steel pot, pemmican, moccasins, the white mans fire and a blanket for Kisikawasan. She threw the buffalo blanket over her shoulder and put the remainder into the small blanket.

She came back down the bank and heard the shaman giving comfort to Kisikawasan.

As she crossed the river, the shaman said, "You must go up the bank and travel south towards Lone Pine's Camp. It will take you several days so you must look for food as you travel. The river winds back this way two days from here and you will have fresh water. Turn west at the river towards the Cypress Hills."

The shaman turned and walked down river. He was never seen again.

The grandmother, with Kisikawasan in tow, began the difficult climb up the south bank. When she reached the top, with Kisikawasan at her side, she viewed the deserted camp below. In the distance she saw coyotes already feeding on the dying and dead bodies. The big birds that eat flesh had also gathered. They turned away from the horror and walked south without ever looking back.

On the second day, before the sun went down, they crossed the river that turned and ran across the plains. Near the edge of the water, the grandmother spread out the buffalo robe underneath a large tree. They drank and ate the pemmican which was almost gone. The grandmother did not want to leave this place for there was water, berries and even fish.

She said to Kisikawasan, "We will stay here my boy and make food before we travel west". She motioned with her hands as she spoke and Kisikawasan understood.

The grandmother looked around and just a short distance from the large tree she saw a dense thicket of saplings which would be shelter from the wind. With the white man's axe, she cleared a small opening into the thicket being very careful not to damage the foliage that covered the opening. There was a small clearing underneath a large sapling and she chopped away the very small shrubs below the level of the ground. With Kisikawasan at her side, she hauled their belongings into the clearing crawling through the small opening as they went. The ground sloped gently to the river to shed the water should it rain. The skin of the great buffalo blanket was tanned with the grease from the buffalo. She spread the blanket skin down and pulled the robe over them. They were both tired and fell asleep quickly.

The next morning, after eating the last of the pemmican, Born in a Snowdrift took her grandson to the river where she washed their clothing in the river. She left them on flat rocks to dry, as they washed themselves in the river. While the clothes were drying, they walked along the river until the grandmother found a small dead tree. She cut a sturdy branch and stripped the rawhide with which she wrapped and tied the centre of the branch. She then cut notches on each end to which she would secured a piece of rawhide. The sturdy wood bowed as she tied the rawhide to both ends. She sharpened one end of a small straight stick and cut a notch on the other end to hold the rawhide. The grandmother drew back the arrow aiming it at the cut bank. The arrow flew through the air and buried into the bank. There was much celebration filled with laughter. It was not a warrior's bow but it would bring in a fish.

For the next two days they fished and gathered berries. The grandmother's bow and arrow brought in several fish which again caused much celebration filled with laughter after each strike. They barbecued some of the filets and ate fresh fish along with freshly picked berries. The remainder of the filets she smoked and dried using the red inards for pounding with the berries. It was the afternoon of the fifth day and before bed, the grandmother, using a piece of buckskin, rubbed Kisikawasin down with the oil she gathered from the fish.

In the early morning of the sixth day, as the sun rose, they left their little camp by the river. Somewhere to the south west was Lone Pine's camp which they hoped to reach in a few days.

The grandmother said to Kisikawasan, "The leaves will turn soon and the evening s are losing their warmth. We will go in this direction towards the Cypress Hills. Do not be afraid."

Kisikawasan was not afraid.

In the six days since leaving the camp, the grandmother did not speak of her grandson's parents and Kisikawasan did not ask about them. It was as though the boy sensed that his grandmother was now his mother and his father. The two walked on stopping periodically for a sip of water and a bite of fish.

A few hours later when the sun was high in the west, the grandmother stopped in her tracks as she stared with disbelief. In the direction of a distant knoll, a lone warrior sat upon his horse outlined against the sun. With her mouth wide open and brushing away tears, she watched as more warriors appeared on the horizon. She began to walk quickly with Kisikawasan towards the distant warriors. She dropped what she was carrying in order to pick up Kisikawasan and walk faster. The grandmother's heart soared as the warriors came down the knoll with great speed towards them.

Out of breath, the grandmother put Kisikawasan down saying "Lone Pine's warriors are here. We are safe now my boy."

The warriors came up the ridge and appeared almost upon them. They were many and she heard their war cries of death. They were not Assiniboine or Cree, these were the most hated and feared by her people. They were Sioux!

The grandmother picked up Kisikawasan and began to run. The Sioux warriors stopped and the leader with his lance, signaled two warriors from each side of him to advance. The four warriors quickly surrounded them. One of the warriors, from his horse, kicked the grandmother to the ground with Kisikawasan crying and falling down on top of her. The young warrior dismounted and motioned for her to get up.

The leader slid from his horse and stood before Kisikawasan and his grandmother. There was fire and hate in his eyes.

In a very low voice, he asked her in Cree, "Where do you come from woman?"

With defiance, she stared into his eyes without answering. With a mighty blow, he slapped her to the ground. With great love for his grandmother, Kisikawasan grabbed his leg to fight him. There was much laughter as the leader kicked him from his leg causing Kisikawasan to roll in the dirt beneath a horse's belly. A young warrior grabbed the boy by his buckskin shirt and held him in the air. The Sioux leader grabbed the grandmother's hair and pulled her to her feet.

"Where do you come from woman?" he asked again.

Born in a Snowdrift feared for her grandson's life and answered, "We have walked three days south from the Lone Eagle Camp. We are lost and hoped you were Assiniboine". The young chief continued staring as he slowly walked around her. Born in a Snowdrift was an attractive young grandmother in her late forty's. She was very stately and of fine features. The grandmother knew he was a chief because he wore the bonnet of eagle feathers. He was the youngest chief she had ever seen which meant he was very ruthless and without mercy.

The grandmother, with Kisikawasan now at her side, raised her head towards the Creator for today they would surely die.

The young chief spoke to one of his warriors in a very loud voice, "Lone Coyote! Take this Assiniboine bitch to the camp of Three Horns. Tell him she is a gift from Grey Cloud for sending warriors to ride with me against the Blackfoot. Take the mare and her colt with you as a gift also."

"What about the Assiniboine brat?"

"Take him with you. The woman will not try to escape when he is alive."

"It is cold in the evening. Should I take a buffalo robe from the horse of no value?" Lone Coyote asked.

The young chief looked at the woman and replied to the warrior, "There is no reason for you to be cold in the night".

There was great laughter as they wheeled and rode facing north. They only went a short distance when the chief raised his lance stopping the warriors abruptly.

He turned and riding a little forward, he spoke very loudly "Lone Coyote! You will remain with Three Horns for you are a gift as well."

There was great laughter from the belly. Some had tears and some fell from their horses. They were many and came for more than stealing horses.

There was a faint smile on the grandmother's face as they rode away for she sent them to their death.

After six days, the only thing left alive at the Lone Eagle Camp were the very elderly and the afflicted. Some were dragged back by elders who put them in their lodge. Some crawled back to escape the wolves and the large birds that eat flesh. They crawled into empty teepees and those who were still alive lit fires as they waited to die.

It was evening when the Sioux war party approached the river below the camp of Lone Eagle. The young chief raised his lance and the war party stopped. They could see the top of teepees with smoke rising. One of the scouts suggested a closer look but Grey Cloud refused for he knew the Assiniboine had wolf dogs. He would regret this decision.

The wind was from the north and the east so Grey Cloud took his war party away from the river to the south and the west. When the war party was down wind, Grey Cloud made camp in a coulee hidden from the Lone Eagle Camp. They made many small fires as they prepared for war. The young bucks drew many skins of water from the river as the warriors were very thirsty. If the young chief had listened to his scout, he would have found the many bodies upstream that lie in the shallow water dead and dying of the sores that kill. They drank the water of death and breathed the wind of death that blew in their face.

It was not yet dawn when the Sioux warriors advanced toward the camp. They crossed the shallow river, through the meadow and up the gentle slope overlooking the Assiniboine camp. The young chief raised his lance stopping the war party. He then signaled to the buck warriors to advance on foot. They would slit the tents and kill as many as they could while the horsemen would wait to hear the yelling before they attacked.

The buck warriors slit the skins and began hacking and stabbing. They screamed their war cries to cause confusion which was a signal for the horsemen to attack.

The Sioux horsemen spread out and attacked the very large camp. There was no resistance as they rode up and down between the teepees. The only things moving were the Sioux buck warriors covered with blood as they emerged. In the heat of battle they did not even notice the absence of wolf dogs and horses. The warriors gathered in confusion. It was light now when the young chief ordered his two scouts to enter the teepees. The scouts came out and stopped a distance from the warriors. The elder scout, with his hands, motioned the chief and the shaman to come forward. They dismounted and walked to speak with the scouts as the warriors watched.

The elder scout, a seasoned warrior, looked into the eyes of Grey Cloud and said, "The camp has only the elderly who are dead or dying from the sores of death".

Another scout confirmed dead bodies in the shallow river below the camp.

The chief and the shaman entered a teepee to confirm the scouts' findings. It did not take very long until they returned to the scouts.

The chief asked the shaman, "Do you have medicine?"

"No" the shaman replied.

The young chief turned to his warriors and said, "The shaman will speak to you".

The shaman, in a very loud voice, told the war party of the sores of death. "We have drank the water and the wind has blown in our face. Many of us will die! If anyone lives, you must not return to our camp.

The warriors stirred but did not flinch or run for they were not children and young mothers. They were warriors!

The shaman continued, "The scouts will take you up river until it turns south. Here you will make camp. Do not gather! Those of you who shiver and have the sores must walk downstream to die. I have spoken."

Grey Cloud spoke to his warriors, "I will remain here. You must leave this place now!"

The shaman turned to Grey Cloud and said, "I will remain here as well."

They watched the scouts lead the war party upstream. The shaman and Grey Cloud then removed a few dying Assiniboines to the centre of the camp and after throwing all their possessions inside the teepees, they mercifully slit their throats. They then began burning the teepees and lodges to the ground. The entire camp was on fire as they rode to the top of the knoll and lit the grass on fire. When the fire reached the half eaten bodies, they turned toward the river where very many Assiniboines lay dead in the shallow water. The shaman removed everything from his horse and set him free. He then sat down on a flat rock beside the river. Grey Cloud then turned and walked downstream. Neither one of them were ever seen again.

It was the second evening and Kisikawasan was asleep in the buffalo blanket. The young Sioux warrior motioned the grandmother to his blanket as he did on the first evening. With a heavy heart and tears, the grandmother spread her legs for the young Sioux warrior. On the morning of the fifth day of their capture, Lone Coyote informed the grandmother that they would reach the Sioux village this day.

It was late in the day, as the shadows grew long, when the three reached a ridge overlooking the Sioux village which was located near a large river that emptied into a marsh. The grandmother was awed by the size of the village. There were lodges and teepees along the river for as far as you could see. This is where Kisikawasan and his grandmother would live for thirteen winters.

As they approached the camp, a small patrol of Sioux very quickly came upon them. One of the scouts recognized Lone Coyote and was glad to see him. Lone Coyote and his two captives were taken to the lodge of chief Three Horns where he told the chief his story. The chief was very pleased with the gifts. He was especially pleased with the mare for she would raise several strong colts. The chief said to Lone Coyote, "I am very happy you are in our camp Lone Coyote for we will soon make war with the Crees to the east. The grandmother I will give to you as a gift for I have several wives and you have none. I am of many winters and have seen many things. The woman will serve you well and the boy will be Sioux before long."

That evening, the three were given food and they slept outside beside a small camp fire. Early in the morning, Lone Coyote informed Born in a Snowdrift that he was leaving to join a hunting party for fish and small game.

He said to her in Cree, "The chief has ordered his wives to help you build a teepee. I will return in a few days."

The grandmother understood Sioux but he never asked so she had not told him. She watched Lone Coyote ride away and considered her position one of fortune for Lone Coyote was a respected warrior and would soon take other wives. He also was a man of humor. The grandmother would do her best for the sake of the boy.

There was tension at first for Born in a Snowdrift but it soon passed. Kisikawasan grew stronger and the older boys would still beat him when they had the chance but the boys of his age became more friendly. After four winters, Kisikawasan spoke much Sioux. In secret, his grandmother kept teaching him Cree and Assiniboine. She told him of his destiny and how they would one day return to their people. Kisikawasan understood the secrecy and would never betray his grandmother.

In the years that followed, Kisikawasan learned much from his captors. He learned about the roots used for medicine, healing and those that gave great sleep. He learned about war, bravery and hunting although he had not yet taken part in the great buffalo hunt. He helped women skin and haul the meat to camp. Every part of the buffalo was used for survival. It was the life blood of the Sioux. Most of all he experienced the peace of meditation. There were those among the camp who had crossed into the spirit world. They would not speak of what they saw except that there was great light and much peace. Kisikawasan danced the tribal rain dance but did not yet dance the war dance. He watched as a warrior died in the sun dance for this was a dance of great penance performed under the hot summer sun.

It was late fall as Born in a Snowdrift walked along the river to gather berries which would soon be gone. Kisikawasan was not with her as he was of sixteen winters and no longer did he gather berries. As she rounded a point in the river, she thought she heard the splash of a horse running in the water. She continued along singing and picking as she went. There was nothing to fear for she thought it was only a Sioux scout looking for strays.

When she neared a thicket of berries, a warrior with his lance raised, rode out quickly towards her. She ducked into the large saplings to avoid the throw of his lance. The warrior slid from his horse and drew his knife. She could see him clearly now and she began speaking in Cree and then in Assiniboine as she dodged around the large saplings.

"I am Cree! I am a Sioux prisoner! I come from the Lone Eagle camp of death!"

The Cree warrior stopped for he knew the history of the camp of death.

"Tell me woman, what is your name?"

"My name is Born in a Snowdrift"

"Before he died, a young Sioux warrior spoke very well of you and your brave grandson. He told us that their Chief died near the water. Where is your grandson and what is his name?" He asked in Assiniboine.

"His name is Kisikawasan and he is with the buck warriors preparing for their first buffalo hunt" she replied in Assiniboine.

"Yes, we have watched them and they will leave early tomorrow as the sun rises. We have come for as many of their horses as we can take. Two winters ago, they took ours so that we could not hunt as many buffalo as we needed to make food for winter. We ate small game and even dug for gophers. We will kill the three Sioux scouts who circle the horses that they will use for the hunt. These fifty or more horses have been cut out from the mares with yearlings and the old horses of no value. These horses are of great value and we must have them to make our herd strong."

The Assiniboine warrior sheathed his knife and gave orders, "In the evening, when the sun turns red you and your grandson must be at this very place. A scout will bring you two of our best horses and he will take you up the meadow to the plains. You must ride like the wind before our buck warriors set fire to the grass behind us. They will not wait! I am Strong Eagle and I fear no man!"

Strong Eagle jumped to his horse and rode into the saplings. There were tears in the eyes of Born in a Snowdrift and her heart soared as she watched him disappear. She wanted to run back to camp to find Kisikawasan but she knew better. She continued picking until her basket was full and walked back to camp slowly as though it were just another day. She waited anxiously for Kisikawasan as the shadows were growing very long.

Finally, she saw a party of buck warriors riding hard toward her. They stopped each at their own teepee until Kisikawasan slid from his horse and put an arm around his grandmother. He was riding the yearling that was a gift to Three Horns.

The grandmother was shaking and tears filled her eyes as she pulled Kisikawasan down beside the small fire. She told her grandson of strong Eagle and the escape. Kisikawasan was in dismay. He dreamed and spoke with his grandmother many times of this very day. He dreamed of escaping and coming back to kill the young Sioux chief who hit his grandmother.

The grandmother knew that he would miss his first buffalo hunt and said to him, "There will be a buffalo hunt this year with your own people my boy."

"It will be worth waiting for grandmother."

"When Lone Coyote comes to the fire we will eat and you will leave to meditate before the great hunt. Do not take your horse! I will remain for a short while and meet you near the place in the river."

Lone Coyote soon approached the fire and they ate heartily. Kisikawasan rose and told them he would mediate before the hunt. Lone Coyote and the grandmother entered the tent. He watched from the great buffalo blanket as she undressed and washed herself down in the dimly lit corner. This is the first time that Born in a Snowdrift ever purposely encouraged Lone Coyote. Lone Coyote was soon without buckskins and he had a somewhat look of dismay which soon disappeared as Born in a Snowdrift spread her legs for him several times for she knew it would make him sleep.

Lone Coyote finally lay beside her and said, "We will have this pleasure again soon Born in a Snowdrift".

Lone Coyote rolled over and went to sleep, not knowing that he would desire this evening for the rest of his life.

Born in a Snowdrift dressed quickly and left the lodge walking very calmly down to the river. She turned upstream until she was out of sight and then ran to where Kisikawasan was waiting. The sun slid over the horizon turning the sky red as they waited for the buck warrior. They did not have to wait long. Over her shoulder, Born in a Snowdrift saw a Cree scout riding hard toward her leading two horses. They each jumped on a horse and followed the Cree scout through the saplings until he stopped near the edge of the meadow. They remained hidden in the saplings.

"When you see the arrow of fire in the sky, we must ride like the wind to catch the horses driven up the slope to the plains. The young bucks will leave a small opening for us to ride through before they close the fire line."

The three well muscled horses danced in the saplings for they heard the noise of the herd. An arrow of fire flew in the darkness and the Cree scout let his horse drive across the meadow with Born in a Snowdrift and Kisikawasan on his heels. They reached the slopes riding hard for the plains. The herd was a short distance ahead when the fires appeared from the north and the south. The fire line started to close to the centre as the Cree scout rode like the wind for the centre of the line. The flames were higher than his horse as he rode through the centre of the fire and stopped. Kisikawasan and his grandmother passed him on either side and the scout ordered the five buck warriors to close the fire line. With his horse rearing and dancing, he ordered Kisikawasan and Born in a Snowdrift to keep riding. He waited for the fire line to close and the six rode hard to the west. They soon caught up to Kisikawasan and his grandmother as the war party turned the herd to the north and into the night.

It was the fall of 1834. There was order and freedom on the plains.

They drove the horses north for most of the night. Strong Eagle ordered two of his scouts to a high knoll just a short distance ahead. The two scouts reached the knoll and stayed below the skyline as the war party and the herd passed. When they were sure the Sioux were not in pursuit, they rode to the skyline and signaled all clear with their lances. Strong Eagle now ordered the herd to be turned west for water. The two scouts rode the high ground until the morning light. There were no Sioux in any direction so they rode down the slopes to join the raiding party as the herd drank from the small stream. They turned the herd north again riding day and night. On the third morning, the Lone Child camp was only two days to the west. Strong Eagle ordered a scout to ride ahead and prepare a great feast. He also ordered him to send the warriors to guard against any Sioux on broken down horses and to help with the herd. There was laughter as the raiding party road easy. Three scouts rode the high ground behind them.

Strong Eagle slid from his horse and began to walk, allowing the horses to graze. The remainder of the raiding party did the same. He ordered the buck warriors to count the herd. They cut out groups and counted them. They returned with great excitement. The herd numbered ninety to one hundred and among them were many mares of great value.

The small raiding party began to speak among themselves. They laughed as each gave embellished accounts of their ferocious deeds. Kisikawasan was very proud to be of the Assiniboine nation.

On the morning of the fifth day, the raiding party could see the Assiniboine warriors riding hard towards them. There was much jubilation and congratulations. Strong Eagle ordered the warriors to bring the stolen horses slowly as the raiding party rode ahead to the Strong Eagle camp.

In the distance, children and buck warriors were walking to meet the victorious raiding party. They wanted to meet Kisikawasan and his grandmother who had been lost for many years. They shouted their names and the name of Grey Owl, the scout who took them through the fire.

The raiding party, followed by the enthusiastic greeting party, reached the place where the plains meet the Cypress Hills. There was a long line of teepees stretched out on the plains just before the tree line. The teepees were very large and beautifully decorated with paintings of all colors and description.

"This is a much smaller village than I imagined" Born in a Snowdrift said to Grey Owl. "You will see the size when we ride down among the trees to the river below. The tents you see are filled with buck warriors, young scouts and young warriors and their wives. They ride out each day in different directions and bring back small game which we enjoy in the summer. They are the ears and the eyes of our village. The young bucks take turns circling the horses while they graze." Grey Owl explained.

Kisikawasan listened to Grey Owl very closely as they descended into the valley down a gentle slope to a flat area, then down another slope to another flat area. On each flat slope there were several small teepees for the very old warriors who were held in high regard. Grey Owl raised his lance in respect as was expected when you passed in and out of the village below. The old warriors touched Kisikawasan and Born in a Snowdrift as they rode by.

Grey Owl took Kisikawasan and his grandmother aside to let the raiding party advance. When they all passed by, he took them forward to the edge of the clearing where they saw the river and the village below.

It was a spectacular sight. Small lodges and teepees lined the river banks for as far as you could see in both directions. Women were busy in the long smoke house preparing the fish and small game for the feast. This lodge was built to prepare the buffalo meat after the hunt. It was here that the women would make pemmican for winter. Another large lodge was where the warriors made weapons for battle. A small area in this lodge was where the warriors and the young would pour water over heated stones to make the water that hangs in the air for cleansing. Then there was a third large lodge where the women did tanning and made clothing. It also had a small area for heating water. Behind the three large lodges was a natural clearing where the village gathered. Tonight a great fire would be built near the trees for the feast and the victory dance.

The river itself was a great thing of beauty. It moved to the north forming small ponds of water as it flowed. There were small plants and foliage lining both sides of the bank. Born in a Snowdrift understood why the lodges were set back for she saw the dead weeds higher up on the small trees. This was how high the river rose in the run-off season and great rains. To the far north, the river turned and formed a small lake. Born in a Snowdrift and Kisikawasan could see the river turn south at the west end of the lake and turn south and then east almost surrounding the clearing where the great fire would be lit. It was magnificent!

Grey Owl said to Born in a Snowdrift and Kisikawasan, "There is always a small stream even in the winter for the river is fed by the water that comes from the ground and does not freeze".

Kisikawasan asked Grey Owl, "Are there fish in that lake?"

"Yes."

"This place is a paradise!" Born in a Snowdrift said.

"There is hardly any wind" Kisikawasan added.

"Near the water there are many of the small animals that swim. The beaver especially are great value for their furs" Grey Owl said.

They rode down the slope towards the village and crossed a shallow part of the stream where the stones were removed. They approached Strong Eagle's lodge where he sat sipping the shaman's water of medicine that gave great peace. Strong Eagle looked to be a man of fifty winters. The three slid from their horses.

"I have ordered the warriors to take the herd to water and let them graze" Grey Owl said.

"Kisikawasan and his grandmother are without horses" he continued.

They may choose one from the herd" Strong Eagle said.

Kisikawasan turned facing his grandmother and spoke to her in Sioux.

"What is it that you speak of that cannot be heard by Chief Strong Eagle?" Grey Owl asked.

Born in a Snowdrift looked at the ground as she replied, "Kisikawasan and me would like to keep the horses that took us through the fire".

Chief Strong Eagle took a long sip of the shaman's medicine and replied, "Your grandson is very young to bargain with a chief. He is also very wise for a horse that will take you through fire is a horse of great value. The mare he rode belongs to me and I will give her to your grandson as a gift. The horse that took you through the fire Born in a Snowdrift belongs to Grey Owl and you must bargain with him."

Strong Eagle rose and as he walked by Born in a Snowdrift, he stopped to look her up and down. A smile came over his face as he turned towards the warriors' lodge where he would sit near the hot water that hangs in the air. Kisikawasan thanked the chief vigorously as he followed behind him.

Born in a Snowdrift continued stroking the head and neck of the horse that took her through the fire as she turned to Grey Owl and asked, "What about this magnificent horse that took me through the fire?"

"Yes, he is a magnificent horse. I raised him from a yearling. Kisikawasan will now live with the buck warriors and you will be lonely. My wife died three winters ago after giving birth. My lodge is empty."

"I am of fifty-nine winters and cannot give you children."

Grey Owl smiled "I am of forty-seven winters and I have enough children."

Born in a Snowdrift rolled her eyes and lifted her head towards the Creator as she agreed to his terms. She walked with her new husband and her magnificent horse to Grey Owl's lodge.

For the remainder of the afternoon, the warriors of the raiding party just wandered around the village telling stories of the raid. There was much laughter and they were given small gifts wherever they went.

One of the warriors exclaimed, "We should call Kisikawasan Peyepot for he made a hole in the Sioux".

From that day forth Kisikawasan was known to the village as Peyepot. When Peyepot learned of his new name he was very pleased. He was also very pleased to learn that he would live near the tree line with the young warriors and the buck warriors of his age.

When he was told of his grandmother and Grey Owl there was no sadness. Peyepot had great admiration for Grey Owl.

The young bucks who gathered near the stream went throughout the camp collecting the raiding party's horses. Peyepot took the two horses outside Grey Owl's lodge and led them, along with his horse, up paths to the meadow surrounded by water. He turned them loose to graze on the lush grass along with the other horses from the raiding party.

It was late in the afternoon and everyone was getting ready for the feast. A young maiden stopped Peyepot and asked him where his grandmother was. Peyepot told her.

"You and your grandmother must come to the lodge where we tan the hides" she said to Peyepot.

Peyepot went to Grey Owl's lodge and did not enter. He asked his grandmother to come out for he had something to tell her. Grey Owl and Born in a Snowdrift emerged from the lodge. Peyepot repeated to his grandmother what the young maiden said to him.

"The women have new buckskins for both of you" Grey Owl said.

Grey Owl almost laughed out loud as he watched them both run towards the tanning lodge.

Grey Owl yelled "Peyepot! Bring your buckskins to the warriors lodge! We will sit beside the water that hangs in the air before you put them on."

The buckskins were magnificent. They were made from the soft hide of the deer. Islets of vertibrae from the fish were dyed in different colors and were sewn onto the buckskins making a picture of two small red flames set against a black sky with tiny yellow stars. Peyepot's flame was sewn onto the left shoulder of his jacket and Born in a Snowdrift's flame was sewn onto the left side of her vest. The hem of Born in a Snowdrift's buckskin skirt was slit into strips and beads dangled from each one.

Peyepot thanked the women many times. He ran from the lodge to take hot water with Grey Owl and change into his new buckskins.

A very old grandmother said to Born in a Snowdrift, "My daughters and me were making your buckskins for my granddaughter who is the wife of Three Killer. She is your size and she wanted you to have them. We added the flames that you rode through on your magnificent horse."

She thanked the grandmother who sat with her two daughters and Snow Child who was the wife of Three Killer.

"When the feast is over, it will be an honor to help make Snow Child new buckskins" Born in a Snowdrift said.

Born in a Snowdrift took hot water that hung in the air. After drying off, she changed into her new buckskins that fit her well. She gathered up her old Sioux buckskins and walked to her lodge receiving many compliments along the way.

Grey Owl and Peyepot sat outside the lodge as Born in a Snowdrift approached. They both looked very clean and Peyepot had changed into his new buckskins.

Born in a Snowdrift said to them, "It is good to be home. Peyepot bring me your old buckskins and we will burn them with mine".

Peyepot returned with his old buckskins and he threw them in the fire with those of his grandmother.

As they watched them burn, Born in a Snowdrift said, "This is the last of the Sioux for us my boy".

Grey Owl said "I hear the drums. Let us go to the big fire."

Many small fires were being lit in order to cook the small game which was a great delicacy. The women soon came to the clearing with the small game. The game was carried on a skin that was stretched between two long poles that were separated by shorter poles tied with buckskin strips at the four corners. Two women, one at each end, carried the game to the edge of the clearing. There were many women carrying skins of game ready for cooking. They placed the ends of the long poles on short logs so the skins would not touch the ground. They did the same with the skins loaded with large baskets filled with various berries. The last to come were skins loaded with small baskets to eat from and pemmican for those who did not wish to cook.

As the drums grew louder, the elders from the small flat areas made their way down to the large campground carrying their lances from the old wars. The tents on the tree line emptied leaving ten to twenty buck warriors who circled the Sioux herd and viewed the plains in all directions.

When the elders arrived, the shaman stood up and made mention of Born in a Snowdrift and Peyepot. Peyepot was with the buck warriors to the south where the river circled and almost met. They closed the small gap where the river almost met. The buck warriors whooped and hollered when the shaman mentioned Peyepot's name.

The shaman gave thanks to the Creator for the safe return of the war party and the herd of Sioux horses. He told them to eat heartily for there was much food. With that, the drums beat and the feast began.

Each small campfire cooked the game of their choice. They roasted the game over the fires using a green willow which would not burn. It had two sharpened points at each end. Some chose fish and others chose ducks, steaks or ribs from the venison and some chose rabbit. Very few chose pemmican.

It was almost dark when most of the tribe had eaten. The flames grew higher in the big fire and the drums grew louder. When the singing started, Grey Owl and Strong Eagle rose to their feet and began to dance around the fire. Toddlers, mothers, grandmothers and just about everyone joined in. Each danced with their own style. The dancing and singing continued without end as some sat down while others joined the circle of dancers and singers.

It was well into the evening when Strong Eagle sent a messenger to tell the buck warriors at their south camp to replace the buck warriors on the ridge above. The messenger gave the buck warriors Strong Eagle's order and they left immediately. Peyepot was among them.

The buck warriors from above soon came running and carried off much meat and berries to the south camp. They ate heartily stopping only to sing and dance around their small fire.

Towards morning, Born in a Snowdrift and Grey Owl walked to their lodge. They talked and sipped the shaman's water of great peace from a small skin. It was almost morning when Born in a Snowdrift removed her buckskin skirt and slipped in between the great buffalo blanket. Grey Owl soon joined her. This time Born in a Snowdrift spread her legs with great pleasure.

In the afternoon of the next day, Chief Strong Eagle called a meeting of the senior warriors and the shaman. He told them that each of the thirty-five members of the raiding party would pick a horse from the herd.

"Myself, along with Grey Owl shall chose two horses each as we gave away a horse to Peyepot and his grandmother" the chief said.

The Chief Strong Eagle continued, "The remainder of the herd will stay with the village to be given to those who need a horse and to the young buck warriors when they come of age. The horses will be picked in turns starting with the eldest to the youngest".

There were smiles and the nodding of heads. It indicated great approval of Strong Eagle's fairness and wisdom.

Strong Eagle then said to Grey Owl "Grey Owl! Tomorrow you will take five scouts and locate the buffalo herds".

"Should I take Peyepot with me to learn our territory?"
"Yes."

Peyepot was excited to learn that he would be part of the scouting party. He went to bed that night and dreamed of the hunt.

Early next morning, the scouts and Peyepot set out. Grey Owl sent two scouts to the south east and two scouts to the north east. Grey Owl and Peyepot rode east.

On the second day, the two scouts from the south east rode north to the top of a high knoll. One of them waived his lance back and forth very quickly. The other scout stuck his lance in the sky three times. Grey Owl, with Peyepot following, rode hard to a high knoll and waived his lance back and forth very slowly. It was a signal that he saw them. Grey Owl looked to the north east to see if the two scouts had seen him. They soon appeared on a knoll and one of them waived his lance over his head very slowly.

"They will soon be here and we will wait for Three Killer for he has found a very large herd" Grey Owl said.

"How do you know these things?" Peyepot asked.

"A quick back and forth motion with the lance means trouble is near. One motion to the sky means few, two motions means many and three motions means very many" Grey Owl replied.

"What if it were the Sioux and not buffalo?"

"If it were the Sioux, the scouts would follow the same procedure. They would ride hard towards me and we would all return to the camp to prepare for war. We are a scouting party and not a war party."

Peyepot did not ask Grey Owl any more questions.

When the scouts arrived, they rode hard towards the camp. They reached the camp the next day before the sun was high. There was great excitement as the scouts rode down to report to Strong Eagle. He was very pleased with Grey Owl's report.

All that day and the day after, the women prepared for the hunt. Any woman who could ride would join the hunting party. They rode the horses of no value. The women would be responsible for all the skinning and cleaning of the buffalo. Their horses carried the tools and dragged the logs for hauling skins and meat.

Strong Eagle remained at the village with more than half of the seasoned warriors. They would not take part in the hunt. Buck warriors were not allowed to ride among the herd. They were ordered to assist the women with skinning and cleaning.

Grey Owl approached Strong Eagle and said, "The Sioux promised Peyepot that he would take part in their hunt".

"What do the Sioux know about raising children. They are people of war. Let the boy ride with you as an outrider."

With a nod and a smile Grey Owl said, "That should be good enough for this year Strong Eagle."

The hunting party left before the sun was high with the scouts leading the way. A short distance away a very deep gorge ran into the plains from the valley. This is where the scouts would run the buffalo. Once the buffalo dropped into the gorge, the warriors would complete the kill. The women and the buck warriors would be ready to skin and quarter.

The hunting party, except the scouts, descended to the bottom of the gorge. They camped for the evening to wait for the scouts to run the herd.

The scouts and Peyepot spotted the herd just as the sun reached the hills. They made camp and waited for dawn.

In the morning, the scouts headed south west and Grey Owl explained to Peyepot how he could help in the hunt.

Grey Owl said to Peyepot, "We cannot run a herd this large. We will take small pockets and run them together to the gorge. We will take the last pocket because this is your first hunt. Stay behind the small pocket and off to one side. These small groups come together fast. If you get caught in between you will die."

"I will do as you say Grey Owl."

The scouts soon came upon the herd. Grey Owl looked over the herd. He pointed out two small groups of about fifty each and a larger group of maybe one hundred and fifty.

Grey Owl said, "We will run the large herd first. Three Killer, you take five scouts and drive the big herd. You four will drive the small herd to the north and I will take the small herd to the south. Follow me Peyepot!"

When the scouts were in place, Grey Owl drove his lance towards Three Killer. They whooped and hollered waiving their blankets as the big herd started to move.

Grey Owl then drove his lance towards the four scouts to the north. They rode hard driving their herd towards Three Killer. Grey Owl saw Three Killer and two of his scouts ride hard to the front and turn the Big Bulls towards the gorge. Grey Owl signaled Peyepot to get their herd moving towards the big herd. The two small herds came together quickly with Peyepot whooping and hollering so loud it made the four scouts ahead laugh out loud.

Within a short distance, the two herds came together and ran off the cliff into the gorge. Everything went exactly as Grey Owl planned. When the scouts gathered there was much laughter.

One of the scouts said, "Peyepot yelled so loud my horse almost followed the buffalo over the cliff."

There was much belly laughing as each of the scouts congratulated Peyepot. This was the proudest day of Peyepot's young life. The scouts returned to the plains to bring in one more herd and after lighting a fire, each had a tall tale.

The next morning the scouts got up early and brought in another herd. Most of the first herd was skinned and being hauled to the village.

Strong Eagle and his warriors waited by the tree line above the village for the scouts as they approached the camp. Lone Eagle ordered the warriors out to guard the plains until the hunt was over.

The scouts, which included Peyepot, followed Strong Eagle down to the village where they would rest and feast on the food that the women prepared for them. The scouts' part in the hunt was over.

After they ate, Peyepot and Grey Owl sat in front of Grey Owl's lodge and talked.

"I would like to be a scout warrior like you Grey Owl."

"You must be strong with your weapons and your heart. I notice that you take time to be alone with the Creator. This you must do at all times for it will make you fearless of death. You must be aware at all times for our enemies to the west and the south are cunning like a fox and will fight you until death. I have killed many of them."

"Will the Sioux come to make war because of the raid?"

"I do not think so. It was not a raid of slaughter and it will take a few winters to build a herd of horses to match the ones we took from them. They lost many young warriors thirteen winters ago when they attacked the Lone Eagle camp. Also, they must fight the Cree to the east and the Blackfoot to the north. They are weak along our territory to the south. If they come north, we will slaughter all of them!"

In the next fifteen winters, Peyepot and his grandmother taught Sioux to those who wanted to learn. Peyepot became the warrior scout he wanted to be for he was very strong with his weapons and became known for his horsemanship. He followed the shaman up and down the river learning of the plants and the roots that healed. He learned how to make the shaman's water of great peace and was able to make it so strong that a wolf could eat your leg off and you would not feel it. The shaman died after five winters.

Chapter Two

Chief Peyepot

"I have seen the future McKay and you were not there!"

It was after the fall buffalo hunt and Peyepot's thirty-first winter when Strong Eagle called the warriors to his fire. He was now more than seventy winters and had much to say.

Chief Strong Eagle spoke, "There are those among us who will leave this place. We are living on the edge of our nation. If we do not establish our people in the north west and the south west, we will be taken over by the Sioux or the Blackfoot."

Chief Strong Eagle continued, "Today I will give you two more chiefs. I have seen more than seventy winters. Those who have seen sixty-five winters and more will remain with me in the village. Those who cannot travel will remain here as well."

Chief Strong Eagle said to Grey Owl, "You will take the warriors who have seen forty or more winters and take them south east to rebuild the Old Lone Eagle camp. You will be safe there for the Sioux are very superstitious and will not return. Your wives and their children who have not seen twenty winters will go with you as well. You will be their chief and from this day you will be called Chief Grey Owl."

Chief Strong Eagle was not finished and said to Peyepot "Peyepot! You speak four tongues and have strong medicine. You will take the remainder of the village and travel to the north east. A few days ride will take you to a large river that flows through the plains. There is much buffalo and small game in coulees and ravines. I have been there. From this day you will be called Chief Peyepot."

Chief Strong Eagle stated further, "We who are left in the village are in need of few horses for many of us ride no more. Many of my horses I will put into the herd that belongs to the village. The two chiefs will divide the village horses with Peyepot taking more mares for his people are young and will have need for many horses. Each chief will take his people and leave the village when the winter is over. I am Strong Eagle and I have spoken."

It was the fall of 1849. There was order and freedom on the plains.

The following day Grey Owl and Peyepot divided the horses into two herds. The herds were kept apart in order for each herd to get established before spring. They would travel better that way. The winter was spent in preparation for the journey.

When spring finally arrived, Peyepot had seen thirty-two winters. Both chiefs were well prepared. As their people began to move, Peyepot watched as his grandmother rode south west with Grey Owl. He never saw her alive again.

It was several days before Peyepot reached the river of which Strong Eagle spoke. He took Three Killer and followed the river north in search of a camp site. From above, they saw a flat area below where the river snaked around it on three sides. The river emptied into a small lake similar to the Strong Eagle village. Peyepot and Three Killer rode down to the river scaring up small game as they went. There was an abundance of dead wood and new trees in the hundreds of coulees. They returned to the camp and spoke of the site with much excitement. They brought the tribe to the site and everyone was very pleased and began unloading the supplies carried by the horses of no value. That night they slept under buffalo blankets with small fires burning across the flats.

In the following days, teepees emerged along the banks of the river and back into the small coulees. Water flowed from the ground and there were many berries. The buck warriors helped the women haul logs to build three lodges - one for the women, one for the warriors and one for the preparation of meat. The scouts brought back much small game while the warriors built the lodges.

Within five years, many children were in the camp and Peyepot had taken his second wife. It was 1855 and Peyepot had seen thirty-seven winters. In those five winters, Peyepot rode out in all directions. He rode north into the sand hills and beyond to a great river that flowed north east. He rode south but did not see Grey Owl's people on the plains for they were too far south. He rode east to the edge of the Cree territory where he met Cree scouts and hunters who told him of a Hudson Bay Trading Post to the north east. To find the post, he had only to ride north east until he came to a large lake with a river that flowed to the east. He was told to follow the river until he reached the trading post where the white man would trade their tools with him for pemmincan and buffalo skins.

It was 1857 and Peyepot had seen thirty-nine winters. By this time he had become a well known horse thief. His young warriors who rode with him were just as wild and unruly as he was. They were great horseman and rode with authority wherever they went. Their long hair blew in the wind and their buckskins were decorated with colorful beads. Small camps in all directions felt threatened with their boldness. Peyepot encouraged small camps for they were good for security purposes.

It was afternoon when Peyepot stopped to visit a camp. The leader of this small camp said to Peyepot, "Your young warriors eat our food and drink our water without showing much respect."

Peyepot, which was his way, rode his horse with great speed towards the leader stopping just short of trampling him. With his knees, he danced his horse to the left and then to the right, stopping once again in front of the camp leader.

He said to him, "It is true that my warriors are young and do not always show respect but when you have great problems, it is me and my young warriors that you come to."

Then Peyepot, which was his way, backed his horse straight back through the ranks of his warriors. He turned and they rode away whooping and hollering as they went.

When Peyepot returned to his camp, he informed Three Killer that in the morning he would take his young warriors north east to find the Hudson Bay Trading Post of which the Crees spoke. Three Killer was the chief scout and in charge of security when Peyepot was gone.

Peyepot said to Three Killer, "Send a few of the young scouts to the north. Have them observe any Blackfoot in the area for one of the camps to the north told me of a small Blackfoot hunting party in our territory."

"I will send them out after you leave in the morning."

"Do you remember the story Grey Owl told us about chasing the fox over a hill?"

"Yes I remember and I will tell the story to the young scouts" Three Killer replied. "There is no greater scout than Grey Owl."

Grey Owl's story was one of great meaning. When you chase a fox over a ridge, the fox will turn sharply to the left or the right. When you reach the bottom and search for him, he is at the top of the hill watching you.

Early in the morning, Peyepot and his young warriors prepared to leave. They loaded several horses of no value with Pemmican and buffalo blankets. They took no women.

Peyepot said to Three Killer, "When the leaves turn, send scouts to bring the camps to the village. We must prepare for the hunt. The women and children to the north and west camps should come to the village immediately."

"These things shall be done Chief Peyepot" Three Killer replied. "Give greetings to my sister in the east camp."

Peyepot gave Three Killer a smile and a nod as he rode away.

Peyepot stopped at Cree camps as they went east. The Crees gave directions and within four days, Peyepot and his warriors reached the top of a sand hill where he saw a large lake to the north as described by the Crees. The lake ran east and west before it turned straight north on the west end. They followed the lake east reaching a river that flowed through a very beautiful valley loaded with small game and there was an abundance of fish in the river. They camped many times for the beauty of the valley caused them not to hurry.

Along the way, Pepepot stopped and said to several of his youngest warriors, "Catch us a few ducks of color for our meal".

There was much laughter and jeering from Peyepot and the remainder as the young warriors spread out along the river bank to bring back ducks of color. Peyepot watched as one of them, with great stealth, approached the edge of the river where a few ducks were feeding. The young warrior waited patiently for a duck of color to dip down and feed from the bottom of the shallow water.

Suddenly, with the speed of an eagle, the young warrior ran through the shallow water and grabbed the duck before it could fly away. The young warrior was totally wet and weeds dangled from his baggy buckskins as he held the bird high to show his prowess. There was much laughter from the hill above. A few hours passed and with enough duck for a meal, the warriors made camp.

In the afternoon of the next day, they arrived at the Hudson Bay Trading Post located at Fort Ellice. There were teepees and lodges everywhere. Peyepot and his warriors were a sight to see. Their long unbraided hair blew in the wind with beaded strands hanging down. Their horses were painted each to his own and the warriors buckskins glimmered with died bangles and beads. They had knives in sheaths tied to their legs and carried strong bows and quivers filled with arrows. Their lances were decorated with dyed feathers. There was no steel in their horses' mouths and no cloth anywhere on Peyepot and his warriors. Peyepot and his warriors rode with great confidence through the large gathering of Crees who wore much cloth. The Crees were standing now as they stared with great awe. Peyepot said to one of them, "I have come to trade with the white man."

Without speaking, the Cree pointed with his nose and finger towards the trading post. Many of the Cree had beside them muskets of great value. This is what Peyepot came for.

Just outside the post, Peyepot saw a young hunter with a beaded buckskin jacket. He was light in color and spoke through his nose.

The young hunter said to Peyepot in Cree, "I am Gabriel Dumont from the east."

"I am Chief Peyepot from the Assiniboine nation to the west. I have come to trade buffalo skins and pemmican for guns."

Dumont went on to explain that he was a buffalo hunter and a gun runner. He went on to tell Peyepot of a very large village below the two great lakes on the prairies just four days ride to the east. He spoke of many white men of Cree blood such as himself who gathered there.

Dumont said to Peyepot, "In this place I have told you of, I can get you the guns you need. This post does not have the guns and ammunition to meet your needs".

"How many winters have you seen?"

"I have seen maybe twenty winters."

Dumont quickly changed the subject and went on to tell Peyepot how the great chief of the Assiniboines was very well known for his horsemanship and bravery.

Peyepot was not interested in Dumont's praise. He smiled to his warriors and stared at Dumont. Dumont spoke no more of praise.

"I am camped by the river in a clearing where your horses can graze. Bring your warriors and I will show you my rifle and how to use it."

Peyepot and his warriors followed Dumont to his camp. Dumont took his rifle from a buckskin rifle case and showed Peyepot and his warriors the loading procedure. He aimed the rifle at a rotten stump much further than any arrow could fly. Taking great aim, Dumont pulled the trigger exploding the rotten stump. Dumont was a deadly shot. Peyepot and his warriors were very impressed.

Peyepot said "Dumont! Will you let me try your rifle?"

"Yes, I will let you and your warriors all try my rifle but I must show you the load or you will blow your hands off."

Dumont took much time explaining the old musket. They wanted to know why it worked with such noise and power. Dumont told them it worked much like the bow and arrow except the power was not in the pull of the bow but in the explosion. Pointing at each part of the musket, Dumont explained that when power explodes, there is much power and there is no place for the load to go except out of the barrel. Peyepot and the warriors understood. They understood because Dumont explained it in simple language when he compared it to the power of the bow.

Dumont watched as Peyepot loaded the musket. He stopped him once or twice until Peyepot had it right. Peyepot lifted the rifle towards a large tree stump in the distance. There was an explosion and Peyepot was thrown backwards to the ground. The shot missed the tree stump and ripped into the river. There was much belly laughter from Dumont and the warriors.

Peyepot rose to his feet and said "I was aiming at that duck in the water. I think I hit him."

There was more belly laughter. Dumont explained that he must hold the gun firm against his shoulder in order to avoid the kick. Each of the warriors took a turn and much was learned. Dumont used small tools to take the musket apart and put it back together. He explained how the barrel must be cleaned and the powder protected.

Peyepot said to Dumont, "The clouds are heavy and it will rain soon. My warriors will take the buffalo skins from the horses of no value and make a long lodge for us to spread our blankets."

"I have some smoked fish to offer but little else" Dumont said.

"With your fish and our pemmican we will feast tonight."

The rain came and they talked and smoked well into the evening. Dumont laughed as he explained to Peyepot that he would give him and his warriors the English words for two things, "Horses of no value are called pack horses. It is true that they are not as young and strong as the buffalo horses you ride but they have great value for they carry your supplies and goods."

The warriors and Peyepot laughed as they kept repeating in English the words, "Pack horses".

"You said two things. What is the other thing?" Peyepot asked.

"Winters in English is called years. The trading post has what is called a calendar that records the days and the months of the changing seasons" Dumont explained.

"Year and calendar" Peyepot repeated.

Peyepot and his warriors repeated these English words many times but they did not laugh. Peyepot shared sips of the water that gives great peace and soon fell asleep.

In the morning, Peyepot offered Dumont a large bull buffalo skin for the powder and ammunition that was used. Dumont refused the blanket and told Peyepot they would talk when he sold his buffalo skins and pemmican. They loaded the pack horses and proceeded to the trading post. The warriors stopped to visit with the Crees camped near the post while Dumont and Peyepot continued on with the pack horses.

When they entered through the gates, a white man who called himself McKay met Peyepot in front of the post.

"I have heard much of you Peyepot" McKay said in Cree.

"I have heard very little of you."

McKay inspected the thirty buffalo skins and ordered two men to take the pemmican inside and weigh it.

Peyepot entered the post that was filled with many tools and items he had not seen before. Peyepot watched the two men weigh the pemmican. When the weighing was completed McKay offered Peyepot thirty £10 sterling. Peyepot looked at Dumont who nodded.

McKay said to Peyepot, "You may use these to purchase the goods you desire."

"I will return with my warriors to trade these flat stones for your goods."

Dumont and Peyepot, followed by the warriors, returned to Dumont's camp. Dumont showed them another weapon called the colt pistol which fired six bullets as fast as you could pull the trigger. It was not as effective for distance as the musket but it was deadly for close in fighting. Dumont dissembled the pistol in order to explain how it functioned.

After firing several bullets, Peyepot said to Dumont, "How many skins and how much pemmican do you need for thirty long sticks and thirty short sticks?"

"Bring me sixty scraped buffalo skins and the pemmican made from the sixty buffalo."

Peyepot held up the ammunition and asked, "How much of these will you give us Dumont?"

"I will give you enough ammunition to start a war."

There was much laughter as Dumont went on to explain the delivery. He showed Peyepot a calendar and marked the current day with a pencil.

"Do you remember the five lakes as you followed the river west?" Dumont asked.

"Yes" Peyepot replied.

Dumont marked August 30th on the calendar and said to Peyepot, "You must mark each day that passes until this day. On this day, me and my family will meet you on the south side of the last lake to the east".

Peyepot took the calendar and placed it in a small water proof pouch. He assured Dumont that he would be there on the day marked.

Peyepot said to Dumont as he pointed to the musket and pistol, "How many flat stones do you need for them?"

Dumont assessed the situation and replied "I will take £10 for the musket, powder and shot. The pistol and a box of ammunition I give to you as a gift Peyepot."

Peyepot nodded his head in approval as he turned to his warriors and then back to Dumont.

"Do you like the buffalo horse I ride?"

"Yes, very much."

"In my herd, I have his brother, a buffalo horse of three winters. When we meet at the last lake, I will bring him as a gift to you Dumont."

"A buffalo horse such as yours is of great value."

"A gun runner of your value deserves a horse of great value."

It was still morning when Peyepot and his young warriors returned to the trading post. They purchased blankets, beads, steel tripods and pots for cooking, axes, and other items for the women. Peyepot managed to purchase one musket and ammunition as well as a very large knife that he would give to Three Killer. The warriors loaded the pack horses and returned to Dumont's camp.

As Peyepot was about to leave, McKay said to him "Chief Peyepot, your warriors are causing resentment among the camp".

"There is resentment because the women, especially those of mixed blood, desire my warriors."

"No matter" McKay retorted, "Keep them under control".

"You keep yourself under control McKay or I will burn this trading post to the ground and you along with it" Peyepot said with a very calm voice.

McKay came from behind the counter and Dumont could see trouble. He stepped between them and said to McKay, "He is from the Assiniboine nation far to the west. I will speak to him".

McKay returned to the counter as Dumont and Peyepot left the post. Dumont spoke to Peyepot along the way.

"Do not worry about this post for it will close soon."

"Why?"

"The buffalo to the east are being hunted out so there will be a new post built on the south side of the five lakes in order to capture the trade" Dumont explained.

"How do you know these things?"

"My family makes it their business to know these things."

When they reached the camp, the pack horses had already been unloaded. A few of the warriors were guarding the camp as the remainder swam in the small lake where the river snaked. "Dumont! Will you guard the camp while we swim?" Peyepot asked.

"Oui" Dumont replied.

Peyepot looked at Dumont with confusion as Dumont laughed and said yes in Cree. They went down to a little sandy area of the shore and joined the other warriors. After washing their buckskins and hanging them to dry, they ran in and out of the water doing belly flops and dives.

It was early in the afternoon when they returned to the camp. Peyepot instructed three of his warriors to remain at the camp. He told all the warriors that they would leave early in the morning before the sun rose. Peyepot and his warriors, along with Dumont, mounted their horses and headed up to the village outside the fort.

When they reached the village, there were many Crees who wanted to meet Peyepot. He saw men of mixed blood making strange sounds with a hollow wood box tied with strings. They danced on a wooden floor and drank water from the white man's bottle. As Peyepot rode through the crowd, people of all tribes reached to touch Peyepot. It reminded him of the Strong Eagle village when he escaped from the Sioux.

McKay watched with envy as Peyepot walked and mingled within the village. He summoned one of his guards and told him to saddle his horse and bring him from the stable. McKay entered the post and loaded his musket. When the guard returned with his horse, he gave him a rawhide target to tie between two stakes in the middle of the village. The guard ordered two of his men to bring two stakes and a cross piece of wood. When they returned, the three proceeded to the flat area of the village and began driving the stakes. Peyepot watched as he sat cross legged in front of a large teepee talking with his Cree elders. The guards drove the sharpened stakes in the ground and nailed a piece of lumber across the top to keep the stakes even a they tightly tied the target to the stakes. When the target was secured, McKay rode through the gate on a pure black.

Peyepot looked at Dumont who was also sitting cross legged beside him.

"He does this now and then to show off his horsemanship and deadly aim" Dumont said. "Today, he is doing it for your benefit Peyepot".

People in the village spread out on both sides to watch the show. The guards and staff encouraged McKay. They called him Richard as did a few of the drunk Crees and those of mixed blood. McKay kicked his horse on both sides with his heels as he drove towards the target. He raised his musket to eye level and fired a shot through the target on the lower left near centre. He turned his horse around waiving his musket above his head to well deserved cheers.

Peyepot and Dumont remained sitting cross legged as did the elders. McKay stopped his horse in front of Peyepot raising his musket up and down above his head.

McKay shouted as loud as he could, for all to hear "I am the future Peyepot".

Peyepot stared at him with narrowed eyes. McKay turned his horse and rode towards his friends. He dismounted and was greeted with much praise and around the shoulder embraces. Peyepot's warriors gathered their weapons for they saw the look in Peyepot's eyes.

Peyepot rose to his feet and motioned with his finger for two of his warriors to come forward.

Peyepot said to them, "Put that water skin on the ground and fill it to the top so that it is round".

Peyepot untied his horse from a tent stake. He picked up his bow and removed two arrows from the buckskin quiver.

"Tie the water skin from the centre of the top cross brace" Peyepot ordered.

The two warriors left immediately. When they finished cutting away the rawhide target and the water skin was secured, Peyepot jumped on his bareback horse. After tying the ends of his reins, he rode to the far end near the celebrating McKay. Peyepot stopped about the same distance from the target as McKay stopped. He drew the reins tight and by using his knees he circled his magnificent buffalo horse in tight circles first in one direction and then the other. When Peyepot knew his horse was ready for the hunt, he placed one arrow in his bow and held it tight by putting his left hand on the centre where the arrow rested on the bow. He placed the other arrow between his teeth and broke towards the target.

With the breakout speed of only a buffalo horse, Peyepot reached the thirty paces in seconds. He fired his first arrow which pierced the centre of the bag and stuck out the other side. With lightening speed, Peyepot raised the front of his right foot up under his horse's neck near the shoulder and hooked the back of his left foot below his horse's left flank simultaneously taking the arrow from his teeth and firing it in to the water skin from twenty to thirty paces as he passed with lightening speed. Water shot out of the skin in four places as a roar rang out from the spectators who lined the side. They blocked his way and shouted his name as he rode through the crowd. The warriors moved to the front pushing the crowd aside. Peyepot saw a clearing and rode with great speed at McKay who backed away with apprehension as Peyepot danced his horse from side to side.

Peyepot pointed his finger at McKay and shouted for all to hear, "I have seen the future McKay and you were not there!"

"You son of a bitch, I am going to reload this musket and blow your head off" McKay shouted. "I am going to shoot those sons of bitches that ride with you too."

The crowd roared calling McKay all kinds of names as the young warriors fixed their arrows.

A burly guard turned to McKay and shouted "I am going to secure this post."

He ordered two guards to move McKay through the gates. McKay was still shouting obscenities as they closed the gates behind him. His favourite obscenity was sons of bitches.

There was great laughter as the crowd shouted obscenities back. The fiddles soon began to play and the drums began to beat. The drums would stop after a loud beat and everyone shouted Peyepot. The warriors moved about the village and were treated as some kind of important people wherever they went. As he walked toward the big teepee, Dumont felt a little guilt for when he sat cross legged with Peyepot against McKay he thought perhaps his young years had betrayed him and did not understand the situation. He knew now that it was worth it.

When he reached the big teepee, Peyepot was there sitting cross legged with the elders. Dumont sat down next to Peyepot and listened as they spoke of the fall buffalo hunt. Peyepot was a modest chief and spoke very little. When the crowd settled down, Dumont and Peyepot moved about sampling barbecued fish and small game.

Before sundown, Peyepot returned to the camp with a fine girl of mixed blood who spoke the language of McKay and also much Cree. Dumont returned with a very attractive Cree maiden. The young warriors guarding the camp whooped it up as they left for the village. The four then sat down on a buffalo blanket sipping and talking until dark. That evening, Peyepot took his third wife.

The next morning, as the sun began to rise, the Dumont camp came alive. Two of the warriors approached Peyepot and asked if they could bring their women with them. Peyepot told the warriors of his new woman and of course had no objection to having their women come as well. The warriors' women were of mixed blood. They both spoke the language of Dumont and much Cree.

Wandering Buffalo, Peyepot's head scout stood to the side talking with four young bucks. Two were Cree, one was Sioux and the other was white who called himself Dalton. Wandering Buffalo approached Peyepot and explained that these four young bucks wanted to ride with the warriors.

Wandering Buffalo said to Peyepot, "All four speak Cree and have been on many buffalo hunts".

"As you know, they are not the first who have asked to ride with our warriors but this is the first time that a Sioux and a white man have asked" Peyepot replied.

Peyepot turned to Dumont and asked, "What do you know about these two Dumont?"

"The Sioux has hunted buffalo with me several times. He is a good shot and has his own musket."

"Do you know why he left his Sioux camp?"

"Yes" Dumont replied. "He killed a Sioux warrior who had an issue with his sister who was before her time".

"And the white man who wears a pistol held up by a belt full of bullets?"

"He comes from the south east beyond the Cree and Sioux nations. He is also a good shot with both a pistol and a musket."

Peyepot mused and said to Dumont, "It is a good day. The woman who comes with me speaks the language of McKay as does the white who calls himself Dalton. The other two wives speak your tongue. There is much to learn of both tongues so yes, it is a good day."

Peyepot then turned to Wandering Buffalo, "Tell the four they may ride with us and live in the Assiniboine nation".

Peyepot walked with Dumont to welcome the four new warriors. After he spoke to them, he turned to Dumont and asked, "McKay and a few of his friends like to call us sons of bitches. What does this mean?"

"It means you are sons of female dogs."

There was a silence and then a burst of laughter. "We are the dog warriors! We are the dog warriors!" was the chant throughout.

Still laughing, Peyepot took Wandering Buffalo aside and gave him instruction. He told him to ride ahead with Dalton and the Sioux for they both had muskets. Peyepot ordered him to take an extra buffalo horse and enough provisions so they would not have to stop. Peyepot picked up one of the muskets and gave it to Wandering Buffalo as a gift from the nation. He picked up the other musket and ordered him to give it to Three Killer as a gift from the nation as well. Peyepot then gave him the very big steel knife in a sheath and ordered him to give it to Three Killer as a gift from the dog warriors.

At the mention of dog warriors there was once again much laughter and dog warrior chants.

Peyepot said to Wandering Buffalo, "With our muskets and much powder, you will not have to run the herd in order to kill the sixty buffalo I need for Dumont. Do not follow the valley for you will make better time on the plains."

The sun had risen when Wandering Buffalo and his two dog warriors rode up the ravine to the plains. Peyepot and the remainder loaded the pack horses and rode out slowly.

"Do not forget to mark the calendar" Dumont shouted.

"Qui monsieur" Peyepot shouted back.

Dumont was astounded that Peyepot would utter a French word. He took his hat off and stomped on it. He repeated saying son of a bitch many times as he watched them ride off laughing as they went.

After almost 2 weeks, Peyepot reached the village. The newcomers were introduced and Peyepot took Three Killer aside for a report on the buffalo hunt. Three Killer was clearly burdened but he gave Peyepot the good news first. He thanked Peyepot for the two gifts and told him how easy it was to hunt with muskets. Not only did he not have to run the buffalo but he could be more selective in taking the old bulls first. He praised Dalton and the young Sioux. Three Killer looked to the west and stared at the ground.

"What is it that bothers you?"

Three Killer looked to the west and to the ground as he told Peyepot why he had such a heavy heart.

"Several days ago, at the north camp, two scouts and several buck warriors came upon a small Blackfoot hunting party. The scouts told the buck warriors they would return to camp and report what they had seen. The buck warriors would not listen and rode after the small hunting party. They yelled back to the scouts that they would scare them to keep them from our territory. When the scouts reported to me, I took the warriors and rode until dark to find them. The next morning, the scouts found them at the bottom of a coulee. The Blackfoot killed them all and took their weapons and horses. Some were killed by arrows and some were shot. The Blackfoot slit their throats and took their hair. I did not chase them for the scouts tracked more than twenty at the bottom of the coulee. I did not know how many more would be waiting if I took the warriors into Blackfoot territory. The small hunting party was a trap. We carried the young bucks on our horses back to the north camp and laid them in the trees on buffalo skins. Your son, Snow in the Summer, was among them."

Peyepot looked west to the Blackfoot territory and now understood why the village was not jubilant on his return.

Peyepot sat down cross-legged on the grass and said to Three Killer, "Sit across from me and do not look at the ground".

Three Killer sat down across from Peyepot and his eyes glistened with despair.

Peyepot explained to Three Killer that his decisions were wise and that the buck warriors were raised to obey the scouts.

"They disobeyed and paid for it with their lives" Peyepot said.

"When will we slaughter the Blackfoot?"

Peyepot explained to Three Killer about meeting Dumont. He told Three Killer to send more warriors to the north camp and to have Wandering Buffalo make a new camp directly west between the two camps. Peyepot explained that he would take several of the buck warriors with him to lead the pack horses and the two Cree as scouts for they knew the lakes well. He ordered Three Killer to remain at the village with the warriors in order to prepared for the hunt and guard against the Blackfoot. Also the women would make a calendar on tanned deer skin. Peyepot rose to his feet and looked west as did Three Killer.

"We will slaughter the Blackfoot when the snow melts and the ice floats on the rivers."

Chapter Three

Preparing for War

"Be careful with the Blackfoot – even their women are warriors."

On the 10th day of September, Peyepot ordered the buck warriors to load the pack horses with sixty skins and pemmican. One of the buck warriors jumped on the three year old buffalo horse that was a gift for Dumont.

Peyepot rode his horse to Three Killer and said to him, "I will be gone many days before I return with the guns. You must begin the hunt soon."

Three Killer pointed to the 20th day of August on the calendar made of skin. He said to Peyepot "I will begin the hunt on this day".

Peyepot nodded and smiled as he turned his horse east. After a short distance, Peyepot ordered his two scouts to the front as he lagged behind. He could not see in the distance for water ran from his eyes as he thought about his son Snow in the Summer.

He raised his head to the Creator and said, "My heart is heavy and I feel I will die."

Peyepot reached the lakes on the 28th day of August. One of the Cree scouts told Peyepot that he knew of a place where the lake bellied and had much sand. With the Cree scouts in the lead, they soon found the sandy shore. They set up camp and allowed the horses to graze. Peyepot ordered the buck warriors out to bring back a deer for they saw many in the coulees as they rode. The two Cree scouts and Peyepot speared several fish while they were gone. In a few hours the buck warriors returned with a deer which they skinned and quartered. There would be no more pemmican today.

The scouts rode out the next day but did not find Dumont. Early in the morning on the 30th day, the scouts rode out and before noon, they returned with Dumont who had with him his father Isodore and his uncle Gabriel. They led several packhorses loaded with guns and ammunition. There was much laughter and after unloading, Peyepot invited them to cook as much fish and deer meat as they could eat. Isodore introduced Peyepot to raisins and bannock.

After eating, the buck warriors assisted Isodore in loading the pemmican hides. The Cree scouts brought the buffalo horse to Peyepot who gave him to his friend Dumont as promised. Dumont could not express his joy. He stroked the three year old and stepped back to look at him. He did this several times. He thanked Dumont with a shoulder hug and much praise for the buffalo horse.

When everything was loaded, Peyepot told the Dumonts what the Blackfoot did to his son and the war that was soon to come.

He said to Dumont, "It was a good time to meet you and trade for these guns".

Dumont immediately turned to his father and said "Peyepot has pack horses with no load. If you give me £10 sterling, I will purchase ammunition from the Touchwood Trading Post and return with him to the west. I will help him train his dog warriors with the guns and stay to fight the Blackfoot".

"It would not hurt to have a little extra ammunition" Isadore agreed. "What about the £10?"

Peyepot spoke up, "When we return to my village, I will have my scouts bring you more than enough skins and pemmican in the trade".

Isadore agreed to meet the two scouts on a determined day at the same place. He gave his son the £10 sterling and said to him, "Do not forget that you have a woman to marry in the summer. Be careful with the Blackfoot – even their women are warriors".

Dumont and one scout each led a pack horse as they rode out with great speed to the Touchwood Trading Post. Peyepot and his party rode up the ravine to the plains.

On the second day, Dumont and the Cree scout reached the Peyepot party. They had the ammunition and brought with them four young Cree warriors who wanted to fight the Blackfoot. Each had muskets and would help in the training.

Dumont said to Peyepot, "When the snow melts, many more Saulteax and Cree warriors will join us at your village".

Peyepot expressed his appreciation to Dumont and the four new warriors.

When they reached the village there was much celebration. With much praise, Peyepot introduced Dumont and the four warriors to the hundreds who came to greet them. The Buffalo hunt was over and the women were busy scraping and tanning the hides.

Peyepot found Three Killer and told him about the ammunition trade. Three Killer laughed and said to Peyepot, "With all these rifles, it will not take long to bring in the buffalo needed for the ammunition."

Early the next morning, Three Killer left with a large hunting party to bring in the Dumont Buffalo. They returned before dark with enough buffalo to pay for the ammunition.

In the next few days, the women and buck warriors prepared a great feast. Dumont and those who knew how to use the muskets, began training the warriors and scouts. It did not take long for Dumont to pick out the best rifle men. Peyepot issued a rifle to each of the best marksmen. He explained to them that they were not gifts and each marksman would be responsible for their care.

Peyepot, Wandering Buffalo, Three Killer and Dumont were a group of four as they walked in the village. Children were everywhere running and playing. Peyepot was amused when he heard his people using the calendar words of days, months and years. There were a few words attempted in French and English. As Peyepot expected, the three wives of mixed blood had an influence in the village. The group of four moved along to the far edge of the village where Dalton was training the warriors how to use the pistols.

The four sat cross-legged and watched Dalton draw his pistol with great speed hitting target after target with deadly accuracy. Three Killer was especially interested for Dalton had taken his daughter for his wife.

Dumont said to Peyepot, "Dalton is very young and does not speak much but he is a killer who the warriors will respect."

"Yes. I notice that the women are making belts like the one he wears to hold the bullets and pistol."

After watching for a while, Peyepot said to Three Killer, "When the feast is over you will have scouts travel to the Chief Grey Owl camp and inform him of the war. I want him to send warriors and weapons. Also I wish to know of my grandmother". Peyepot continued, "Send two scouts and several buck warriors to the old Strong Eagle village. I would like to know how many are still alive and how many wish to come here to the village. Take two pack horses and load them with much pemmican and buffalo blankets".

"I will go with them" Three Killer replied.

Peyepot nodded and the four continued sitting cross-legged watching Dalton train the warriors.

Before long, a young buck warrior approached the four and informed them that hot rocks were ready in the warriors lodge. The four proceeded to the warriors' lodge where they would enjoy the hot water than hung in the air.

Dumont exclaimed with much delight, "That steam is going to feel good!"

The other three looked at one another and laughed. Another word was given to them from the white man. As they walked along they repeated the word "steam" with much laughter. Peyepot realized that the white man's culture was creeping into his village and he did not think it was all bad. The four stopped to observe the young wives who washed and played with their children in the small lake.

After taking steam, the four proceeded to the flat area where the drums were beginning to sound and small fires burned everywhere. The four sat down on buffalo blankets around a small fire and where soon joined by the wives and children. Dumont had met a young maiden who sat beside him. She seemed quite honoured to be in such great company.

When the camp ground filled, Peyepot rose and spoke to his people. He told them there would be no talk of war at this feast. After giving thanks to the Creator for the buffalo and the abundance of the plains, he once again introduced the new dog warriors. There was much whooping and hollering when he introduced Dumont as a gun runner of great value.

The feast began and continued for two days. On the third day, Three Killer and Wandering Buffalo set out in different directions to the old Chief Strong Eagle village and to the village of Chief Grey Owl. Peyepot remained in the village to await their return. Dumont and the buck warriors were busy loading the pack horses with skins and pemmican as Peyepot approached.

"There is much more skins and pemmican than needed" Dumont said.

"Yes" Peyepot replied. "There is some extra to purchase more steel bowls and what is needed to make you bannock."

Chapter Four

Dalton Meets the Renegades

"You will turn and ride south or you will die."

There was laughter from the buck warriors as Dumont accused Peyepot of wanting the bannock for himself. When the pack horses were loaded, Peyepot put Dalton in charge of the buck warriors. Dumont and Peyepot wished them well as they headed east.

It was in the afternoon of the second day when one of the buck warriors saw two riders on the top of a small hill. Dalton watched as six more appeared and rode with great speed towards them. Dalton ordered the buck warriors to prepare for battle. He checked the pistol in is holster and the one shoved down in his belt for a left hand draw. The buck warriors placed an arrow in their bow and one between their teeth. They tied the ends of their horse's reins and removed the covers of the knives that were strapped to their legs. They let the pack horses graze as they lined up three on each side of Dalton. Dalton moved a little forward as the eight approached. One of them carried a lance making him the leader. Dalton saw two muskets.

Dalton said to the buck warriors, "When they come into the range of your arrows, I will order them to stop. When I draw my pistol, fire your arrows and charge. We will slaughter them all."

Dalton watched the buck warriors spread the line and there was no fear in their eyes. When they were in range, Dalton ordered them to stop.

They came to a stop as the leader moved to the front and yelled at Dalton, "Where are you going with the little boys and the horses of no value?"

The eight Crees laughed. Dalton looked to his left and to his right. He could see the fire in the buck warriors eyes.

"Where we are going is none of your concern" Dalton yelled back. "You will turn and ride south or you will die."

The Cree leader raised his lance to throw as Dalton drew his pistol with lightening speed and fired two shots blowing the leader off his horse. Arrows began to fly as they charged the Cree renegades. Dalton fired both pistols at the two Crees with muskets and they fell to the ground before they could shoot. One of the renegades jumped up behind Dalton and was about to stab him when a buck warrior drove the dead leader's lance through his throat. Dalton kept firing and it was over in minutes. One of the renegades jumped on a horse and made a run for it. A buck warrior picked up a musket and blew him from his horse before he could reach the ravine. The buck warriors whooped and hollered for the good shot.

Dalton slid from his horse to take a look at two buck warriors who took arrows. One had an arrow that entered above the right rib cage, coming out under his right shoulder. The other buck warrior had an arrow stuck in his right thigh. There was very little blood.

Dalton ordered three of the buck warriors out to gather up the horses including those of the dead renegades. He ordered the two wounded to remain where they were. Dalton and Big Man Walking headed to the ravine to make sure the shot renegade was dead and to gather wood. When they approached the renegade, Dalton drew his pistol and slid from his horse. There was a hole in his back and as Dalton turned him over, his intestines rolled out on the grass. The renegade had just enough life in him to move his hand and draw a finger across his throat. Dalton aimed his pistol and shot him between the eyes.

Dalton turned to Big Man Walking and said "I know that you have studied the medicine of the elders."

"Yes I have."

"Did you pack the medicine to heal the wounded?"

"I have the medicine and I can heal the wounded."

In a short time, Dalton and Big Man Walking returned to the wounded dragging much firewood. They waited with them while the three buck warriors gathered all the horses and anything of value the renegades had with them. When they were finished, a fire was lit and Big Man Walking brought the medicine from one of the pack horses.

Dalton watched as Big Man Walking gave drink to the warrior who took an arrow above the rib cage. In just seconds, the warrior's eyes rolled as Big Man Walking cut the narrow end of the arrow and pulled it through. He stripped a piece of buckskin from a tanned hide and placed a portion of the medicine that heals in the centre of the strip. He put the medicine that heals over the front wound as a warrior held it in place. Big Man Walking then pulled the strip tight across the chest and under the right arm continuing tightly across the back. When he reached the other wound, he covered it with the medicine that heals and drew the buckskin tight under the left arm, finishing with a firm knot. In order to keep the buckskin from slipping down from sweat, Big Man Walking cut two strips of rawhide and tied them from the front to the back on either side of the buck warrior's neck.

Big Man Walking then turned his attention to the leg wound. "Is there much pain?" he asked.

The young warrior nodded his head up and down.

"I will give you a drink of the water of great peace before I give you the water the makes you sleep."

Big Man Walking gave him a drink and walked with Dalton towards the trees. They found a thin branch that crotched half way up the tree and Dalton cut it with his knife.

"What is this for?" Dalton asked.

"We will squeeze the ends together at the top to make a small circle and wrap it with trips of skin" Big Man Walking explained. "When I remove the arrow and burn the wound, I will place the circle in position before tying the doe skin. It will help stop the blood."

When they returned, the first wounded buck warrior had his eyes open. Big Man Walking gave the second wounded buck warrior strong drink as Dalton put wood on the fire and heated the knife.

The eyes of the second wounded buck began to close when Big Man Walking turned to Dalton and said, "There is very little blood so I will remove the arrow at the same angle it entered the leg."

Dalton was proud of Big Man Walking as he stooped watching him remove the arrow and burn the wound. Big Man Walking spread the medicine and wrapped the doe skin over the circle.

"I think he will be healed" Big Man Walking said to the party.

Dalton gave Big Man Walking a shoulder hug and said to the buck warriors "There was no fear in your eyes today." Dalton continued "when we return to the village I will ask Chief Peyepot to make you dog warriors so you can ride with me when we fight the Blackfoot. I will not ask for Big Man Walking. He is far too valuable to ride with dog warriors."

There was much laughter and praise for Big Man Walking. Dalton looked around at the dead renegades and ordered them brought to the fire. The buck warriors brought them to the fire and laid them in a row.

Dalton said to the buck warriors, "Place all their possessions in a pile before them. We will take only their horses and those things made by the white man."

These things were done immediately. Dalton explained that the two wounded should be left at the village of Three Killer's sister.

Dalton asked, "How far is it to the camp?"

One of the young warriors replied, "It is just a little to the south and not very far. We can reach it before the sun disappears."

Dalton walked slowly towards his horse and then came to a stop. He turned and walked back to where the dead renegades were laid out in a row. The young warriors watched as Dalton stretched his hands in front of him and raised his head to the sky.

Dalton said in a loud voice "Creator of all the plains! These dead warriors came to kill us and to steal our possessions. We have no hate for them. Their spirits belong to you."

There was silence as the party rode south towards the Chief Thunder Eagle village. However, it did not take long before the young warriors started bickering among themselves. Dalton was only 24 years old but had never been in the company of young men before. He was amused at how they constantly insulted one another. Dalton ordered two of them to ride ahead to the Thunder Eagle village.

Many rode out to meet them as they approached the village. Thunder Eagle had the wounded taken to the warriors' lodge. He told Dalton that the Crees they killed were renegades who rode the prairie killing and causing trouble. Dalton gave Thunder Eagle the two muskets and powder as a gift.

Thunder Eagle said, "These muskets will be good for hunting and we will bring them with us when we join Peyepot in the spring."

They spoke of the wounded and Dalton agreed that the two buck warriors should stay in the village until the party returned from the five lakes. Dalton told Chief

Thunder Eagle that he would offer a horse each for the help of two warriors from the village. Thunder Eagle sent for two scouts who readily agreed to take the party to meet the Dumonts as they knew the lakes very well. The village prepared food of great delicacy for Dalton and his buck warriors. After eating, the party retired for the evening.

Early the next morning, the scouts picked a horse each from the eight renegades' horses and the party rode out to the lakes. With the scouts in the lead, the Dalton party reached the lakes on the second day and the Dumonts were there waiting. The pack horses were unloaded and the deal was completed. Dumont gave Dalton a bag of raisins for the trip home. Dalton sent the two scouts to the Touchwood Hills to trade the left over buffalo skins and pemmican for the various items the women needed back at the village. They left immediately and took two pack horses with them.

Dalton turned to Gabriel and spoke to him about the violin that he carried wherever he went. "I wish to trade you for your violin. The young girl of French blood who is now a wife in our village knows how to play your violin. I have heard her play many times"

"What have you got to trade?" Gabriel asked.

"I will give you one of my colts when the war is over. If I die your nephew will still bring it to you."

"What if you both die?" Gabriel asked.

"Then I guess you're just shit out of luck."

There was much belly laughter from the Dumonts.

Gabriel said to Dalton "I do not want your colt. I have several violins and if Chief Peyepot can give my nephew a magnificent buffalo horse for a gift, then I can give you this violin as a gift."

Gabriel took the violin case and handed it to Dalton.

"There is much rosin and spare strings in the case. My nephew knows how to use horsehair for the bow if needed."

Dalton was surprised by the gift and was very gracious to Gabriel. The two parties visited for awhile and then rode out in different directions.

When Dalton reached the Thunder Eagle village, the two scouts were already there. The two wounded were in good spirits and ready to ride so Dalton sent them ahead with the pack horses. He told them to leave the violin with his wife. There was no deadline to meet so Dalton and the four buck warriors remained at the Thunder Eagle village for a few days and made many friends. Three Killer's sister asked many questions about her brother and Dalton's daughter. Dalton promised he would bring her for a visit.

Early the next morning, the two scouts brought the six renegades' horses and the Dalton party drove them west. In two days the party arrived at the village with many coming to greet them. They all wanted to know about the encounter with the renegades. The party split up and Dalton rode directly to sit cross legged with Chief Peyepot and his warrior scouts. The council asked many questions as Dalton gave a full report. Chief Peyepot asked no questions.

Chief Peyepot spoke to the council, "The six buck warriors will each take a renegade horse. Dalton will choose a buffalo horse from my herd."

Chief Peyepot rose and motioned Dalton to walk with him. They stopped on a high place overlooking the small lake.

Chief Peyepot turned to Dalton and spoke. "You killed four renegades to protect six of my young warriors. It took much courage but not as much courage as it took to speak in a mighty voice to the Creator. You have made a place for yourself in this nation. Paint your lodge and the buffalo horse I have given you with your mark. I have spoken."

Dalton knew that "I have spoken" meant there was no more to say. He turned and walked through the village to take steam. When he finished taking steam, Dalton left to meet his wife who was waiting for him beside a small fire. They talked and ate the fish and berries that she prepared.

Dalton turned to her and said, "We must have a mark!"

There was much laughter as each suggested several marks but could not agree. Dalton now felt that he belonged somewhere. It was a good day to be alive.

"What is in this hard case?" Little Tree asked. "One of the young warriors brought it to me."

"It is a violin. Gabriel gave it to me as a gift for Red Feather's wife. Let us walk to their lodge and give it to her.

They walked through the village to Red Feather's lodge and Dalton gave the case to Madeline telling her it was a gift from Gabriel's uncle.

"Is there really a violin in this case" Madeline asked.

"Open it."

Madeline opened the case and her eyes widened. "It is beautiful!" she exclaimed. "I did not think I would ever see a violin again."

"Play for us" Red Feather said.

Madeline began to play and a crowd began to gather in front of the lodge as she played with great feeling.

Dumont yelled, "Play us a step dance!"

Madeline picked up the pace as Dumont began to step dance. Soon the very young wanted to step dance. They took their turns and did a few steps which soon turned into a war dance.

Chief Peyepot and a few warriors sat cross legged in a line watching from a little knoll.

One of the scouts spoke "pack horse – steam – calendar – bannock – violin. What is next?"

The next day, Three Killer and his party returned to the village. Peyepot and the council took steam as Three Killer told them what was happening at the old village.

"Chief Strong Eagle is still alive and in good health?" Three Killer said. "We decided his age to be 79 years. The old warriors in the small tents along with more than half of the elders have died. The shaman is still alive. The elders did not have enough strength to lay the dead high in trees and some were swept away by the spring water. The buck warriors found most of them and we laid them in the trees. Most of the elders are getting too weak to hunt and to fish. None of them wanted to leave the old village so we made the warriors' lodge and the tanning lodge bigger and moved them all to these two places for the winter."

"You are missing four buck warriors" Peyepot stated.

"Yes" Three Killer replied. "I left the four buck warriors to help them get through the winter until you decided what should be done. They have much pemmican and the four buck warriors I left are good hunters. The four will return to our village when the snow melts and give you a report."

"You did the right thing" Peyepot said.

The council of scouts and warriors agreed with Chief Peyepot. The council members each took turns telling Three Killer about Dalton's trip to the lakes and the eight dead renegades. Three Killer tried not to appear proud of his daughter's husband.

"The buck warriors were very brave" Three Killer said.

There was a great silence from Peyepot and the council.

"So was Dalton" Three Killer added.

With a burst of laughter, they all teased and gave Three Killer many shoulder hugs.

It was several days before Wandering Buffalo returned from the Chief Grey Owl camp. He took his place in the council and gave them a report.

"I will tell you about your grandmother first Chief Peyepot" Wandering Buffalo said. "She died four years ago at the age of seventy-eight. The village put her high in the trees overlooking the river and valley that she knew so well."

There was a great silence among the council.

"Yes, she took me to the river many times" Peyepot said. "Those were good days. I would like now to know of Chief Grey Owl and his village."

"Chief Grey Owl is of 70 years and does not ride in the buffalo hunts. There are many young warriors in his village who will come to fight the Blackfoot and they will bring many weapons of war."

"I notice that the scouts did not return but you brought several young maidens" Peyepot said.

"Chief Grey Owl thought the trade would be good for both villages and the scouts will return in the spring."

The council looked at one another and began laughing with much loudness.

"I like the trade" Peyepot said as the laughing continued.

The leaves fell and the days grew shorter as the war games continued. Dumont, the Sioux and the Crees who came with muskets created many sharp shooters. They taught the buck warriors how to load for each shooter would have three rifles and two buck warriors for reloading.

Dalton continued training the dog warriors with the colt pistols. The drill was about accuracy and not the swiftness of the draw.

"When you are reloading, make sure you have time for when the chamber is open the pistol is of no use to you" Dalton said. "Do not look away from the chamber when you decide to load. If a bullet drops on the ground just leave it and take another from your belt."

Peyepot met with the council almost every day. Today he wanted to know where the Blackfoot village was located and an idea of their strength.

One of the council spoke. "The Blackfoot will not be on the plains. They have finished with their hunt and will now prepare for winter. We could send scouts deep into their territory without resistance."

Peyepot and the remainder of the council agreed. They decided to send two seasoned scouting parties. One party led by Wandering Buffalo would follow the tree line east and the second scouting party led by Three Killer would follow the big river. They agreed to leave early in the morning and travel with great speed in order to locate their village before the winter season.

The two scouting parties left early the next morning and the training continued.

At one of the council meetings, Peyepot put forward that the old village should be maintained for the elders of all the villages including the village of Thunder Eagle. Peyepot said to the council, "The Dumonts say that in the east the buffalo are thinning out. Even the Crees take many more buffalo than they need in order to trade".

One of the council members spoke. "And if this is true, the buffalo hunters will move west into our nation. They will bring with them those of mixed blood and the white man who will trade their water for our buffalo".

"Yes" Peyepot said. "It will be no different here than it is in Fort Ellice. Already we have killed more buffalo than we need in order to trade for the white man's tools."

Peyepot explained that one summer, many years ago, when he was a buck warrior, Grey Owl took him and several others southwest deep into the trees.

"What did you see?" one of them asked.

"There was wild life everywhere. We saw red bears fishing in the streams for fish that we do not have and there were deer twice the size of our deer. W came to a place where we could see, far off in the distance, hills that reached the clouds. Grey Owl said that in those hills, there are places where no man has ever gone."

"We should go there!" one of the council exclaimed. "We could use the old village as a camp for our scouts."

"That is true" Peyepot agreed. "We could use the old village and at the same time make sure the elders are not abandoned and left without food and the respect they deserve."

Peyepot agreed that the council should continue the discussion of about the big hills soon after the war.

As Dalton and Dumont walked by, Peyepot asked them to join him at the practice area located in a nearby ravine. The three walked towards the ravine where the buck warriors were practicing loading the muskets.

Peyepot said to Dumont, "There will be many rifles here in the spring. Do we have enough buck warrior trained for reloading?"

"We have trained over one hundred" Dumont replied. "With two buck warriors for each shooter we should have enough for fifty to seventy rifles."

"What about the colts?" Peyepot asked.

"The dog warriors are ready" Dalton replied.

The three continued to the ravine where Peyepot practiced with his colt and musket.

The scouts returned in late October as indicated by the marks in the calendar. The village wanted to know the size and location of the Blackfoot camp but they would have to wait for Peyepot told the scouts to take much steam while the women prepared a feast for them.

The steam did not take long to make because it now came from the white man's huge steel pots that hung on a steel rod above the fires burning in the lodge. So great was the appreciation for the scouts that Peyepot ordered cooked delicacies into the lodge for them.

When the scouts were finished eating and taking steam, they left for the village to find Chief Peyepot. Peyepot told them to bring their families to enjoy Madeline's violin and they would meet to study the blackfoot village in the morning.

Early the next morning the council made their way to the warriors' lodge. They took with them their buffalo blankets and sat cross-legged around a small fire lit by the buck warriors. Three Killer untied a small piece of doe skin which located the blackfoot camp. He handed the doe skin to Peyepot who passed it around to the other members of the council and waited for them to speak from his left to his right.

One of the council spoke "I see a small river that flows from the north and meets the big river that flows to the east through our nation. Their village is located on the big river just south of where the two rivers meet. Let us go outside where you and Wandering Buffalo can show us the length of this village."

The council moved outside to a high place overlooking the ravine and the river below.

A councilor asked, "If this is the centre of their village, how far would it be in that direction?"

Three Killer pointed to place in the river. The council asked many more questions and determined the Blackfoot village to be almost twice the size of the Chief Peyepot village. The council moved back into the warriors' lodge and the talking continued.

Peyepot asked Wandering Buffalo "The banks above their village; are they steep or long flowing?"

"They flow down with certain speed but they are not cut or steep" Wandering Buffalo replied.

"Can the rifles reach the village from the ridge?" Peyepot asked.

"Yes."

"With accuracy?"

"Yes."

"Three Killer. How many days ride is it to their village?" Peyepot asked.

"My scouts did not travel with speed on our way to their village. After several days, Wandering Buffalo rode north and joined our party as they could see from a high place that there was no village on the plains or near the big river. We traveled together following the big river until we found the Blackfoot village. After we observed their village for several days, we decided to ride back in different directions with great speed. I followed the big river and could have reached our village in less than 3 days. We stopped and waited for Wandering Buffalo who took the long way riding south to the trees and east to meet us as we agreed."

One of the councilors asked, "Wandering Buffalo, how many days did it take you to reach our village?"

"My scouts could have reached our village on the fourth day" Wandering Buffalo replied.

"On this map, the big river turns south with much sharpness! Does their village turn with the river?"

"Yes" Wandering Buffalo replied.

The weeks passed and winter fell upon the village. Dalton and his wife took their mark. In the spring they would paint their teepee with the black outline of a white hand and a smaller brown hand painted in the centre. Yellow flower made a very small beaded mark on doe skin for Dalton to tie on the main of the buffalo horse given to him by Chief Peyepot.

During the winter months, the council met many times and just before the snow began to melt, they agreed on a battle plan.

Twenty shooters totaling sixty rifle positions fifty paces apart alone the south and west ridge. One hundred and twenty bows divided in pairs with quivers of arrows would run down the ridge until they were in range and position themselves between the rifles and the ridge.

One hundred and fifty warriors would line themselves from the bottom of the east ridge to the river bank backed up by ten pistols and fifty riders. Wandering Buffalo would lead them.

Three hundred warriors, fifteen or more pistols and one hundred or more riders would be positioned at the bottom of the west ridge between the river and bank. Three Killer would lead them.

Peyepot and fifty dog warriors would be mounted on the south ridge to lead the charge or to assist Three Killer and Wandering Buffalo if necessary.

Many buck warriors were given only one assignment. They would round up all horses and drive them up the slopes to the prairie and take them west where those who heal are positioned. If word came of defeat they would drive the horses west with great speed for the Blackfoot could not pursue without horses.

When the snow melted, warriors began arriving at the village. They came from the east as far away as the Qu'Appelle Valley and beyond. Bush Crees came down from the north and Grey Owl came from the south with many weapons. Peyepot was especially pleased with the rifles which would bring the total to more than eighty instead of sixty. There were a few more colt revolvers as well.

The leaders of those who arrived were told of the plan for battle and there was much agreement.

Peyepot enjoyed sitting cross-legged with Chief Grey Owl. They spoke of Born in a Snowdrift and the days in the old village where Grey Owl made Peyepot a scout warrior. There was much laughter when Peyepot thanked Grey Owl for the maidens he sent in the fall.

"I knew you would be pleased" Grey Owl said.

For five days, the war party travelled west following the trail of Wandering Buffalo. The war party would approach the Blackfoot village from the south. Peyepot sent several scouts ahead to observe the village. Three Killer and Wandering Buffalo were not among them.

Dalton was pleased that Peyepot gave his buck warriors the title of warriors. He felt good that five of them would be in charge of rounding up horses and driving them west to where Big Man Walking was waiting with those who heal.

On the fourth day, the war party reached a place south of the Blackfoot village where they camped in a ravine and prepared for war.

The next morning, the scouts arrived at the camp and gave their report. They reported that the Blackfoot village was very active. They were busy fishing and enjoying the warm weather.

"Was the river high?" one of the leaders asked.

"Yes" the scout replied. "The river is high and the ice floats quickly."

"Are there many horses?" Peyepot asked.

"Yes" the scout replied. "There are hundreds of horses grazing in the tall grass where the river turns south and they do not have scouts anywhere in sight."

"That is because they are so feared that they think scouts are not necessary" Peyepot stated.

Later in the day, Peyepot gave his final orders to the leaders.

"Remember! Do not drive towards the Blackfoot until I lower my lance and point it forward. When you have reached your position, send your horse back in the direction you came. The young bucks will round them up along with those of the Blackfoot. The riders to the east and the west along with me and the dog warriors on the south and west ridge will lead the attack on the village. I will let the rifles from above and the pistols on the ground deliver the first blow. Let the warriors with bows advance slowly in order to keep them within distance. I have spoken."

Grey Owl, who would remain with those who heal, listened with great pride as Peyepot spoke.

Chapter Five

The Blackfoot Massacre

*"You are the greatest warrior and Chief on the Plains.
I would save you if I could."*

Early the next morning, the war party rode with great speed towards the Blackfoot village. Dust rose in the air as the buffalo horses' hooves pounded the dry soil. In the distance, small Blackfoot hunting parties watched as death rode towards them. They turned and rode hard towards their village.

The Peyepot war party passed many Blackfoot horses that grazed on the plains. Many more could be seen from the ridge grazing in the flat area where the river turned south. The Blackfoot village was alive as they ran in all directions gathering their weapons.

The Peyepot war party took their positions and those who would fight on the ground turned their horses loose.

Arrows from the east, west and above rained on Blackfoot warriors. Rifles from the ridge and pistol shots on the ground sounded many times. The Blackfoot were lying everywhere dead and dying. They attacked the south bank killing several but were blown off the bank by the rifles and many had arrows and lances driven into them. They fought like mountain lions but could not gain the high ground. Their Chief ran to the centre of his warriors and ordered them to the east and west. A rifle shot hit him in the shoulder spinning the Chief around knocking him to the ground. He got to his feet and ordered the women and children to the river bank. Peyepot looked down at the Chief and could tell he was an elder and had no fear.

The Blackfoot warriors advanced towards the east and west taking many arrows and bullets. Dumont raised his rifle with both hands signaling he was out of powder. Peyepot lowered his lance and pointed it forward.

Peyepot and his dog warriors rode with great speed down the bank into the centre of the Blackfoot. The warriors on the lower level left their bows and charged behind Peyepot with a knife in one hand and an axe in the other. The shooters and the buck warriors above took their places to protect the south bank.

Peyepot drew his colt and fired three shots killing two and wounding a third. As Peyepot's horse wheeled, the wounded Blackfoot leaped from the ground and drove his knife into Peyepot's leg. Peyepot fired a fourth shot into the side of the Blackfoot's head. Peyepot looked to the east and to the west and could see the riders driving hard to the centre killing Blackfoot as they rode.

From his horse, Peyepot saw the Blackfoot Chief fighting with one arm. He drove his lance into a warrior before an arrow hit him in the stomach taking him to his knees. The Chief rose to his feet and split a warrior's head with his axe. A lance flew through the air hitting the Chief in the throat driving him to the ground. He moved but he could not rise.

Peyepot slid from his horse getting off two more shots and killing two Blackfoot. Peyepot threw his pistol to the ground and drew his knife. A Blackfoot drove his knife towards Peyepot's throat and Peyepot blocked it with his axe. He drove his knife into the Blackfoot's stomach and hit him in the back of the head with his axe.

Peyepot saw his warriors advancing closer from the east and the west killing Blackfoot as they came. The Blackfoot in the centre saw the warriors coming and ran towards them to die in battle. Dumont's shooters and the buck warriors came down the south bank to help kill the few remaining Blackfoot. With Dumont at his side, Peyepot took his time reloading his colt as he walked towards the Blackfoot Chief. Peyepot stood over the dying Chief and said to him in Blackfoot, "You are the greatest warrior and Chief on the plains. I would save you if I could."

The Chief tried to speak but could not as the blood poured from his mouth and stomach.

Peyepot lowered his colt and shot him in the heart.

Dumont and Peyepot walked to the river while the leaders went throughout the village killing the wounded Blackfoot. Blood seeped through the leg of Peyepot's buckskins and rolled down his leg into his moccasin. There were hundreds of women, children and a few elders.

A shaman dressed in red stood with his arms folded. Peyepot spoke to the Blackfoot women and elders who stood on the bank near the river.

"Your Chief was a great chief! He did not order warriors to kill little boys! It takes a proud shaman to put this into the heart of a warrior."

Peyepot turned and shot the shaman between the eyes.

"You should get a new shaman that knows the Creator and what is expected from great people" Peyepot said.

A white woman with golden hair holding the hand of a white girl came forward and spoke.

"We would like to go to your village."

"Bring them" Peyepot ordered.

The leaders gathered to discuss the battle while their wounded were taken to those who heal. Peyepot was not among them.

"How many of our warriors have we lost?" Peyepot asked.

"We are still counting but it is less than one hundred" Three Killer replied. "Over five hundred Blackfoot warriors are dead."

"A few took to the river and only a small number made it across" Dalton added.

The rest of the day was spent healing the wounded and gathering weapons. The buck warriors had all the horses gathered on the plains above and they brought buffalo horses for the warriors who were on foot. The owners would claim their horses as they travelled west.

"How many Blackfoot horses are there?" Thunder Eagle asked.

"Over five hundred" a buck warrior replied.

Chief Grey Owl looked at the Blackfoot children and young warriors who stood by the river. Peyepot knew by the look in Grey Owl's eyes that he had to make another decision.

Peyepot said to a group of buck warriors, "Bring down the pack horses and all the pemmican. Bring also five muskets with powder and many bows and quivers filled with arrows. They will need horses and weapons to hunt with. If I wanted them to starve to death I would have killed them."

Grey Owl looked at Peyepot and gave him a smile of approval.

After Wandering Buffalo cleaned Peyepot's wound, the victorious army headed west.

It was the spring of 1858 and Chief Peyepot was forty years old. There was freedom and order on the plains.

After a distance, Peyepot ordered all the buck warriors to ride ahead to the village and hunt game for the women who would prepare a feast of delicacies with much fish. The war party travelled very slowly stopping to let the horses graze and the wounded be attended to by those who heal. The dead were dragged on poles and hung in the trees when the west border of the Assiniboine territory was reached.

Soon after the burial, a rain storm began. The war party camped in the coulees and waited for it to pass. Many fires burned as the war party ate what was left of the pemmican and spoke of the great courage shown by the Blackfoot warriors.

Several days passed before the war party neared the village. Many came out to greet them but they soon retreated to the village when they saw the hundreds of horses driving hard towards them. The Blackfoot horses were cut out and driven north of the village where they would graze on lush green grass and drink the cool clear water from a stream that ran slowly on the prairie. The village horses were taken to the south of the village and turned loose near the lake.

The warriors immediately went to the lake and bathed in the shallow water heated by the sun. The council and their guests went to the warriors' lodge where the young warriors prepared much steam and brought delicacies. Among the guests were Chief Grey Owl, Chief Thunder Eagle, Dalton, Dumont and a fierce Cree warrior from the north called Big Bear. They ate the delicacies of berries, fish and deer meat that were placed on very large leaves that grew under small trees in the coulees and ravines. They were told by those who heal that they could eat the leaves for the buck warriors who were sent to the old village learned of this from the shaman. They ate the leaves and each looked at one another and nodded their approval for the juice from the berries and the meat made the leaves very delicious.

"These young medicine men are of great value" Dumont spoke out.

Everyone except Dalton and Dumont looked at one another as laughter broke out among them.

"Medicine men?!" Peyepot shouted. "We have another word from our white friend."

The council decided to meet the next day before the sun was high. They changed into clean buckskins brought to them by the young warriors and left for the village to meet their women. They did not walk directly to the village as the council wanted to say a few words to several of the warriors who were still at the lake. Along the way, Big Bear and Thunder Child were shown a shallow holding pond filled with fish. The holding pond was made by putting logs one on top of the other between big rocks. "This we must have in order to supply fresh fish for the village" Three Killer explained.

Peyepot joined his three wives and children who sat around a small fire waiting to hear about the war. He did not say much except to honor the Blackfoot Chief and the bravery of his warriors. They wanted to know more but Peyepot changed the speaking to the young "medicine men" who knew as much as he did and more.

"Where is the white woman and her daughter?" Peyepot asked.

"She is in my teepee resting" Peyepot's first wife replied. "I found them buckskins and they have taken steam."

"I have just come from the lake and have spoken with Wandering Buffalo. I have given her to him for one of his Buffalo Horses."

There was great silence among them. Anne, Peyepot's third wife, broke the silence and said to Peyepot "Wandering Buffalo is much younger than her".

"Wandering Buffalo is a great dog warrior and scout. He will sit in my council at a young age."

Where are my daughters?" Peyepot asked.

"They are with Madeline. That is where they have been each day since the violin arrived" one of them explained.

"I will stop there on my way to speak with the white woman."

Peyepot walked to Madeline's teepee and found the three of them sitting on a bench. The girls ran to him and there was much hugging and violin talk.

"Madeline, who made this bench for you?"

"Me, Annette and your three wives."

"The logs you sit on are flat."

"Yes, it took a little time but it was fun using the axe you brought from the trading post" Madeline said. "Sit down, I have something to show you."

Madeline went inside and returned with the violin. Peyepot's daughters took turns playing and they played very well. Peyepot was so proud of his daughters he could hardly bring himself to speak. After he got over the shock, Peyepot gave Madeline and the girls much praise. He asked the girls to play more and stayed until a crowd began to gather.

Before leaving, he said to Madeline "I will get more violins!"

"And axes."

There was much laughter as Peyepot left to speak with the white woman and her daughter. He found them sitting with Annette who spoke English as well as French. Annette visited with Peyepot for a short time and left.

Peyepot asked the whites in Blackfoot, "Do you speak Blackfoot?"

"Yes" the mother replied.

"What are your names?"

"I am Beth and my daughter is Anne."

"How many years are you?"

"I am thirty-two and my daughter is eleven years."

"Why did you wish to come to my nation?" Peyepot asked.

"Because you were going east" Beth replied.

"Now tell me how you came to live with the Blackfoot."

Beth explained, "We are from the south east where land ends and water as vast as the prairie begins. My husband wanted to make a fortune in the fur trade and six years ago we followed the Missouri north. Along the way, we were attacked by Sioux who killed my husband. We lived with them for two years until the Blackfoot attacked our small camp taking us captive and took us north to the big village where we lived for four years until your war party attacked."

"I have spoken to Wandering Buffalo about you. He admires you very much and I have agreed that you and your daughter will share his lodge. He is twenty-three years old and will soon sit in council for he is a great warrior and scout" Peyepot explained.

"Is he the warrior that has a Buffalo with no eyes painted on his horse? Anne asked.

"Yes" Peyepot replied.

"He is very handsome" Anne said.

There was a silence and Peyepot almost laughed for he was very amused. Beth was not amused.

Peyepot said to Beth, "When I permitted you to come, I would decide what would become of you and your daughter. I gave you to Wandering Buffalo for one of his fine buffalo horses. He will come for you this evening."

Peyepot left to speak with Wandering Buffalo.

"My God! He sold me for a horse!" Beth exclaimed. "We should have stayed with the Blackfoot!"

"Hell no! There is laughter and violin music here" Anne replied.

"I suppose we must learn Cree and Assiniboine. Why in hell did that father of yours drag us to this God forsaken part of the world!"

"It will get better mother. You are lucky to get a warrior as handsome as Wandering Buffalo."

"Fine! When you turn sixteen, I will sell you to him for a buffalo horse."

There was much laughter as Beth wrestled Anne to the grass.

"I wonder if he has that crazy buffalo painted on our teepee?" Anne asked.

There was more laughter as mother and daughter continued wrestling on the grass.

That evening, before dark, Wandering Buffalo arrived and took Beth and Anne to his large teepee which had the crazy buffalo painted on it. Beth told Anne to visit with Madeline while she spoke with Wandering Buffalo and they would come for her shortly. There was not much speaking for Wandering Buffalo understood very little Blackfoot or English. Beth closed the cover to the teepee entrance and crawled between two buffalo blankets where she spread her legs for Wandering Buffalo several times.

The next morning, Peyepot and the council arrived with the same guests to discuss the horses and weapons taken from the Blackfoot. In very private conversations, Peyepot and his council agreed that there would be no discussion about the journey towards the big hills to the south west. The council agreed that each warrior who came from outside the Assiniboine nation would take two horses each including two horses for each of their warriors who died. The total number of horses to be taken by the warriors of other nations totaled four hundred and ten. The remainder of the horses would be given to the Assiniboine nation for it was the entire nation that went to war. It was agreed that the other items taken from the Blackfoot such as muskets, powder, lances, quivers, arrows, knives, axes, buffalo blankets and the hides from most of their teepees would be given to those of other nations who were in need of such items. The remainder of the items would stay with the Assiniboine nation.

Big Bear spoke, "All the muskets and powder taken should stay with the Assiniboine nation for if the Blackfoot should ever come, they will attack the Assiniboine nation first."

This was good to hear from Big Bear and there were no arguments. The sun was high when they all left the warriors lodge to take part in the feast and celebrations.

After several days of feasting, celebrating and visiting, the warriors returned to their villages. Peyepot thanked Dumont for his help and agreed they would likely meet at Fort Qu'Appelle sometime in the summer.

Soon after everyone left, Peyepot and his council met to decide several issues. It was decided that the three scouting camps to the west would be maintained and the scouts would be replaced at the beginning of each month in order for them to spend time in the village. A new camp would be started between the three camps to the west and the village. This camp would be run by young warriors and buck warriors who would do only one thing. They would maintain fresh horses for any of the scouts from the three west camps who must travel with great speed to the village.

It was also decided that the old village would be re-built and renewed by buck warriors and young maidens. Dalton would take his wife who was expecting a child and he would be in charge of the re-building. The old village would be a place for the scouts to camp for their journey to the south west which would begin in the next year.

Peyepot said to the council, "I will spend much time on the plains and at the fort in the Qu'Appell valley. The dog warriors will ride with me as we go where we are needed. Tomorrow we will take many pack horses loaded with the hides that we took from the Blackfoot and trade for the white man's tools such as axes, saws, steel cooking pots and maybe even some violins. I will always return for the buffalo hunt and Three Killer will be in charge of the village when I am gone." Peyepot continued, "Grey Owl! Your camp has many elders. You and those who wish to go should move to the old village for at least the winter months. The young people who will now live there could learn much from you."

The warriors left the lodge for the village. Peyepot walked with Three Killer and Dalton.

Peyepot said to Three Killer, "There is something I learned from the war. You must relocate our village in a place above the river where the banks are steep and there is a view of the plains".

"I will look for a new place right after you leave tomorrow for the fort" Three Killer replied.

Peyepot said to Dalton, "Pick the buck warriors and maidens you will take to the old village and wait for the pack horses to return with the white mans' tools".

"I understand Chief Peyepot" Dalton replied.

Early in the morning, Peyepot and his dog warriors loaded the pack horses and rode east to the fort. They reached the fort in a few days and traded for what they needed. They even managed to trade with the buffalo hunters of mixed blood for three violins in cases filled with new strings and rosin.

The Crees and Saulteaux near the fort invited the Peyepot party to their village and gave them much food. They wanted to know everything about the war. Peyepot told them he was grateful for the young warriors who came from their villages. Peyepot and his warriors spent the night at the Cree village and moved out early in the morning.

Peyepot sent five of his twenty dog warriors back to the village with ten pack horses loaded with everything from Hudson Bay blankets to gun powder.

Peyepot spoke to one of them. "I have many pounds sterling in this pouch. Give them to Three Killer to keep for the village. We are riding to the Thunder Eagle village and then to Grey Owl's village before we stop at the old village to talk to Dalton."

"I will tell Three Killer of this" the warrior replied.

For the next fifteen years, Peyepot rode the plains visiting the camps, stealing horse and spending much time at the fort before returning to his village each fall to join the hunt.

One summer when Peyepot was at the fort, the Sioux, who had heard of Peyepot's power, sent for him to bring rain to their land for there was a great drought. Peyepot went to their territory and brought rain. There was a great peace and from that day the Assiniboine nation would no longer have anything to fear from the Sioux.

As the years went by, white men who called themselves Canadians were everywhere in the east. They were dividing up the land and moving west with great speed. The buffalo were disappearing east of the fort just as the

Dumonts warned and the white man changed Peyepot's name to Piapot.

Chief Piapot was asked to sign off his rights to land in the east and he tried to negotiate with the Canadians for land in the Qu'Appelle Valley. There was much discussion but in the end the Canadians refused to give him the land he desired. Chief Piapot left the Qu'Appelle Valley in 1872 and returned to the Cypress Hills in the summer of 1873.

Everyone spoke of the whiskey traders and wolf hunters who killed over thirty Assiniboines including women and children.

In the old village, almost all the elderly were dead including Grey Owl, the shaman and Strong Eagle. Two days ride to the south of the old village, Dalton was working his way south west to the mountains and had already established two camps and working on a third. Each camp took a two day ride to reach. Dalton sent Chief Piapot word that it would take two more camps before reaching the mountains.

Chief Piapot sent word to Dalton that he was to continue building the third camp and many more warriors, with food and tools, would be sent after the hunt in order to complete the camp before winter.

Piapot spoke with his council and Wandering Buffalo was among them. They ordered the scouts and buck warriors in from the four camps located north of the Cypress Hills. When the scouts returned, they reported that Blackfoot were seen one days ride to the west of the camps. Piapot told the scouts that he would ride out to determine their intentions.

It was decided that the Piapot village would be divided. Piapot and all those over the age of 55 except Three Killer, would remain at the Piapot village.

Piapot said to the council, "Three Killer will move to the old village with those under 55 years and from this day, he will be called Chief Three Killer". Piapot continued, "In the last fourteen years, I have seen the buffalo disappear in the east and the white man appear dividing the land for a country they call Canada. What has happened in the east will soon happen here and that is why Dalton is building the camps that will lead our people to villages in the mountains and what is left of freedom. The Grey Owl village will be moved to the old village where the buffalo hunt will take place. My village will be the only village on the plains and I will bargain with the white man for our land and rights. The white man does not have to know about the villages in the mountains. When the outcome is clear, our people can return to the plains or remain in the mountains. I am Chief Piapot and I have spoken!"

The council left the warriors lodge and walked towards the village. Piapot stopped Three Killer and Wandering Buffalo at the top of a high place where they sat cross-legged.

Piapot said to Three Killer "I have been riding on the plains for almost fifteen years and I have not noticed the great number of children. Many of them speak English and French."

"Yes" Three Killer replied. "There are many children in the village. I have quit counting my grandchildren."

"Me too" Piapot replied with much laughter.

"Beth and I have four children and my step daughter and Big Man Walking have four" Wandering Buffalo added. "They all speak English and Beth has made me speak English also".

Three Killer and Piapot laughed for they knew that Beth was in charge of the Wandering Buffalo teepee.

"I will be sending four of my youngest six wives and all the children and grandchildren to the old village" Piapot said.

"You will see them each year at the buffalo hunt when you come to visit" Three Killer added.

Piapot said to Wandering Buffalo "In the morning, you will take two scouts to the Grey Owl village and have them move to the old village. You do not have to return."

"I will find two scouts and leave early in the morning."

"Three Killer! It is July on the calendar and with more than fifty muskets, the buffalo hunt, the first week in September, will not take long. When you have moved to the old village, send scouts to Dalton's third camp and have him bring everyone to the old village for a September feast. I will bring my village for the feast as well. It will be the first time in many years that our nation has been together."

"It will be good for everyone" Three Killer replied. Piapot rose to his feet and the three left in different directions.

The next morning, Three Killer and his party began removing the hides from their teepees and sent them ahead to the old village. After a few days, the remainder of their belongings were tied to pack horses and his party rode south. Three Killer stopped to visit with Piapot and gave him the £ sterling that Piapot left with him for the nation. Before leaving, Three Killer agreed to have sixty buffalo hides ready for trading.

In the days that followed, Piapot took several scouts with him and rode west to observe the Blackfoot and to locate whiskey trading posts called whoop-ups. They did not locate any Blackfoot from the sand hills to the Cypress Hills but did however, locate several whoop-ups near the border of the Blackfoot territory. Piapot told his warriors the Blackfoot observed by the camps were probably just hunting in the area. The scouts also agreed with Piapot that the Blackfoot were a little bolder because they killed many Assiniboines a few years earlier in a very poorly planned battle which Piapot did not approve.

Piapot said to his scouts. "The Blackfoot are no longer a threat for they still fear the Sioux and will soon have a problem with the white man. Gabriel told me at the fort that a Canadian army called police will build a fort in the Cypress Hills to help the white settlers steal our land. I do not drink but I know that some of our people go to the whiskey traders for whiskey. For the whiskey traders' part in the spring massacre, we will slaughter them along with the wolf hunters and freighters."

The scouting party returned to the Piapot village and waited for word from Chief Three Killer.

It was the middle of September when two scouts arrived from the old village and reported to Piapot that the buffalo hunt was successful. Early the next morning, the two scouts and the remainder of Piapot's entire village rode south to the old village.

When they arrived, the plains above the village were lined with many teepees and everyone wanted to speak to Piapot. It took much time before Piapot could ride down the slopes to the village below. Three Killer and Dalton found Piapot and the three of them along with the elders walked throughout the village speaking with everyone. There were many from the Grey Owl village that Piapot met for the first time.

Piapot said to Three Killer, "Tomorrow the feast shall begin and with this many people, there will be no time to talk. I will bring my council and meet you at the warrior's lodge with your new council".

"It is a good idea" Three Killer replied. Piapot and his council walked directly to the warriors' lodge and were pleased with the work Dalton and his buck warriors had done. There was a long table and benches with flat boards, the steam room was bigger and several more benches were placed around huge steel pots that gave off much steam from the fires that burned below them. Piapot and his council took steam as they waited for Three Killer.

Three Killer and his council soon arrived. Wandering Buffalo, Big Man Walking and Dalton were among them and their council did not take steam. When Piapot and his council finished taking steam, they all sat on benches around the long table.

Piapot said to Dalton, "You and your buck warriors have made fine improvements. How did you make the trees flat?"

"We used our axes to make cracks in the trees and then drove sharp flat stones into the cracks. The trees fell apart as the flat stones thickened and we used the axes and saws to make the pieces smooth. The long two man saws and one man saws were of much help in cutting the ends. We used the nails to put them together."

All the councilors spoke at once with much praise for Dalton.

"Does anyone here know of a fort to the south called Fort Benton?" Piapot asked.

"Yes" Three Killer answered. "Some of the buck warriors have attended trading post to trade for flour and supplies for making bannock. The whiskey traders and wolf hunters are from the Fort Benton area where you can trade for just about everything including whiskey, guns and ammunition."

"Good!" Piapot exclaimed. "Fort Benton is much closer from the camps that lead to the mountains. Are we having bannock?"

There was great laughter from everyone.

Piapot went on to explain once more why the camps and villages in the mountains were being built. There was great understanding and everyone approved of the move.

Both councils agreed that some of the hundreds gathered in the old village should be moved to the camps.

"Dalton! Will the third camp be completed before the snow comes?" Three Killer asked.

"Yes."

The councils decided that those of seventy years and older would move to the first camp as it was the shortest distance to travel from the old village and the easiest to supply.

"It is wise" Big Man Walking stated. "There will be much coming and going at the first camp and we will know at all times the condition and needs of the elderly."

There was a great silence among the council and then much laughter and shoulder hugs for Big Man Walking.

"You are truly a great medicine man!" Three Killer exclaimed.

It was decided that the wives, children and husbands would move to the second camp and the remainder would move to the third camp. Three Killer would remain in the old village with one hundred dog warriors and those who came with Piapot would return with Piapot.

It was agreed that the whiskey traders and wolf hunters would return to the plains by October on the calendar. Three Killer and his one hundred warriors would scout the plains and let them through. The nation would be instructed to continue trading at their posts. It did not matter how many hides were traded for the nation would get them all back in the early spring.

Piapot spoke "In March on the calendar, before the traders and wolf hunters return to Fort Benton from the west, we will first slaughter the small traders north and south for their goods and hides". Piapot continued, "The small whiskey traders will have much ammunition and many repeating rifles which we will use to slaughter the big traders, freighters and wolf hunters to the west."

It was agreed Three Killer will divide his warriors to attack the posts sending fifty south to meet Dalton and take fifty north to meet Piapot who would ride south attacking the posts north from the big river and the sand hills. Dalton would take fifty of the warriors along with buck warriors for reloading the muskets and attack the whiskey trader's posts from the south to the north until he met the fifty warriors riding south. They would then return to the old village

Everyone at the posts including wolf hunters would be killed and their horses and wagons used to haul the goods, whiskey, firearms and ammunition to the old village. If any of them were killed outside, their bodies would be dragged and thrown into the trading post which would be burned to the ground. Everyone agreed that there would be many repeating rifles and much ammunition in order to destroy the freighter, traders and wolf hunters who would in the month of April or May, make their way east from the very large posts located to the west in the Blackfoot nation.

"How will we attack the posts?" Dalton asked.

"The best way would be to have four or five enter the post carrying hides in both arms, hiding colts in both hands" Wandering Buffalo suggested. "The remainder of the warriors should remain out of sight until the shots are heard."

"That is the way it will be done" Piapot agreed.

"If there is a window to escape from, make sure there is one or two shooters outside to stop an escape" one of the councilors added.

"Yes" Piapot said. "Also have five or more warriors with muskets ready for distance." Piapot continued, "When the war on the traders is over, I will send scouts to the Dumont family. The goods we do not keep we will sell to the Dumonts for Canadian and Yankee money. They will not have to bring horses or wagons for we will sell them the horses and wagons as well."

"What about the white police?" another councilor asked.

"When the white police arrive next winter, they will be pleased to say that they drove the whiskey traders and wolf hunters from the plains" Piapot answered.

There was great laughter from the council.

"Do all war parties start on the same day?" Dalton asked.

"Yes." Pointing to a calendar, Piapot continued "We will begin on the day marked 15 of this calendar month called March."

There was nothing more to speak of so the councils left to walk in the village.

As they walked, Piapot who had not eaten, stopped to sit cross legged and eat various delicacies and bannock offered to him by the wives. Dalton and Three Killer who sat with him watched Piapot dip the bannock in the clay bowl filled with hot meat juice.

Piapot held up the clay bowl and said to Three Killer, "Where did the village get these bowls?"

"Annette and Madeline found good clay near the river. They showed the women how to shape and heat the bowls."

"I knew those girls would be good for the nation!" Piapot exclaimed.

Piapot stopped a young warrior who was walking nearby and asked him to bring Rain Cloud. As they waited for Rain Cloud, Piapot mentioned that when he was in the Sioux nation and asked the Creator for rain, he met Chiefs and warriors of great position.

"I told them of a brave Sioux warrior called Rain Cloud who lived in our nation and killed many Blackfoot" Piapot said.

"Did they know him?" Dalton asked.

"They did not know him before the ceremony but after the rain came, an elderly chief called Many Horses came forward and spoke of Rain Cloud. He said that Rain Cloud's family lived in his village less than one day's

ride west of Fort Benton. I asked Chief Sitting Bull if
Rain Cloud would be allowed to visit his family who lives
in the village of Chief Many Horses. Chief Sitting Bull
told me that Rain Cloud could walk with much freedom
in his nation for taking women before their time was not
allowed in the Sioux nation. I told Chief Many Horses
that Rain Cloud would come soon to visit his family."

Rain Cloud soon appeared and Piapot told him of his
family who lived just west of Fort Benton in the small
village of Chief Many Horses.

Rain Cloud said to Piapot, "My heart soars with this
report Chief Piapot. I will go alone to visit my family
but my home is here in the Assiniboine nation and I will
return to help you destroy the whiskey traders and wolf
hunters when they return from the west."

"You must take one horse from the nation's herd as
a gift to Chief Many Horses." Piapot continued, "Also,
you will take two buck warriors with you to help along
the way and to learn the location of Fort Benton. Your
sister and her family may return with you if they so desire."

"With or without them, I will return and I will not
speak of the villages in the mountains. They are the
future for the nation and my wife and children!"

Dalton walked with Rain Cloud to his large teepee.
They rode the plains together before joining Piapot and
were good friends. Dalton wished Rain Cloud a good
journey and left to visit with his wife and children.

The next day, the buffalo hunt celebration began and
there was much food and music. Along with the violins,
there were now big violins played with the fingers and
small pieces of metal put to the mouth. This celebration
was bigger and better than any in the nation. Piapot

could see the changes as he watched people eat out of bowls with forks and spoons. Steel kettles filled with pieces of meat and chopped roots, steamed over fires and several ducks speared by a steel rod were being turned over the heat of red coals.

As Piapot walked, several warriors and scouts came to walk with him. They stopped several times to watch the step dancing for it amused them.

"Some of the elderly are not here" Piapot said.

"They are gathered on the second level and I have sent them roasted fish and berries" Three Killer stated.

"Let us go up and visit. I will send for my daughters and they will play for them."

Three Killer sent a young buck to bring Piapot's daughters and the Piapot party continued walking to the second level where they sat cross legged with the elderly. The girls soon appeared with their violins and played much music. There was great laughter as Chief Piapot, Chief Three Killer and the warriors took turns step dancing.

After several days, the celebration was over and the village began to empty. Rain Cloud went south. Dalton left for the third camp and Piapot took his people north west to their village.

When Piapot returned to his village, he sent several warriors west with the £ sterling to purchase ammunition, flour and cloth for the women.

It was late October when the old warriors returned from the fort. The Piapot village took what supplies and ammunition they needed and sent the remainder of the supplies and ammunition to Three Killer at the old village.

The trading party managed to buy several repeating rifles and colt revolvers which they left with Chief Piapot.

Chapter Six

The Wolf Hunter Massacre

"Now I know why they call these places Whoop-ups!"

The fall soon became winter and the old warriors in the Piapot village prepared for war against the whiskey traders and wolf hunters. Much time was spent practicing with rifles and colt pistols for this was a war of firepower and not bows and arrows.

When it was early March on the calendar, Piapot gathered his warriors to speak of the war.

"The first two posts to the north are close together and should be attacked at the same time" one of the warriors stated.

"Yes" Piapot agreed.

"The best time to attack would be towards evening before dark when the wolf hunters and those who drink are in the post" another warrior spoke.

"Yes. The more of them we kill the more repeating rifles and ammunition we will have" Piapot added.

Another warrior spoke, "Most of our outside firepower should be to the east for that is the direction they will ride if any Blackfoot or wolf hunters try to escape."

"Yes! And we will put two muskets at each window" another warrior exclaimed.

When most of the battle plans were discussed, Piapot spoke to his warriors. "In our village, we have many brave scouts and warriors who have felt the heat and have done much killing for our nation. When I speak of this war, I see the fire in their eyes but time has weakened their eyes and their hands are not steady. Some will reload the muskets and some will guard the horses of those who do not enter the post. When the first shot is fired, some of those hidden outside will come through the door and some will kill whoever is outside. When we have slaughtered those at the north post, we will ride south with the wagons and goods. I put Two Horns in charge of those who attack the south post. I am Chief Piapot and I have spoken."

In the early evening of March 15, Piapot and four of his warriors, walked by several drinkers and entered the door to the trading post carrying buffalo hides draped over both hands. Piapot dropped his hides and fired a bullet into the head of the owner. Outside the muskets began to fire with great speed as warriors inside put bullets into the heads of four wolf hunters sitting at a table. The muskets outside stopped firing and several of Piapot's warriors came through the door and fired at two Blackfoot who tried to make it to a window. Four women of no value ran through the door and were cut down on the planks. Piapot emptied one of his colts into a wolf hunter who tried to crawl behind the counter and with his other pistol, he shot the wolf hunter's women in the heart as she came at him with a knife.

It was over in minutes. The four warriors with pistols walked through the post and killed those who were dying on the floor. Piapot stepped outside and saw bodies lying everywhere. He ordered one of the four warriors to ride out and bring in the horses and the warriors who guarded them.

Piapot then ordered his warriors to drag the dead inside and place their weapons and ammunition on the planks.

"Little Calf! Did we lose any warriors?" Piapot asked.

"No" Little Calf replied with a smile.

Piapot stepped back into the post and walked behind the counter. He ordered the warriors to remove the weapons and ammunition and place them on the planks beside the others. A warrior entered the post and reported to Piapot.

"There are four wagons and sixteen heavy horses in the corral along with twelve horses that must have belonged to the dead wolf hunters and the post owners. There are twelve saddles, bridles and saddle blankets as well as harnesses for the horses. The warriors are herding the remainder of the horses which number fifteen to twenty."

Inside the post there were many buffalo hides along with the tanned hides of small animals. Also there were many of the white mans' blankets, rolls of cloth, cooking pots, tools, and small items for the women.

Piapot spoke. "There is more whiskey then this. Look for it under the floor."

It did not take long to find two doors on the floor. One was to the left of the counter covered by a smaller counter and the second was underneath the trader's bed. There were only two wooden boxes of whiskey under the first door. When the wooden cover of one boxes was removed, Piapot saw twelve sealed bottles of whiskey divided by wooden sleeves. The hole underneath the second door was not as big but it was full of boxes of whiskey.

"Place the open box of whiskey on the counter beside the unsealed bottles and take the remainder outside" Piapot ordered.

Piapot and the warriors moved outside to count the weapons. There were thirty-two repeating rifles and most of them had cases made of soft leather with great design. The colt revolvers numbered twenty-five and there were many belts filled with bullets and hard leather holders for the pistols. Many boxes of ammunition lay on the planks. There were nineteen old and new muskets with much powder and shot.

Piapot then sent four scouts to the south trading post to return with a report.

Piapot spoke to his warriors, "Those of you without a repeating rifle will take one and the remainder of you will take pistols. The warriors who guarded the horses and reloaded the muskets have no need for these weapons. You will take the muskets and powder along with the horses, hides and goods to our village. Those without saddles will take one before everything is loaded. Load your weapons and belts with bullets and have the remainder put on a pack horse to take with us as we ride south. We will soon be a nation of repeating rifles and colt revolvers."

The weapons were loaded with great speed for the shadows were growing long. The old warriors left just before the sun turned red.

Piapot stood on the planks and invited his warriors inside. He smiled as he stepped behind the counter and began placing small glasses on the counter top.

"Many years ago, when I first met the Dumonts at the fort, they told me about the white man's whiskey. They empty half the bottle and add water and poison. It burns the stomach and the throat. If too much poison is added it will kill you for it is the same poison wolf hunters use to poison the wolves, fox, coyotes and their pups. Dumont told me never to drink from a bottle that is not sealed." Piapot continued "Do you see these large bottles? They are filled with poison and have been used to poison these bottles without the seal."

Piapot gave the poison and poisoned bottles of whiskey to a warrior and said to him, "Pour them over the bodies lying in the centre of the room for they look like they could use a drink". There was much laughter as Piapot took a sealed bottle from the case and began pouring whiskey into the glasses.

"I do not drink the white man's whiskey but I know there are drinkers in my village." Piapot continued, "Warriors who drink in front of children and the very young are warriors of no value. There are no children here for I am the youngest among you."

Piapot poured a small amount of whiskey into a glass and raised it for all to see.

"I invite you to share with me a drink of real whiskey in honor of all the brave warriors who have died for our nation."

There was much whooping, hollering and praise for Piapot as the warriors came forward for a drink of real whiskey.

"Now I know why they call these places Whoop-ups!" an old warrior exclaimed.

That brought a roar of laughter as Piapot continued to pour real whiskey for his warriors. The four scouts who rode south returned in time to share a drink of real whiskey from the last bottle.

One of the scouts reported, "The post to the south is burning and there is much weapons and goods."

This brought more whooping and hollering.

The scout continued, "Two Horns said he will wait for your war party to arrive."

There was much pemmican in the trading post which was divided among the warriors. The remainder was taken outside to be loaded with the ammunition in the morning. The white man's paper money was placed in a deerskin water bag along with the coins and given to Chief Piapot.

"Take all the counters and anything that will burn" Piapot said. "We will use them to make small fires for the night."

When this was done, the post was set on fire.

Early the next morning, the Piapot raiding party rode south and joined with Two Horns. Armed with repeating rifles and pistols, they rode south plundering and burning the posts until they met the Three Killer raiding party. The plundered hides and muskets were sent to the Piapot village and everything else would be taken to the old village where Dalton would be waiting.

It was late in March when Three Killer and Piapot arrived at the old village. Dalton could hardly believe the great number of weapons they brought with them. There were twelve wagons loaded with goods for the camps and this did not include wagons that were sent to the Chief Piapot village. The wagons were left on the flats above the village and horses were unharnessed and put out to graze.

Three Killer and Piapot found Dalton who gave a report on the raids to the south.

"We raided four trading posts and took away much more than we thought we would." Dalton continued, "We took one hundred and six repeating rifles, forty-two colts, five wagon loads of hides, eighty-four horses, thirty-six muskets, eight wagon loads of tools and goods for the women, twenty-seven cases of whiskey and more ammunition than I can count. There is also a bag of Canadian and Yankee money."

Three Killer and Chief Piapot looked at each other and laughed.

"Is that all you got!" Chief Piapot exclaimed.

There was much laughter and shoulder hugs as the three walked to the warriors' lodge for steam.

As they walked, Chief Piapot asked Dalton, "Did Rain Cloud and the buck warriors return from the Sioux nation?"

"Yes" Dalton replied. "He brought his sister and her two daughters and son. He also brought his sister's twenty-four year old friend who is white and has hair the color of snow. Her name is Victoria and she has a seven year old daughter called Cathy. I met them at the first camp and Rain Cloud rode south with my raiding party. He is now taking Cathy, his sister and her family to the second camp and will return soon to help us slaughter the traders and wolf hunters from the big post to the west."

"What about his sister's husband?" Piapot asked.

"He did not come" Dalton replied. "The Yankee soldiers are making great pain and suffering on the Sioux, much like what happened to our people last spring. The Sioux nation will make a stand against them on the Little Big Horn and the husband wants to be there."

"And where is Victoria?" Piapot asked.

"Victoria is on the practice range. She does not like to make bannock or haul wood" Dalton continued. "Her father and her Sioux husband, who died crossing the ice taught her how to use a rifle and pistol. She has her own weapons and is a deadly shot, fast too!"

"Did any of your warriors get killed!" Chief Three Killer asked.

"Yes" Dalton replied. "One of our warriors shot through a window and killed another warrior inside the post."

"We must give much thanks to the Creator for our success" Piapot said.

After taking steam, the Chiefs and council sat at the big table and discussed the war with the traders and wolf hunters who will soon come from the west.

"How many repeating rifles are now in our nation?" a councilor asked.

"There are over four hundred and fifty and there is much ammunition" Wandering Buffalo replied.

"How many pistols are now in our nation?" another councilor asked.

"There were over three hundred and fifty pistols with very much ammunition" Wandering Buffalo replied.

"How many horses from the raids are grazing above on the plains?" Three Killer asked.

"Four hundred and sixty are grazing" Wandering Buffalo replied.

"We must take all the goods to the third camp as soon as possible" Dalton stated. "We now have enough pack horses and young buck warriors to move them quickly for we no longer need our young bucks for reloading muskets."

The council agreed with Dalton. Piapot gave orders to load and move out in the morning. Chief Piapot spoke, "All the hides and whiskey will be sent to my village for it will be less distance for the Dumonts to travel. They are now settled north of the big river and I will now send scouts to speak with them. I do not think they will have enough Canadian money to purchase all the hides and whiskey but we have enough pack horses and wagons to take the remainder to the fort."

"What will we do with all the hides and whiskey we get from the raid on the wagon train from the west?" a councilor asked.

"These will be taken and stored at the third camp" Three Killer replied. "We cannot sell any more at the fort for there will be questions asked."

"And we cannot trade at Fort Benton for the disappearance of the white traders and their goods will be on everyone's lips" a councilor added.

"There are enough fair and mixed bloods in our nation now for us to purchase goods for cash anywhere next year" Dalton added.

"Dalton! Tell us about the camps" Piapot said.

"We have a place to begin the fourth camp" Dalton stated. "The fourth camp is eight days ride from here. It is across a big river and into the rolling hills before the mountains. With all the tools we have, we will be done the fourth and fifth camp and into the mountains before winter."

"What about all the wagons?" a councilor asked.

"They will be of great value in the mountains" another councilor replied. "We can take them apart and use just two wheels closer together for one horse to haul small loads of building materials, goods and tools. We will make two small wagons from each wagon."

"Let us now speak of the battle" Piapot said.

The council agreed that small scouting parties would ride west in the morning to wait for the wagon train and send back riders each day to report their progress. Once the wagon train was located, they agreed that scouts would find a place on the trail which has trees on one side and a high spot on the other side, This is where the battle would take place.

"In the morning, the repeating rifles and colt revolvers will be divided and much training will take place" Three Killer stated.

Before leaving, Piapot spoke to Three Killer and Dalton. "I will need one hundred dog warriors to ride the plains with me." Piapot continued "Some wolf hunters from Fort Benton may ride north seeking revenge when they begin to realize that their friends will never return.

If they come north to the plains, I will slaughter them. Also Chief Pound Maker, the Bush Cree north of the big river has sat cross legged with the Blackfoot and I will speak to him of this. The warriors who ride with me will not wear the white man's cloth but will have the white man's saddles. Also, give me two of your young bucks who worked in the camps" Piapot added.

Dalton and Three Killer smiled for they saw the fire in Piapot's eyes.

"I would like to ride with you Chief Piapot" Dalton said.

"I would like to have you but you must return to the camps" Piapot stated.

"I understand" Dalton replied. "Me and Chief Three Killer will bring you the very best warriors".

The next morning scouts were sent in different directions to bring the Dumonts to the old village and to look for the wagon train from the west. The weather was warm as the pack horses were loaded and sent to the third camp. Rain Cloud returned from the second camp and sat cross legged with Chief Piapot. After speaking briefly, they walked to the large meadow and took part in the training.

As the days passed, the councils met to discuss strategy for the villages. It was agreed that the nation now had several whites and many of mixed blood who could take entitlement for free land offered by the Yankees and Canadians. Also, much of the cash the nation accumulated could be used to purchase the additional land in order to block white settlement near the villages in the mountains.

"The purchased land will be attached to the given land?" a councilor asked.

"Yes" another councilor replied.

"How much will the purchased land cost?" Wandering Buffalo asked.

"It is grazing land and will cost very little" Dalton stated enthusiastically.

"The Dumonts will advise us of this for many of mixed blood have taken land below the two big lakes east of the fort" Piapot added.

When the council meeting ended Piapot and Three Killer walked to a quiet place and sat cross legged.

"When I arrived at the old village after the buffalo hunt, the number of young and very young surprised me" Piapot said.

"There will be many in our nation soon" Three Killer added.

"Yes and just about all of them speak French and English" Piapot continued. "The council is not good enough as it sits now. I think that each who sits in council should be in charge of a certain thing. I will be done better and the council will have more power. I would not want to do everything in the new village."

"I have also given this much thought" Three Killer replied.

The two spoke until the shadows grew long and agreed about a division of power. They agreed that those who were responsible for the most serious of the nations business would be called Chief Councilor and those of everyday responsibilities would be called Councilor for whatever he or she is responsible. Three Killer would be Chief of Chiefs in the village and say yes or no.

"Beth wishes to build what she calls a church and read from the white man's book of creation. She says the white man's Creator and the nation's Creator are the same" Three Killer explained.

As they walked, Piapot spoke. "When I was east of the fort, I saw men dressed like women and they had two pieces of crossed sticks tied around their necks." Piapot continued "Every Sunday on the calendar, people filled the church which Beth speaks of and they paid to hear him read from the white man's book. The white man's words can not move our nation away from the Creator. Tell Beth she will have her church but we will not pay her to read from the white man's book."

There was much laughter between them.

It was the twelfth day of May on the calendar when scouts arrived from the west and reported to Piapot. They reported that the traders' wagons were three days ride and moving fast on the old trail.

"How many wagons?" Piapot asked.

"Sixteen" a scout replied.

"How many people are there?" Dalton asked.

"There are thirty-two freighters, twelve traders and twenty-one wolf hunters" the scout continued. "There are several Blackfoot women who ride in the wagons."

"What is their fire power?" Dalton asked.

"They all have repeating rifles and some of the traders have colts" the scout answered.

"Have you located the place for the battle?" Piapot asked.

"Yes" the scout answered. "Less than one day's ride from here, there is a place where the trees belly as a river and there is a high place to the north. The old trail does not belly but goes straight just below the high place.

"Do they have scouts?" Three Killer asked.

"No" one of the scouts replied.

"We will leave early in the morning and take our positions" Piapot said.

It was late the next day when the war party reached the place of battle. They did not proceed past the east end of the battle field, taking care not to disturb the grass or leave any marks on the trail. Most of the horses were left a distance east of the battle field with the buck warriors. The remainder of the horses were taken up the banks and away from the crest of the bank which overlooked the train below. The wagon train was estimated to be seven hundred and fifty paces. Seventy-five warriors armed with repeating rifles and pistols were positioned along the top of the bank, twenty riders were positioned at each end of the bank and at the sound of the first shot, would ride down the slope to stop anyone trying to use the trail to escape. Almost one hundred warriors positioned themselves in the trees that bellied from the east to the west end of the battle field. The firing would come from all directions.

Late in the day, two more scouts arrived from the east and reported to Piapot who was positioned at the top of the bank.

"The wagon train will be here when the sun is high" the scout continued. "The last of the scouts will observe the wagon train until it reaches a short distance from here."

The scouts left to report to the remainder of the warriors and took position in the trees as two buck warriors came through the trees to lead their horses away.

Three Killer said to the buck warriors, "Remember to tell the buck warriors not to stop each wagon until it clears the battle field".

"We will keep our pistols aimed and kill anyone who is wounded before we stop the wagons" one of the bucks stated.

Three Killer nodded and the two buck warriors rode away through the trees with the scout's horses.

In the morning, before the sun was high, the remainder of the scouts rode up from the plains behind Piapot and gave their report.

"They will be here soon" one of them said.

Piapot sent the scouts to the east and to the west to join the other riders who were hidden back from the ridge. Piapot waived his rifle to signal to all the warriors below.

Piapot watched as the wagon train approached the battlefield. When the centre of the wagon train was below him, Piapot raised himself to one knee and blew a driver from his wagon seat. Rifle fire came from all directions as the drivers were hit several times. Those who were wounded jumped from the wagons and ran for the trees. They were cut down along with most of the wolf hunters and traders. The wolf hunters who survived jumped from their horses and took cover in the tall grass. The traders who were driven by greed, chased after their wagons on horseback and were slaughtered immediately. The rifles on the bank pounded the wolf hunters who hid in the tall grass below. Two of the Blackfoot women who jumped from the wagons, threw up their hands and were cut down where they stood.

Joseph, the youngest son of Three Killer, came from the trees and walking beside him was Victoria. As they walked, a wolf hunter, with rifle raised above his head, jumped from the tall grass and yelled "I was not at the massacre!"

"You are at one now!" Joseph shouted.

Before the wolf hunter could lower his rifle, Victoria drew her pearl handled colts and fired two bullets into his chest. Joseph walked closer and put a bullet into the side of his head.

The riders from the west rode to the meadow and put a bullet into the head of everyone on the ground. The riders to the east of the trail rode to both sides of the wagons and shot the few who were alive and dead in the driver' seats. Piapot and his warriors came down the slope to meet with the warriors who came from the trees. The battle was over in less than thirty minutes and not one warrior was killed or wounded.

"What will we do with the dead?" Wandering Buffalo asked.

"Let them float down the river as a gift to the Blackfoot" Piapot ordered.

After anything of value was taken from them, the dead, totaling seventy-two, were hauled away in wagons and thrown into the river. There were seven Blackfoot women among them.

Everything was taken to the old village to be taken to the third camp to supply the fourth and fifth camp. The buck warriors returned with their pack train and the goods were loaded.

"How many horses were taken?" Three Killer asked.

"One hundred and forty-nine" Wandering Buffalo continued. "Also, one hundred and thirty-four repeating rifles, sixty-two muskets, seventeen wagons including two cooking wagons, one hundred and fifteen saddles and bridles, very many coins and some paper money, fifty-six boxes of whiskey, much cloth and more ammunition than we know what to do with."

"The muskets we can use for hunting and save on bullets" Dalton stated.

"The wagons can take the long route south and avoid the trees" Rain Cloud said.

"Yes and the horses can be herded with them" Wandering Buffalo added.

"The old village will be used for the buffalo hunt" a councilor said.

Piapot spoke, "Yes and I will return for the hunt whenever I can." Piapot continued "Three Killer will explain the new power that will control the nation in the mountains. Dalton will be Chief Councilor in charge of what the white man calls land development. The two young builders that come with me, I will send to the fort where they will learn from a white man called McDonald, the secret of splitting stones. You will need less buffalo skins for the buildings will be made of trees and stones. Agriculture will be most important for land must be bought for the cattle I steal from the white settlers and there will be much growing. In the new village, Three Killer will be Chief of Chiefs. I am Chief Piapot and I have spoken."

Additional pack horses were loaded, and after eating, the pack train left for the camps. The buck warriors used the two cook wagons and made food for the warriors. Piapot took two small bags of coins and left the remainder of the money with Three Killer. Chief Three Killer and Chief Dalton rode to the meadow below and returned with the one hundred warriors. They wore no cloth and there were bangles in their long hair and knives were laced to their legs. They had leather belts that held many bullets and a pistol. Each had a repeating rifle in a white man's case attached to a white man's saddle and ammunition in belts that hung crossways from their shoulders to their waist. Among them were two warriors with strong medicine, Joseph, the youngest son of Chief Three Killer and Victoria who had long hair as white as the snow.

Piapot smiled at Dalton and Three Killer as he turned and drove his buffalo horse to the north east. Dalton was disappointed as he watched the one hundred ride behind Piapot with their hair blowing in the wind.

It was the spring of 1874 and Chief Piapot was fifty-six years old. There was freedom and order on the plains.

Chapter Seven

The Sell Off

"I think the women want to run away with you Gabriel!"

In a few days, Piapot and the dog warriors reached his village. The old warriors wanted to hear what happened with the traders and wolf hunters from the big post to the west. There was great celebration filled with much praise when it was told that traders and wolf hunters were killed to the last man. Several of the dog warriors were sent out to hunt small game, several were ordered to remove the saddles and bridles from the horses and guard them as they drank and grazed while the remainder gathered wood for the fires.

The old warriors and the women asked about Victoria. Piapot told them about her Sioux husband and white father who called himself William McLeod.

"Is she a warrior?" one of them asked.

"When we slaughtered the traders from Fort Benton, I watched from a high place as she drew her pistols and put two bullets into the chest of a wolf hunter before he could lower his rifle. She walked in the tall grass with Joseph and put bullets into the heads of the living and the dead. She is a born killer!" Piapot exclaimed.

Piapot's two wives took Victoria to the women's lodge for steam and no one asked any more questions about her.

Piapot sent for the two builders that worked with Dalton in the camps. When they arrived, Piapot told them about the two brothers at the fort called McDonald who had native wives.

"They will teach you how to build with stones" Piapot told them.

"Where will we find them?" one of them asked.

"Just ask for them by name. They said they would even pay you but here is £5 sterling to buy food and the tools you will need to split the stones if it is not so." Piapot continued. "If they pay you, leave the remaining coins at my village when you return."

"We will leave first thing in the morning Chief Piapot" one of them stated.

The two builders left early the next morning and the dog warriors continued to hunt small game.

It was noon near the end of May on the calendar when Pitpot's scouts and the Dumonts rode into the village. The Dumonts knew of the wagon train slaughter and were amazed at the dog soldiers' fire power.

"Bonjour Chief Piapot" Gabriel shouted.

"Bonjour" Piapot replied.

It was for the first time that many of the dog warriors met the Dumonts but the old warriors knew them well.

After much story telling and laughter, the Dumonts and Piapot sat cross legged to discuss the value of the goods.

Gabriel spoke, "The goods you have are of great value. The white man needs the hides for more than blankets for in the east, they have machines that are driven by the tough skin of the buffalo. The bush Cree still value the old musket and powder which I will trade for hides. The horses and wagons we can use in our settlement. Especially the horses for they are trained and have harnesses."

"What about the whiskey?" Piapot asked.

"Whiskey? You have whiskey?"

"Much whiskey" Piapot answered.

"Yes! I will take all the whiskey you have" Gabriel continued. "Also, I will take any blankets and items used for cooking and eating."

"Each person in our village will have a white man's blanket along with a buffalo blanket and you can have the remainder" Piapot continued. "The women will decide what other goods we will trade."

A woman approached the group and told them there was much food ready on the tables. The Dumonts were impressed with the tables, bowls, utensils and the variety of food including soft bannock.

"We are hunters and cannot show up at the post with traders' wagons. Where will you trade the hides and goods?" Piapot asked.

"We will send half the wagons north and the remainder west to the fort" Dumont continued. "Most of the hides will be taken to the fort. The muskets, powder, whiskey and other goods will be taken north to trade with the bush Cree. I do not like trading whiskey but if I do not somebody else will. From me they will at least get real whiskey."

After eating, the group sat cross legged to discuss the value. Dumont wrote down the number of each item and what they would sell for. A total value was arrived at which amazed the Piapot group. Dumont drew a straight up and down line on the paper. He drew a line across the up and down line near the top.

"This represents sixty percent of the value of these items and this is what I will pay" Gabriel explained.

"Send Victoria to me" Piapot ordered. Victoria soon appeared and sat cross legged with the group. The Dumonts could not help but stare for Victoria had great beauty.

"Tell me Victoria, how much is sixty percent of this total value?" Piapot asked.

Victoria took the pencil and multiplied the figures. "Sixty percent of $3,600 leaves $2,160 for the nation. Is that correct Mr. Dumont?" Victoria asked.

"Yes! Where did you learn all this?" Dumont asked.

"I was educated in the east until I was fifteen years old and my father was a trader" Victoria replied.

Piapot thanked Victoria for her help and she left to join the warriors.

"This is much money Gabriel" Piapot said.

"Yes! There is now paper money in the west but I have coins as well. I can give you $1,500 and will need $660 credit until I sell the hides" Dumont stated.

Piapot spoke, "Almost twenty years ago on the calendar, your family gave me credit to purchase the firepower I needed and you helped our nation fight the Blackfoot. Your word is good in my nation Gabriel".

Gabriel nodded and said to Piapot, "If you send a few warriors to the fort with us, I will give them $660 when I sell the hides. I will get as many coins as I can."

"This will be done" Piapot said.

Gabriel gave Piapot four bags of coins and much paper money. "I do not have any Yankee money" Gabriel said. Piapot nodded and they walked to the warriors' lodge where they took steam and did much talking.

"What do you know about free land?" Piapot asked.

"Free land is available in the east near the Fort Garry area" Gabriel continued. "You must be what is called a British subject which includes the mixed bloods. There are certain things you must do to get title or complete ownership of the land which the whites call one quarter section."

"What must you do?" Piapot asked.

"Things like putting up a white man's house and working the land" Gabriel continued. You must live on the land for two years. It will cost twenty dollars before you start."

"There is a white woman in our nation who knows much about what she calls vegetables" Piapot continued. "The buffalo will soon be gone from the plains as your family has warned. We must grow our own food and raise the white man's cattle. There are many of mixed blood in my nation and they will use their English and French names to take the free land and buy more land when the time comes. We will need grazing land for the cattle I will steal from the white settlers to the south and to the east."

There was much laughter as Piapot and Gabriel dressed and walked through the village.

As they walked Piapot asked, "Is it true that Chief Poundmaker sits cross legged with the Blackfoot?"

"Yes" Gabriel replied.

"I have the Blackfoot to the west and I do not need them to the north as well" Piapot continued. "I would ask that when you return to your settlement, you send a scout to tell Poundmaker that I will meet with him below the big river on the last day of the next month."

"That will be June 30 on the calendar" Gabriel confirmed.

"Yes! June 30 on the calendar" Piapot repeated.

Gabriel could feel the heat and said to Piapot "My people and Chief Big Bear will ride with you if it comes to war."

"You have before and I know your worth" Piapot replied. As they walked, they came to a high place where it was quiet.

"Let us sit cross legged for I have something to tell you" Piapot said.

They sat down on the grass and Piapot spoke. "When I brought rain in Montana, I had a great vision" Piapot continued. "The sun gave much heat and before the sticks tore the flesh from my chest I saw the white light. The Creator did not want my spirit but showed me an evil monster made of steel that would travel through our nation bringing much hardship to my people. It was higher than three buffalo horses one on top of another and smoke that would burn you, came from the head and two nostrils. It travelled on a trail made of steel. I saw this monster once before shortly after we fought the Blackfoot almost twenty years ago. This monster I must kill."

Gabriel stared at Piapot and said nothing.

"Do you know what this monster could be Gabriel"" Piapot asked.

"Yes" Gabriel replied.

"What is it?" Piapot asked.

"It is a steam engine made of steel and has wheels on each side and they travel on steel tracks" Gabriel continued. "The smoke you saw is from the burning of wood and coal that makes the steam which drives the engine. It does release steam from both sides and it will burn you. The engine pulls many smaller wagons with steel wheels and travels behind on the same track. This monster is nothing you can kill and it will bring supplies, animals and settlers from the east. The whole thing with the wagons connected is called a train."

"How do you know this?" Piapot asked.

"I saw it when I went south east of the Missouri with my family to talk guns with the Yankees" Gabriel replied.

Piapot rose slowly and looking east, he said to Gabriel, "I will stop the train."

The two walked back to the village where the Dumont family sat cross legged with several dog warriors and they were speaking much French.

"This is so good" one of the Dumonts said. "Your dog warriors speak much French."

"Yes All the warriors who ride with me speak either French or English and many speak both" Piapot replied.

"I have two gifts for you Chief Piapot" Gabriel said. Gabriel walked to one of the pack horses and returned with a new Winchester rifle.

"This is the Winchester 73" Gabriel continued. "There is no lever action. You place the bullets here and it fires as fast as you can pull the trigger."

Piapot placed the bullets in the chamber and pulled the trigger several times. "This is truly a repeating rifle of great value!" Piapot exclaimed.

The dog warriors gathered around and took turns firing the new Winchester.

"How many of these rifles do you have?" Piapot asked.

"Just a few" Gabriel continued. "I will let you know if I get more from the Yankees."

Gabriel laughed and ordered one of the family to bring a bag of potatoes. The family member quickly returned and laid a large bag of potatoes on the wooden table.

"This is called a potato which is part of your second gift. I will now cook for you" Gabriel said.

There was much laughter as the old warriors and the women gathered around to watch Gabriel cook.

Gabriel peeled several potatoes and cut them into several small pieces. He then took a large steel pot with a lid and added water and salt. He placed half the pieces of potatoes into the pot and put them on the fire to boil. One of the family members attended the boiling potatoes while Gabriel cut the remaining potatoes into smaller pieces. "Bring me fish, grease and two large fry pans" Gabriel asked.

Gabriel prepared the fish with a flour batter and added grease to both fry pans. By this time, the potatoes were boiled and Gabriel drained away the water. He mixed a white powder with a little water and poured them over the potatoes adding a little more salt as he squashed the potatoes with a large spoon until they were just right. Gabriel placed a spoonful on a small plate and handed it to Piapot.

Piapot picked up a fork and tasted the mashed potatoes. His eyes grew in size and a great smile came to his face as he tasted the potatoes.

"These potatoes we must have!" Piapot exclaimed.

The women gathered and tasted the potatoes. They were very excited and gave Gabriel many hugs.

"That is called mashed potatoes" Gabriel continued. "Now we will fry them. It is faster and water is not required."

Gabriel added more wood to the fire that burned below the white man's thick steel plate that laid level on four stones above the fire. He placed the two large fry pans on the steel plate and added salt and pepper as he turned the fish and potatoes as they fried. When they were done he placed a piece of fish and potatoes on a plate and gave it to Piapot.

"This is even better!" Piapot exclaimed as he wolfed down the potatoes and fish.

The women tasted the fried fish and potatoes. They were amazed and gave Gabriel more hugs and kisses. "I think the women want to run away with you Gabriel" an old warrior said.

This brought much laughter.

"I have also two bags of seed potatoes that I kept in a warm dark place" Gabriel said.

Two members of the family brought the seed potatoes and Gabriel explained the planting.

"You see this potato" Gabriel continued. "It has little green spots. These are called eyes and you cut each potato in about half making sure there are about four eyes in each half. We will plant them not too deep with the flat sides down. They will take about two weeks to come up and will be ready to dig when the leaves begin to turn. These two bags will make you fifteen to twenty bags of potatoes. You must give them water and make sure nothing grows around them. Also, I have seeds called corn. They grow in rows not too far apart and will be ready about the same time as the potatoes. You will see something grow on them with fine hair like my whiskers. When the kernels turn yellow, they are ready to boil or eat raw if you like. Both of these vegetables are very good for your nation. Let us go down by the river where rich soil has fallen from the banks and washed up by the river. The soil there will not be as hard as the soil on the prairie."

Piapot ordered the dog warriors to cut the potatoes as Gabriel said and bring them to the river. When this was done, the whole gathering, except the women, walked down to the river with many of the white man's shovels. Gabriel found a flat spot and showed the dog warriors how to work the soil.

With a hundred young dog warriors, it did not take long to work the soil. Gabriel took a shovel and showed the dog warriors how deep and how far apart to dig the holes. They started several rows and Gabriel placed a seed potato in a hole. The dog warriors followed the shovels placing seed while other warriors who came behind filled the holes.

When this was done, Gabriel took a shovel and cut a shallow line in the soil with one edge. He placed several corn seeds showing the dog warriors how deep and far apart to put the seed. The dog warriors cut more lines and warriors came behind planting seed and covering them with soil. Several dog warriors went up the bank and came back with many of the white man's pails. They went to the river and took turns watering the planted potatoes and corn seed.

Several women, who helped prepare the food, came to the bank and told them it was time to eat. The dog warriors ran up the bank and feasted on potatoes, fish, deer steaks and berries.

The old warriors lagged behind and spoke with the Dumonts about vegetables and the new Winchesters.

"Just when we catch up to the white man's fire power, he finds something better" one of the old warriors stated.

"Maybe it is time for peace" another old warrior added.

"It will be time for peace when there is fairness" Dumont stated.

"There may be peace but there will never be fairness for I see their greed" Piapot said.

They spoke a little longer and decided to go to the tables before the dog warriors ate everything. The dog warriors were excited about the potatoes and thanked the Dumonts many times.

When everyone was done eating, the old warriors brought out their drums and the Dumonts rosined up their bows and drank wine. Piapot ordered up several small sipping bags. There was much step dancing and the celebration went on long after the sun went down.

In the morning, several dog warriors travelled west to the fort with the wagons and the remainder of the Dumont family went north to their settlement. The dog warriors who remained at the village continued hunting small game, repairing the lodges and watering the potatoes and corn.

The warriors went in different directions to scout the plains as well as hunt. Piapot gave Victoria the recipe for wine that Gabriel left him.

"Guard this recipe well for they will make it in the new village. This is alcohol that I approve of for my nation" Piapot said.

"I can hardly wait for the village to be built" Victoria stated with much excitement.

Time passed quickly and within ten days the dog warriors returned with the money and the two young builders were with them. They complained about missing the potatoes which brought much laughter and teasing from the dog warriors. One of the dog warriors gave Piapot the money which consisted of some dominion paper and many coins.

Piapot sat cross legged with the builders and asked them, "What did you learn?"

"We learned much Chief Piapot" one of them answered. "We know how to split and square the stones and this we can teach the builders. Also, we can build what the McDonalds call partitions and arcs. We know how to construct chimneys and fireplaces for warmth and cooking. The McDonalds, who know nothing about the mountains, advised that one great hall be built to feed the people. Smaller rooms should be built off the great hall which put the warriors' lodge, women's lodge and the room where the food is stored and prepared under one roof. This great room, when it is not being used for eating, could be used for gatherings, teaching, church and any other occasion with the proper use of water, there is no need to go to the trees to empty the stomach."

"These things must be done in the new village!" Piapot exclaimed.

"The McDonalds paid us for our work and fed us as well. They sold us the tools we needed and we had some money left over which we have given to the dog warriors" the other builder added.

Piapot nodded and smiled.

"Chief Piapot! We ate potatoes everyday" one of the builders said. "Dog warriors should never laugh at a builder."

The dog warriors looked at one another and shouted threats and insults at them.

Piapot raised his arm and said, "It is true! We must never laugh at a builder".

There was much laughter as Piapot and the old warriors gave the builders many shoulder hugs.

Piapot met with his council and decided that Piapot and his warriors would keep fifty dollars in dominion coins and the remainder of all the money would be sent to Chief Three Killer. All the warriors would ride south with the builders and the money. Piapot would remain in the village.

Piapot said to Joseph, "You will take fifteen scouts, five to a party, and keep a good distance ahead of the warriors". Piapot continued, "Ride straight south with a good distance between the scouting parties. If there is no trouble wait for the warriors to reach you before you ride west with the scouts. The warriors will wait until there is distance between you before they follow. You will leave early in the morning."

"This will be done Chief Piapot" Joseph said.

In the morning, the sun was on the plains before the horses were saddled and the warriors were ready to leave. He told Victoria to give the recipe to the French girls and he reminded the warriors they must return before June 25 on the calendar. Joseph and the scouts left first with much whooping and hollering.

"It is good that the Dumonts have taken everything from the raids" Two Horns said.

"Yes. If the white police come when I am gone, give them a potato" Piapot joked.

"I like the idea of several chiefs with one duty Chief Piapot" an old warrior said. "Tell us again how it will work."

"Chief Dalton, chief council for land development. Chief Big Man Walking, chief council for medicine, Chief Wandering Buffalo, chief council for money, chief Beth, chief council for what the white man calls education. These will be a few of the chiefs. Chief Three Killer is chief of chiefs and will say yes or no to everything."

"We should have built everything under one roof and done this a long time ago" Little Calf stated.

"It has been said before and now you know it to be true. We are never too old to learn" Piapot concluded.

The days passed without any scouts returning to the village and this was good because they would only bring a bad report. Piapot and the old warriors enjoyed hunting small game. Many fish were caught and put into the shallow water surrounded by wood. After several rains, the potatoes and corn began to grow and this brought much joy to the village.

Before noon, on the 23rd day of June, two scouts rode into the village. One was the grandson of Chief Thunder Cloud and was called Alexander. The other one was the youngest son of Little Calf and was called Wild Fire.

The two scouts sat cross legged with the council and gave their report.

"We have delivered the money and the builders to the second camp" Wild Fire said. "We are to report that the fourth camp is completed and Dalton has moved the builders to start the fifth and last camp."

"Also, everyone has moved one camp further west" Alexander added. "The elderly in the first camp were moved with wagons and horses. There is nothing standing in the first camp. You would never know it was even there. Big Man Walking did not want to leave them more than one camp away".

"Did you see any whites from Fort Benton?" another councilor asked.

"No" Alexander replied.

"How much money is in the camps?" another councilor asked.

"Wandering Buffalo does not know the true value of the British £ but knows the money will be more than $4,000 dominion dollars and there will be much more when the remainder of the goods are sold next year" Wild Fire stated.

"Three Killer has named his chiefs and everyone wants to go to the mountains as soon as possible!" Alexander exclaimed.

"Who is the chief that will talk to the Creator?" Two Horns asked.

"Three Killer said it will remain the same. Each will give thanks to the Creator in his own way" Alexander stated.

"Where are the warriors?" Piapot asked.

"They will be here before the shadows grow long and they hope the potatoes are ready" Wild Fire said.

There was much belly laughter as the village began to start cooking for the dog warriors.

It was not long before the warriors arrived and there was much talk about the mountains. Half of them sat down to eat and the other half unsaddled the horses and put them out to graze. The warriors kept their weapons at their side which was the Assiniboine custom.

Piapot approached Alexander and said, "In the morning, you will take five scouts to the big river and report the location of the Poundmaker camp."

"This will be done Chief Piapot" Alexander stated.

The scouts left the next morning for the big river and the warriors kept busy with building, hunting and fishing.

Chapter Eight

The Poundmaker Smackdown

*"Your Blackfoot friends with the repeating rifles are telling
you in Blackfoot that they are going to kill me."*

On June 27, when the sun was high, two scouts returned
to the village and reported to Piapot.

"Chief Poundmaker and his warriors have arrived and
are camped between the big river and the sand hills" the
scout continued. "He has one hundred twenty-five to
one hundred fifty warriors armed with muskets, some
repeating rifles and we saw no colt pistols. They are
camped in a low place and easy to observe. With the one
eye and two eye glasses, we counted the hairs on their
heads."

Piapot laughed and told the two scouts to take steam
and return for food.

The dog warriors heard the report and took their weapons to the practice range. Piapot practiced with his new rifle.

After the warriors took a few shots at the targets, they sat cross legged and cleaned their weapons.

When the warriors finished reloading their weapons and belts, Piapot spoke to them about the meeting with Poundmaker.

"At this meeting with the bush Cree, I will sit cross legged with Chief Poundmaker for there is much peace in my heart. I will ask Poundmaker why he brings the Blackfoot to his nation. If they fire one shot, we will slaughter them to the last warrior."

Piapot looked around at the dog warriors. They chewed the seeds that grew wild on prairie and fire was in their eyes. They were ready.

The next morning, the war party drove their horses north and west towards the Poundmaker camp. That evening, just a short distance from the Poundmaker camp, the war party stopped and set up camp. Piapot sent the two scouts ahead and ordered them to join the other scouts.

"Have one of the other scouts return with a report" Piapot ordered.

One of the other scouts returned the next morning and gave Piapot a report.

"We scouted the Poundmaker camp to the west, the east and the north and there are no other bush Crees in the area." The scout continued, "The scouts will remain in these places until the meeting with Poundmaker is finished. There are several Blackfoot in his camp. They have repeating rifles. But not the kind you and Victoria have."

Piapot told the scout he did not have to return to the Poundmaker camp and would ride with the warriors in the morning.

At sunrise the next morning, the horses were saddled and Piapot gave them his final orders.

"We will be divided into four war parties" Piapot said. "Twenty-five warriors will sit cross legged behind me with distance between you. Twenty-five warriors will spread about and sit cross legged a short distance up the slope. Our horses will be left on the ridge above and our repeating rifles we will carry cross ways. Fifty warriors will remain on the ridge. Twenty-five to the east and twenty-five to the west. Stay on your horses and let them see you. If a battle begins, the warriors to the east and west will ride down from the ridge with great speed and attack from both sides. No matter what words are spoken, do not attack until I raise my rifle high. The Blackfoot have no fear and will be the first to attack. Joseph! Take the rifle Dumont gave me. Victoria has the same one. She will position herself to my right. You will position yourself to my left. Both you and Victoria will pick two warriors to sit close to you. Kill the Blackfoot if they point their rifles."

Piapot's war party soon appeared on the ridge. They watched as Poundmaker put the glass to his eyes. As though in disbelief, Poundmaker made several excited gestures with his hands. He gave the glass to a warrior who became excited as well. What they saw on the ridge was one hundred killers dressed in buckskins and with great fire power.

Piapot's fifty warriors tied their horses reins and slid from the saddles carrying their rifles cross ways as they walked down the slope. As they walked down the slope. Halfway down, twenty-five of the warriors stopped and sat cross legged ten paces apart. Joseph and Victoria looked for the Blackfoot, who they knew would not be near to the front of Piapot. They located all seven of them and they would be the first to die.

Piapot stopped a short distance in front of Poundmaker and his twenty-five dog warriors two or three paces apart. To his left was Rain Cloud and to his right was Thunder Child who drove a lance through the neck of a renegade who attacked Dalton.

"Your warriors wear a lot of buckskin" Poundmaker said.

"Yes. Our women still know how to make them" Piapot replied.

Poundmaker wore much cloth and knew this was an insult. He heard that Piapot was a chief of few words but had a tongue that could sting you. Now he knew.

"Let us sit cross legged and discuss the fall buffalo hunt" Poundmaker said.

"Or how many buffalo hunts are left" Piapot added.

Both chiefs walked forward and sat cross legged while the front row warriors sat cross legged behind them. They spoke of the dwindling buffalo herds to the east and other small items of concern.

"What do you think of the white police who come from the east?" Piapot asked.

"What police? I have not heard of this!" Poundmaker stated. "What do they want?"

"They are coming to help divide up the land for the whites. They are gathering below the two big lakes east of the fort and will be on the plains as the leaves turn" Piapot answered.

Poundmaker and his warriors looked at each other with disbelief.

"Chief Poundmaker, I have not come here to speak to you of the white police. I want you to tell me why you bring the Blackfoot into your nation." Piapot stated.

Poundmaker, with shock and anger, rose to his feet and said to Piapot "I do not need permission to bring the Blackfoot into my nation. You have brought the Sioux into your nation and I did not ask you to explain it. It is time to make friends with the Blackfoot and heal the wounds you have inflicted."

Piapot rose to his feet and said to Poundmaker "The Sioux have never bothered the bush Cree. My nation has fought them many times when we stole their horses and they stole ours. They never desired our land and my nation has never desired their land. This is not true of the Blackfoot for they have expanded their nation south to the Sioux plains, west to the mountains, north across the big rivers and east to the Assiniboine nation. The Blackfoot know they cannot defeat the Assinboine and the plains Cree. They make friends with you so they can bring your warriors and their warriors against us from the north while they bring their warriors from the west."

The bush Cree warriors who sat cross legged listened with great interest to Piapot's words for many did not approve of the Blackfoot.

The Blackfoot behind Poundmaker began to stir and speak with a loud voice against Piapot. Poundmaker turned and ordered them to be quiet.

Victoria and Joseph looked across at each other and nodded.

The three on each side moved their rifles from cross ways to a ready position.

Piapot continued, "Your Blackfoot friends with the repeating rifles are telling you in Blackfoot that they are going to kill me. Let me tell you this Poundmaker! If you bring one more Blackfoot south of the big river, I will bring three thousand warriors from my nation, the plains Cree nation, the Sioux nation and drive you and your Blackfoot friends north across the two big rivers to a place where the ice never melts. I am Chief Piapot and I have spoken."

The Blackfoot yelled their war cry and raised their rifles. The sound of repeating rifles came from the second level and the Blackfoot fell, the bush Cree moved away from them as the repeating rifles from the second level put bullets into the ones that moved.

Piapot did not raise his rifle as he moved it to his left hand. The Poundmaker and Piapot warriors remained sitting cross legged. There was a great silence.

Piapot said to Poundmaker, "You gave them orders not to fire. Learn from it Chief Poundmaker!"

Poundmaker was without words as he watched Piapot take his warriors back up the hill. Chief Poundmaker, great speaker among the Crees, now understood the difference between talking and killing.

Piapot danced his magnificent buffalo horse from one side to another. He stopped his horse and looked down on the bush Crees before driving south to the great sand hills. Rifle fire could be heard above the Assiniboine war cries and their long hair blew in the wind.

Chapter Nine

The Visit with Walsh

"This is a time for peace and we will find another way to fight the white man."

For the next five years, Piapot and his dog warriors roamed the plains stealing horses in the north and selling them to Yankees in the south. They rode the south plains near the Cypress Hills looking for wolf hunters but did not find any.

As their reputation grew, they became known to the NWMP who established Fort Walsh in the Cypress Hills in the fall of 1875. The Fort was named after the builder and commander, inspector James Morrow Walsh, who spoke openly about his admiration for Piapot and his dog warriors. He watched them with his binoculars and was taken by their burckskins, magnificent horses and their long hair blowing in the wind. To James Walsh, they represented a kind of freedom which he envied and desired. He was so taken with Piapot and his warriors that before long he had the native women make him buckskins. He let his hair grow long and he learned their language.

Chief Piapot signed Treaty Four in 1875 and received land near Qu'Appelle.

Big Bear and Poundmaker, who no longer sat cross legged with the Blackfoot, came south of the big river to hunt what was left of the buffalo.

The first village in the mountains was completed in 1876 and after the fall buffalo hunt, Joseph and Victoria went to the mountains where she would have their first child.

That same year, Sitting Bull defeated General George Custer at the Little Big Horn and many Sioux travelled north to Fort Walsh seeking refuge. The husband of Rain Cloud's sister was not among them for he was killed at the Little Big Horn.

In the years that were to follow, the buffalo all but vanished from the plains forcing Poundmaker to sign a treaty that took him north of the big river to his reserve.

In 1879, Piapot decided that it was time for his dog warriors to go to the mountains. They gathered at the Piapot village where Piapot would meet with his council.

Piapot said to Rain Cloud, "Have the warriors help the women prepare a feast for it will be the last feast in my village".

"This will be done Chief Piapot."

Piapot and his council walked to the warriors lodge and took steam.

Piapot spoke, "In the morning, I will leave for the mountains and return to the village in one or two years. Is there any in our village who wishes to ride with us to the mountains?"

"We have spoken of this in the village and have decided that we are too old to ride that far" Two Horns answered.

"Yes! It is a long ride and if I were a little older, I would not ride that far either."

One of the councilors spoke, "With the buffalo gone and the Sioux still here in numbers, there is hunger on the plains. We are not hungry for we have our fish traps and much vegetables. Also, in the lodges your warriors built, there are still new Hudson Bay blankets, much cloth and buffalo blankets."

"I will leave you many Dominion dollars but I want you to wear old clothes when you go to the posts."

"There are women of great beauty at the posts. Could we wear our good cloth every now and then?" an old warrior asked.

This brought much laughter!

"We will miss the young warriors and the women they have left with us" the old warrior continued. "They are of white skin."

"Yes some of their women are full whites, but most are of mixed blood. The new village in the mountains will be a strong nation" Piapot replied.

"Will you be signing the white man's treaty?" Little Calf asked. Piapot spoke. "There have been talks of a treaty desired by myself, Big Bear and Poundmaker for land near the Cypress Hills. This will fail for the white man wishes to divide our nations. The treaty I signed in 1875 will probably be the only treaty needed."

"Will you slaughter the white police at Fort Walsh?" an old warrior asked.

"I do not think so" Piapot continued. "Even though we have the warriors and the fire power, it would not be wise to slaughter them. I have travelled east beyond the Fort and lived near a place called Fort Gary. I can tell you that the white man is there in the thousands. We do not have enough ammunition to kill them all. If we slaughter the white police at Fort Walsh, we will have to travel south and ask the Yankees for food and shelter as Sitting Bull had to travel north to do the same after killing Custer. This is a time for peace and we will find another way to fight the white man."

"How will we fight them?" one of them asked.

"The white man speaks much about their laws and fairness for all people. We will fight them every day with their own laws" Piapot continued. "The white man wishes to steal our land with much speed for they have problems with the French and the mixes bloods. Also the Yankees are moving west just below us and the Canadians fear delays. It is a good time to trade with them"

Piapot and the elders let the dog warriors eat first. After the dog warriors finished eating, they gathered in groups and lit many small fires. The sound of guitars and mouth organs could be heard from fire to fire. They sang in French, English and Cree.

When they were done eating, Piapot and the elders walked from fire to fire and listened to the dog warriors play and sing. The village was alive and the elders knew they would not see the dog warriors again in these numbers. It was a glorious evening.

In the morning, the dog warriors prepared to move out. The elders told Piapot to take the buffalo horses to the mountains for they only needed a few pack horses. The dog warriors rounded up the buffalo horses and waited for Piapot's orders.

Piapot spoke, "I will take twenty-five warriors with me to Fort Walsh" Piapot continued. "It is said that Inspector Walsh will leave next year and I will sit cross legged with him for the last time. Little Calf! It is possible that I may stay in the mountains for more than one year. I will return to the village no later than 1882 on the calendar."

Little Calf replied, "We have money, food and good clothing. We will be comfortable in the village."

Piapot and his warriors rode out towards Fort Walsh and the remainder rode towards the mountains. Piapot felt a sadness as they rode west. The buffalo that used to roam by the thousands were now seen in small pockets scattered on the plains. The white mans' thirst for hides and the thousands of Sioux at the Fort had taken their toll. It was good that most of the Sioux returned to their land.

Two days later, Piapot and his warriors reached Fort Walsh just after the sun was high. Only Sitting Bull and just two or three hundred of his people were at the Fort. Piapot and his warriors rode among them until he found Sitting Bull. They sat cross legged and talked about many things.

"The Canadians want us to return to our land" sitting Bull said.

"You should stay one more year until the sting of Custer's death is forgotten."

"Yes! We did the Canadians a favor when we fought the Yankees! They owe us something for that" Sitting Bull stated.

"The Canadians do not want to feed my people so they will not feed your people much longer."

Piapot spoke with Sitting Bull and left with his warriors when the shadows grew longer. They rode to the top of a slope overlooking the gates as the white police watched them with binoculars from the top of the stockade. They slid from their horses and began gathering wood for the fires. They took turns herding the horses s they grazed while Piapot and several warriors walked down the slope to a flat place where the gathered stones and wood for Piapot's fire. When the stones were put in place and the fire started, the warriors walked back up the hill and left Piapot by himself.

Piapot sat cross legged smoking his pipe and sipping from the small bag.

Before long, Walsh appeared at the top of the stockade and approached his recruits. He took the binoculars and watched Piapot as he sat cross legged by the fire.

"There are only a few warriors. We could kill some of them from here" one of the recruits said.

"Where are you from?" Walsh asked.

"I am from Toronto sir."

"When you are done your hitch, you should get the hell back to Toronto just about as fast as you can!"

"Yes sir" the recruit replied as he looked at his boots.

Walsh turned to his sergeant and ordered him to bring his horse to the gate along with twenty men mounted. Walsh descended from the stockade and headed for his quarters. He returned to the gate carrying a small buckskin bag. Walsh said to his sergeant, "Do not let anyone in or anyone out unless I tell you."

Walsh and the twenty police rode through the gate towards Piapot. At the bottom of the slope, Walsh dismounted and ordered the recruits to remain where they were until he returned.

Walsh walked up the slope carrying his small buckskin bag over his shoulder. When he reached Piapot, he sat down cross legged across from him.

"It has been a long time since we have sat cross legged Chief Piapot" Walsh said to him in Cree.

"You have been very busy with the Sioux."

"I saw you with Sitting Bull. Did you tell him to go home?"

"No."

"Why not? They are killing what is left of the buffalo."

Piapot spoke, "It is not the Sioux that have made the buffalo disappear. The hunters to the south kill the buffalo by the thousands for sport and for hides. They do not eat the meat. The buffalo will disappear from our plains because there will not be enough to travel back and forth from south to north which is their custom. You cannot stop what is happening to the buffalo and neither can I. If the white man kills our buffalo, you kill the nations of the plains. There are no white man's law to stop it so I think you must want it. I told Sitting Bull that he must stay another year until the Yankees forget some of the heat which was caused by killing Custer. I told him I would ask you to feed them for this short time."

Walsh looked at this soft spoken Chief who was known in the east as far as Ottawa and Montreal. He reached into his bag and took out a small bottle of whiskey. He removed the cap and took a big swig.

"I will feed them."

"Why are you leaving the Fort next year?" Piapot asked.

Walsh took another swig and replied, "They want me to leave because I wear too much buckskin and I speak too much Cree." Walsh took another swig. "How did you know I was leaving?"

"My warriors and me have just come from the east" Piapot continued. "I was told in Fort Qu'Appelle by a Frenchman who speaks from both sides of his mouth."

"A lawyer?"

"Yes."

Walsh took another big swig and threw the empty bottle to the ground. He took another small bottle of whiskey from his bag as Piapot put a few logs on the fire.

"This will be the last time we will sit cross legged. Let us share a drink of whiskey" Walsh said.

"I will share a drink of whiskey with you if you will share with me a sip from the small bag."

"What is in that bag?" Walsh asked him with slurred Cree.

"It will bring you the peace you require."

Piapot took the small whiskey bottle and passed the small bag to Walsh. They looked at one another and each took a drink and a sip. They drank and sipped until the shadows grew long.

"Chief Piapot! You have many warriors with repeating rifles and small arms. I think I know where you got them but nobody seems to care and neither do I. Chief Piapots, I mean Chief Piapot" Walsh was drunk. "I know you could burn this Fort and kill us all. What is stopping you?"

Piapot was also drunk and he took a bullet from his belt and showed it to Walsh.

"You see this? You see this? I do not know how to make them but when I do, I will burn your Fort and all the Forts on the plains."

"I believe you" Walsh continued in an even more slurred voice. "You have been to the east and you have whites in your nation both English and French. Why can you not speak English Chief Piapots?"

"Who told you I could not speak English Fort Walsh?"

"I am Superintendent Walsh, not Fort Walsh. Say something in English then."

"Piapot looked straight at Walsh and said to him in English "Superintendent Walsh eats buffalo dung and drinks horse piss."

Walsh was in the middle of a swig and the whiskey shot out of his mouth and he began to cough and could not stop. When he finally stopped coughing, he spoke words of no meaning. "I am an officer of the Queen … I am an officer of the Dominiion … I am an officer of the Queen. You cannot talk to me like that."

Piapot gave the small bag to Walsh and he took a sip. They looked at one another and there was great laughter.

"You son of a bitch! You made me struggle with Cree when you knew English all along. Why do you not speak English then?"

"I will speak English when I feel it is necessary Fort Walsh."

There was much laughter between them.

"Let me tell you this Chief Piapot" Superintendent Walsh continued. "There is something coming to the plains that will change everything. It is made of steel and has steel wheels that travel on a steel trail. It is called a train and it carries settlers, soldiers and ammunition. With it will come wires that speak and nothing will be the same. You must return to your reserve before the train arrives. Because after it arrives, your position will be weakened."

Piapot took a swig and said to Walsh, "I will stop the train."

"I must return to the Fort before they shoot you. This has been my best day on the plains and I wish you well Chief Piapot."

Walsh rose to his feet and began to walk down the slope. His body moved forward but his feet would not keep up. Inspector Walsh tried to stop the speed but could not and fell to the ground rolling for a distance, got up and rolled again. Piapot laughed as the recruits galloped towards Walsh. He told them to stay back as he tried to mount his horse. Every time he tried to put his foot in the stirrup he fell backwards to the ground. The recruits put him on his horse and took him through the gate.

Piapot lost his footing half way up the slope and slid down a ravine into a small bush.

The next morning, as the sun rose, the recruits were at the top of the stockade looking for Piapot and his warriors but they were nowhere to be seen.

Chapter Ten

Piapot Goes to the Mountains

"What you and the builders have done here is bigger and better than anything I have ever seen!"

Piapot and his warriors took much time as they made their way to the mountains. They saw only one small herd of buffalo near the old village and not one more buffalo on the plains.

After six days, they reached the third camp which was left standing. Some of the warriors hunted small game while Piapot and the remainder picked berries and caught several fish for a small feast. There were many pots and bowls left at the third camp which came in handy for cooking and eating.

The Piapot party left early the next morning and reached the fifth camp four days later and to their surprise, there were many from the new village waiting to greet them. There were many who had not met Piapot and reached out to touch him as Three Killer led the Piapot party to the warriors' lodge to take steam.

"This is a very large steam room" Piapot said.

"Wait until you see the one in the village!" Three Killer exclaimed.

"It was wise to leave the last three camps standing" Piapot continued. "We have made good use of them along the way."

"We also make good use of them" Three Killer replied.

After taking steam, the Piapot party changed into new cloth which their women brought for them. Piapot was a buckskin warrior but he could not refuse the cloth. There was much laughter as the warriors complimented each other on how good they looked in their new cloth.

Three Killer took Piapot to a large lodge where they filled their plates with food. As they ate, Piapot asked Three Killer about the food he never tasted before.

Three Killer spoke, "This is cucumber and these are called beets. We grow much more at the first village. When we cleared the forest for timber, the soil was very black and good for growing."

"This meat has a different taste" Piapot continued. "Where did it come from?"

"It came from one of the stolen steers you and the dog warriors delivered to the first camp" Three Killer stated.

There was much laughter from Piapot and the dog warriors.

The next morning everyone got busy cleaning the camp and after loading pack horses, they left for the first village.

As they neared the village three days later, a war party of young children and grandchildren came to greet them. They were all dressed in buckskin with beautiful bead work. Their faces were painted and they had colorful feathers in their hair.

Piapot's heart soared as he dismounted for his grandchildren were among them. The dog warriors and Piapot walked with the children towards the village. When they were just a short distance from the village, the sound of drums could be heard and the children began to dance as the party advanced.

They walked up a gentle slope to a high place where the village came into view. Piapot and his dog warriors were without speech. The village followed the forest line near the mountain rock and stretched as far as the eye could see. In the meadow, two small lakes joined by a small river could be seen. On one side of the lake there were buffalo and on the other side there were cattle.

"What is that very large building in the centre?" Piapot asked.

"It is the great lodge for eating with many rooms attached for the Chiefs who run the village" Three Killer replied.

"I notice that there are many teepees."

"There are still those of us that like our teepees" Three Killer replied with an ear to ear smile.

The party continued to the village. Along the way, Three Killer explained that they would rest and feast for a few days before showing the entire village. Piapot and his dog warriors readily agreed for it was a long ride.

When they reached the village, the dog warriors' women were there to greet them. Piapot's four wives and his sons and daughters came to embrace him and spoke much about how happy they were to see him.

After several days of touring the village, Piapot and Three Killer called a meeting of Chiefs and their councils in the great hall. All the Chiefs arrived from their various locations including Dalton who came from the second village.

"Dalton. What you and the builders have done here is bigger and better than anything I have ever seen!" Piapot exclaimed.

"By the time we finished building five camps, the building of the village was not that difficult. We have the best of the white man's equipment. The steam driven engine we bought before starting the village made it much faster to saw the logs. Also I spoke to the right person in a place called Great Falls who showed a few of us the art of using a thing called dynamite. I will also mention Chief Piapot, that over 400 builders took part in the building of this village and much thanks is given to the hunters and the women who fed us while we worked. Also, the elders cared for our children and showed them the old ways which they must learn and never forget."

There was a silence and then a roar of approval for Dalton's words.

Big Man Walking rose and spoke "All the strong medicine we had on the plains is here in the mountains. We have the Canadian and Yankee money to purchase the white man's medicine but some of it we do not trust. The whiskey we took from the post we did not sell. We have learned how to make it more powerful and use it for cleansing wounds. The pure whiskey is also fuel for the lamp we carry in the food storage caves that have been built into the mountains. In the winter, we have ice from the lake and put them layer on layer into the caves which will allow us to store food in the hot months."

There were nods of approval and Piapot was proud of Big Man Walking and his wife Anne.

Three Killer said to Piapot, "Except for wine, we do not allow the drinking of alcohol in the village".

"Wandering Buffalo. Is this village in the Yankee territory or the Canadian territory?"

"I do not know."

This brought such a roar of laughter that even the women came from the kitchen.

"Does anyone know?" Piapot asked.

"We do not care!" a young councilor exclaimed..

There was another roar of laughter and Piapot said in a loud voice, "That is what I wanted to hear".

After all the Chiefs spoke, everyone left the great hall for the outdoors. Piapot, Dalton and Three Killer walked to a flat place and sat cross legged.

"I must know about the water" Piapot said. "I will have to explain it to the elders when I return to the plains. There are several pools of water with cut stones around them and they are of different depths. I notice that even in the night and early morning the water is always warm. Where does this water come from and how do you keep it warm?"

Dalton spoke "The Creator must have told you to send the nation to the mountains for he has been very good to us Chief Piapot. When we looked for a location for the second village before the building of the first village started, we looked for a hidden canyon just as we did for the first village. A little higher and less than a days ride, we went into a hidden canyon and the air smelled damp as we continued. We came upon a huge flat ledge that overlooked a deep valley and on the ledge were pools of water with much steam. I put my hand in the water and it almost burned me. The water from the hot pools formed a river and ran back into the mountains through a large cave. We followed the large cave and the boiling hot water disappeared under a ledge. We returned to the outside ledge which grew bigger and turned into a meadow that made its way down slowly to the bottom of the canyon and a very big lake with many fish of all kinds. The lake was fed by cold clear streams and not hot water. We followed the lake from one end to the other and there was no river to release the water. We found many small caves near the side of the lake that touched the mountains. When we looked inside the caves we found that the caves were the river's overflow. We knew this because we found water lines on the walls. I immediately sent a young builder to bring back the many builders who broke stone."

"What did the stone breakers have to say?" Piapot asked

"When the stone breakers arrived, they could hardly believe what they saw. I asked them if they could take the hot water to the first village and they all agreed that it would be easy. The plan was easy to understand. The stone breakers' plan was to remove dirt down to rock to form a small pond and build stone walls to keep the dirt out. They decided they would build two stone arches leading from the bottom of the large pond. The two arches dug down below the level of the pond would take boiling hot water to the first and second village."

"How long did this take?" Piapot asked.

Dalton continued "It took every stone breaker and over 400 young and old warriors all summer to build stone arches to the first village."

"How did you get the water into the stone pond?"

"We dug a trench from the large pond to where the hot water entered the cave. When the stone breakers arched the trench with stone, we were ready to dynamite the distance between the trench and the river. When this was done all the boiling hot water ran to the large pond and then underground to the first village. We installed what the white man calls a valve on each hot water line that leads to the buildings and the pools from the large holding pond behind the buildings. There is a large valve located at the holding pond which can turn off the hot water whenever we want. This is necessary for repairs and bringing hot water to a new building. The same thing is done with the cold water trench. Both trenches are covered with dirt higher than two buffalo horses in order to keep the cold water from freezing and the hot water boiling hot. The small pipes which lead to each building and pool can be turned off and on in order to make the water as cold or hot as you want."

"Where does everything go when we use the small stalls that are in each building?" Piapot asked.

"This is another line called a sewer line which runs downhill to a place where you don't want to go" Dalton explained.

Piapot shook his head and laughed.

"How hot can you make that small pool?" Piapot asked.

"As hot as you want" Three Killer replied.

"Good! Turn on the hot water for I must sit in the water. There is dynamite in my head."

After Three Killer turned on the hot water, they took off their cloth and sat in the small pool laughing and talking until the women came and told them it was time to eat.

For the next few days, Piapot and the Chiefs walked through the second village. The beauty of the valley below made Piapot just want to stand in one place and look down all day. Piapot viewed the boiling hot water pools that had trenches leading to the hot water holding pond which fed the water to both villages. The upper ledge ran down gently to a ledge so huge it turned into a meadow of trees and grass. As they walked along the huge ledge, there were many small caves where the young warriors lived. The front of the small caves were built up with stone, a wood door and windows.

"The buck warriors fight over these caves" Big Man Walking continued. "We built on the lower ledge in order to supply hot and cold water."

"I can see that for a young warrior, this would be a new and desired place to live" Piapot replied.

Beth, Chief councilor for education spoke "Each child in the first village must learn to read, write and know how to use the white man's numbers and be 18 years on the calendar before they are allowed to live in buck warrior village. Also, they must have great wilderness skills for they do not eat in the big village except on special days. The young maidens must also be 18 years and have the same education and wilderness skills as the buck warriors."

Three Killer spoke, "In the buck warrior village, there is also one chief and eight warriors and their wives who live here at all times."

Piapot asked about the caves where the buck warriors lived and was taken into one of them. There was a beautiful wood floor decorated with skins and several beds made of wood. The cave had a stall and a rock basin for washing. From the front construction entrance the valley and mountains could be seen for miles. There was a small fireplace for cooking and warmth.

Piapot exclaimed "I wish I could have lived here when I was a buck warrior!

With much laughter, Piapot and the Chiefs were proud of the buck warrior village and showed Piapot the bulding where the game was prepared for the kitchen and many other buildings used for shoeing horses, storing weapons and ammunition, barns and corrals for the horses and a building for hand to hand fighting.

When it was almost time to eat, the Piapot party entered the great hall. It was magnificent with many doors leading into rooms from the great hall. There was a room for warriors, young maidens and women, education and strong medicine, Chief and councilors, a men's room with stalls and a women's room with stalls.

There was a door on each side of the kitchen that led to individual sleeping rooms for those who required them. There were two doors to the rear of the kitchen where food was bought in for storage from the connected room where meat was prepared and a door from the connected room where the fruit and vegetables were stored and the wine was prepared.

"The storage cave is so large and goes into the mountain so far that we have not been to the end of it yet? Beth said.

"I noticed that the walls of the cave I saw were smooth as skin" Piapot said.

"Yes. We believe that water ran through them many years ago and smoothed the rocks" Beth explained.

It was time to eat and the Piapot party took seats in the great hall. When the elders were finished taking their plates of food, the Piapot party took plates and helped themselves to the fine food prepared entirely by the young maidens. Piapot was impressed and ate heartily.

"Tell me Chief Wandering Buffalo. Where does the nation get the money to buy the white man's tools?"

"With our new saws driven by steam, we are able to sell timber north and south. Also, we grow more potatoes than we need and these we sell to the trading post in a place called Lethbridge. We have spent very little of the money we received five years ago and will soon add to it and have more than when we started" Wandering Buffalo continued.

"In the village, it is the custom for the elders to take the boys under fifteen up the streams to pan for the white man's gold. They take no food. The rifles they carry are used only for protection and not for hunting. The children learn wilderness skills and when they get a piece of gold in their pan, I am sure they can be heard back at Fort Walsh."

Wandering Buffalo continued above the laughter. "This is done in the summer months and one month in the winter in order to learn winter skills. Except for that one month, Chief Beth and her councilors teach the children from November 1st on the calendar until April 1st on the calendar."

"Yes and when they become eighteen years on the calendar, they come here to the young warriors village" Piapot added.

"That is right" Wandering Buffalo continue. "And the reason I speak of panning for gold is because much to our pleasure, the children and elders pan enough gold to more than pay for all the books and everything else that is needed to teach."

Three Killer added, "Also, in the winter, we take wagon loads of fish north and south. The store owners sell as much fish as we can bring them."

"Wandering Buffalo, where is the wealth for those who work?" Piapot asked.

"The nation has pulled together like teams of horses but now that the nation is strong in the mountains, we will on the first day of January on the calendar, pay the workers eighteen years of age good money. There will be two kinds of workers. Those who work in the village and those who work to sell. Those who labor for the village such as builders, women who feed us, the women who sew cloth, those who herd animals, teachers, hunters, growers and many more, will receive $2.00 per day for themselves. Those who provide timber for the nation and sell timber north and south will also make two dollars per day or fifty percent of what they sell to divide among themselves. It will be the same for anyone who sells. The nation will provide all things needed to produce and haul whatever is being sold. Those who sell will use some of the nation's money to purchase items that are not made in the mountains. These items will be put into the nation's store for our people to purchase. The store will have much cloth, guitars, violins, knives and much more."

"Fifty percent is half?" Piapot asked.

"Yes" Wandering Buffalo replied. "This may be too much or too little. We will not know until the end of each year. One thing we know, money must come into the nation for us to keep up with the Canadians and Yankees."

Beth spoke "Chief Piapot! Your two daughters are in the east learning music. When they return, they will give us great music from what are called pianos and organs. They will be valuable music teachers for the nation and this is money well spent."

"And this is more valuable than buffalo horses?" Piapot asked.

There was a tremendous roar of laughter as the Chiefs raised their wooden cups and took a drink of wine.

Winter was just around the corner so for the next few weeks, Piapot went panning for gold with the elders and grandchildren. When they returned, the young gold panners had many nuggets for Wandering Buffalo and it was almost time for school.

Piapot said to Wandering Buffalo, "This was the best time I have had in years and you are right these nuggets will bring in much money!"

Two winters passed and by the end of the second winter, Piapot shook the hand of everyone in the two villages and knew most of them by name. One of the big things Piapot noticed was that the winters were not as cold or lasting as the winters on the plains. Within a few steps, there was shelter everywhere. The buffalo and cattle in the meadows grew in numbers and there was an abundance of wild game, birds and fish.

In the first week of May, 1881 Piapot held a meeting with the Chiefs and told them he would leave the mountains August 1st on the calendar.

Chapter Eleven

Piapot Days

"I am not Chief of Chiefs for nothing!"

Without Piapot knowing, Three Killer and the Chief councilors began to organize what would be called Chief Piapot Days. Every year on the calendar, for seven days beginning the second Monday in July and lasting until Sunday in the evening, there would be feasting and tests of skill to honor their great Chief. It was agreed by all the Chiefs that Beth would be in charge.

After a few days, Beth sent for Three Killer and spoke with him. "It would please me and my assistants if Chief Piapot was not in the village until the second Monday in July. Piapot's two daughters, who returned from the east five days ago and are hidden in the fifth camp, could come to the village and practice their music."

"The piano and organ. Are they here?" Three Killer asked.

"No, they are not here yet but they will be soon. Two scouts have returned from the south and have reported that the two wagon loads of timber have been delivered and the piano and organ loaded. They will be here in less than two days" one of Beth's councillors stated.

"It is June 14 on the calendar" Three Killer continued. "I will ask Piapot if he would like to take our grandchildren on one last wilderness trip for gold."

"That is a great idea!" Beth exclaimed.

"I am not Chief of Chiefs for nothing!"

There was great laughter among them.

Three Killer left and found Piapot swimming in the large warriors pool with a few elders and several Chiefs. Three Killer left his cloth in the change lodge and joined them in the warm water with a belly flop which brought much laughter from everyone.

After their swim, Three Killer mentioned the wilderness trip and panning for gold with their grandchildren. Piapot thought it would be a good way to end his stay in the mountains. Three Killer and Piapot told their grandchildren between ten and eighteen years of age to get ready for the wilderness trip. The children were very excited and the next morning Three Killer, Piapot and four warriors left with the grandchildren for the mountain streams. They took with them four pack horses.

The piano and organ soon arrived and Piapot's two daughters, Josephine and Roseanne, came from the fifth camp to the village. They were surprised with how much bigger the camp had become. They especially liked the store that was owned and operated by the nation. Anne, the wife of Big Man Walking, gave them ten dollars each for Piapot days. Anne informed the daughters that their children went to the streams to pan for gold and the husbands were with them.

"Our husbands and children will be surprised to see us" Josephine said.

"Yes, so will your father" Anne replied.

Piapot's daughters thanked Anne for the ten dollars and left for the store. They were well amazed when they went inside and saw all the goods that were for sale. There was a section for women that had just about all the things women needed such as paint, personal health items that came in small boxes and much clothing, both buckskin and cloth, the white man's shoes, moccasins, hats, jewelry, cloth for making clothes, sewing supplies and much more.

"Where did you get all goods?" Roseanne asked.

"All the clothing is made by the women in the village. They sell to us and we sell to you." one of the assistants answered.

"There is a section for men and children as well" Roseanne said.

"Yes. The men like to buy the white man's pocket watches and gold chains" another assistant added.

"I like the toys and cradles" Josephine stated.

"The sales are a little slow. Everyone is working hard and saving their money for Piapot Days" the operator stated.

After buying much clothing and essentials, the girls walked to the women's lodge to clean up and change into their new clothes. Josephine bought buckskin and Roseanne bought cloth.

The freighters had placed the organ and piano underneath the overhang on the planks outside the great hall and covered them with the white man's canvass. When the girls arrived, the canvass was removed, and they began to play. Many in the village had never heard this kind of music as they gathered to listen and look at one another with dismay. There was much whooping and hollering as the girls played classical and step dancing tunes.

On the practice range, the top ten shooters in the village were shooting targets from various distances with colts and repeating rifles. Cathy, the daughter of Victoria, who was seventeen years old, was among them. She was a little taller than her mother and had black hair, blue eyes and fair skin.

Joseph spoke, "Slow it down a little Cathy. You are very fast but your accuracy has to match your speed. Give one a chance to catch up with the other and you will soon be fast and accurate."

Cathy holstered her colts and said to Joseph, "Thank you father. You are a great teacher and I will be ready for Piapot Days."

Joseph smiled and left for the rifle range to practice with Victoria. They both were among the top ten with repeating rifles and they would compete on Piapot Days.

For the next few weeks, the village was busy getting ready for Piapot Days. The competitions would include everything from horse training to timber sawing.

The wilderness party was having good days. The wild game and fish were plentiful and the children were finding color in their pans. They whooped and hollered every time a little color appeared in their pan. One of the warriors, who was in charge of panning, would slip a little color in a pan to make sure they all found a little gold.

"These have been good days. If I stayed another year, I do not think I would ever leave" Piapot stated.

"Why not stay Chief Piapot?" one of the warriors asked.

"I want the nation to have a choice of two homes."

Three Killer spoke "We have asked several of those who are fair to move near the white man's towns to operate stores to sell what we make and there is very little interest. The nation has offered to build the stores and give those who work there half of what comes to the top. Wandering Buffalo has even told them that they could buy the stores at their value at any time."

"This will change when the white man's villages grow big like those in the east" Piapot said.

It was almost the second Monday in July when the Piapot party left the streams for the village. Three Killer sent two warriors ahead to prepare for Piapot's return. A short distance from the village, Piapot heard strange music which caused him to ride a little faster. He saw two girls playing magnificent music and he knew it was his daughters. As he arrived on the planks, his daughters came to embrace him.

Piapot pointed to the piano and organ and exclaimed "This is much better than buffalo horses!"

There was a roar of laughter from the crowd and even though Josephine and Roseanne did not quite understand, they thought it was humorous and laughed along with them. The girl's children and husbands soon arrived and there were many more hugs and tears.

Piapot spoke with a young warrior in the crowd and asked him what all the commotion was in the village. When the young warrior told him what it was all about, Piapot did not know what to say. Beth soon found Piapot and explained further.

"We have put these days together because you are the Chief of the nation and when you leave the mountains, we may never see you again" Beth stated.

"It will be a good memory for me and I will have much to tell the elders when I return to the plains."

"Tomorrow is Monday and your grandson, Adam, competes in horse training" Beth said.

"I will be there!" Piapot exclaimed.

The Monday horse training competition was won by Broken Wing with Adam coming in second. Piapot was proud of Adam and told him so.

In the days that followed there were many competitions.

"It is Saturday on the calendar and the gun competition is the day for which I have been waiting" Piapot stated.

Piapot, the Chiefs and their assistants all walked to the gun range where they sat cross legged and waited for the competition to begin.

The quick draw colt and rifle shooters each had 16 shooters that won in eliminations during the week.

The target was brought out from the forge and the steel post was placed into a greased canister like container. Two three foot pieces of steel were welded on both sides of the post like arms. The thick steel target which was welded to the end of each arm was twelve inches in diameter and five feet off the ground. Whoever hit the target first would cause the target to spin in the direction of their opponent and lock. If the target was just nicked and did not make the half turn, the opponents would shoot again.

Chief Wandering Buffalo and his assistants arrived to explain the betting and how much the competitors would receive as they did in all the competitions.

A young assistant spoke "The first eight shooters who are eliminated will collect one dollar each. The four shooters eliminated from the second round collect two dollars each. The two shooters eliminated from the third round will receive three dollars each and the two finalists will be paid five and ten dollars. The payout to the pistol and rifle shooters will be the same. The final will be two out of three for both the rifles and colts."

Another young assistant, who knew numbers, spoke to those who wished to make a bet. "The rules are simple. The nation has decided who is best to win. On a dollar bet, you will collect one dollar and fifty cents if a great shooter such as Dalton wins and as much as twenty dollars, if Cathy wins. The names of the shooters, both rifle and pistol, are written here on this paper and it shows you what you could collect on a dollar bet. This paper you can see on the boards throughout the village. After the first round, there will be only one more bet on the remaining eight and the amount you could win on a one dollar bet are cut in half. You may bet as little as one dollar."

"Do we win anything after the first round?" a young person asked.

"No. Only after the second round when a winner is named" another assistant explained.

"Is everything the same for the rifles?" someone asked.

"Yes" the assistant replied.

"How much can we bet?" a young builder asked.

"As much as you can pack" Wandering Buffalo shouted.

There was a roar of laughter.

The young assistant continued. "The rifle 'shoot-out' will begin in almost one hour when the little arrow is at ten on the clock. There are several assistants here and at the store who will take your bet. If you want to bet, then you better get started."

Most of the women went to the store to make their bets.

"This piece of paper has a ticket number, a shooter number and the amount of your bet" the young assistant continued. "You will need this piece of paper to collect".

"I understand" the young woman stated.

"Grandfather, we are collecting coins to bet on Cathy."

"Here is twenty-five cents" Piapot said.

Piapot's grandchild ran off with his friends to raise another seventy-five cents.

Everyone made their bets before the little hand reached ten and the "shoot-out" began. Just before the little hand reached twelve, the first round was over. Victoria was among the eight rifle winners and her daughter Cathy was among the eight pistol winners.

An assistant spoke, "The shooting will start again when the little hand reaches two. The rifle shooters will be moved back thirty paces and the pistol shooters will be moved back fifteen paces. For those who wish to make a final bet, you have until the little hand reaches two."

Most of the Chiefs and assistants left for the planks outside the great hall where sellers were cooking different foods. Piapot paid twenty-five cents for a large bowl of stew and two bannock biscuits which was his favourite dish. Three Killer paid fifty cents for a large plate of baked trout, wild nuts, berries and fried potatoes.

At two on the big clock, the rifle shooters drew names from a little wooden box as the target was moved back thirty paces. It did not take long to get the rifle finalist down to four. Victoria was among the four but Joseph lost to Alexander. The four drew names and Victoria would shoot first against Raincloud and Alexander would shoot against Wandering Buffalo. When it was over, the two finalists were Raincloud and Wandering buffalo. Three Killer reached into his pouch and drew out his ticket. He looked at Piapot and tore it in four pieces.

"Who did you have?" Piapot asked.

"Victoria" Three Killer replied.

"Who have you got?"

"I have the winner. I have Wandering Buffalo!"

"How much did you bet?"

"I bet two dollars. If he wins, the nation will owe me six dollars. I bet Wandering Buffalo on the second round."

The entire village was whooping and hollering as the finalists sat cross legged with their rifles held crossways in front of them. An assistant hit down hard on the large drum. The shooters moved to one knee and fired. Wandering Buffalo hit the target with his second shot spinning it half way around.

Piapot jumped to his feet whooping and hollering. "One more time! One more time!" Piapot shouted.

The shooters loaded their rifles and waited for the drum. At the sound of the drum, the shooters moved to one knee and fired. Raincloud hit the target with his first shot but only nicked it and the target did not move to the half way stop. There were moans and groans from the crowd as the shooters reloaded. At the sound of the drum, Raincloud moved swiftly and missed with his first shot. Wandering Buffalo, who moved just a little slower, fired and spun the target to the lock position.

There were cheers from the crowd as Beth ran forward and hugged Wandering Buffalo.

"I am rich!" Piapot shouted as he did a little war dance.

The young assistant shouted above the crowd "Let the rifle shooters and winning betters come forward and collect your money. The pistol 'shout-out' will start at four on the big clock."

I bet a dollar and so did Anne!" Beth exclaimed.

"On the first round?" Wandering Buffalo asked with a loud laugh.

"Yes!" Beth shouted above the crowd. "The nation owes twelve dollars."

Wandering Buffalo turned to Raincloud. "You are a great shooter. If I did not take my time, I would not have beat you."

Wandering Buffalo gave Raincloud a shoulder hug as they went to collect their money.

"It is good to see Wandering Buffalo win. He has been a good warrior for our nation" Three Killer said.

Piapot looked at Three Killer and could see the lines of age on his face.

"So have you" Piapot continued. "Let us get a mug of wine and bannock biscuits. I am going to buy."

As they walked through the crowd, there was great celebrating. Even the ones tearing up their tickets were enjoying themselves. Music filled the air with the sound of drums and guitars. The girls entertained on the planks and there was much dancing.

A young assistant spoke from the planks, "The target has been moved and the pistol 'shoot-out' is about to begin."

Dalton removed his waist pistol that he used in the first round and hung it on the end of a bench near the Chiefs and elders.

"I have some money on you Chief Dalton" one of the elders said.

Dalton spoke "Do not count your money yet. I can outdraw and kill just about anybody with my waist pistol but the targets have been moved back fifteen paces. I will have to draw from the leg for accuracy."

The shooters drew names and when the second round was over, Dalton and Cathy were among the four remaining.

In the third round, Dalton was outdrawn but won with accuracy.

When Cathy came to shoot, the assistant had to quiet the crowd.

Strong Eagle, the grandson of Grey Owl, named after Chief Strong Eagle, said to Cathy "You had better win for I fear they will take my hair."

There was laughter between them as they turned and faced the target.

On the sound of the drum, Cathy hit the target with her first shot and the young crowd roared. Torn up tickets flew in the air as several assistants came forward to move the young crowd from the shooting range.

When the young crowd was moved back, Dalton and Cathy took their place for the two out of three final.

The drum sounded and Dalton hit the target with his first shot. Cathy nicked it with her second shot but not enough to stop it from moving slowly half way around. There were cheers and moans from the crowd.

On the second try, Cathy hit the target with her second shot and spun it around with the sound of steel on steel. The roar from the young crowd drowned out Piapot and his party as they encouraged Dalton.

On the third try, Dalton hit the target with his first shot and Cathy hit it with her second shot. Dalton moved the target toward Cathy but not enough. This time, scouts on horseback came in to clear the crowd.

"I think he moved it half way!" Three Killer exclaimed.

"We wish he moved it half way!" an elder stated.

Cathy took a doe skin glove from her belt and put it on her left hand. The glove fit skin tight.

On the sound of the drum, Cathy drew with blazing speed and fanning her pistol with her left hand. Dalton hit the target but Cathy hit it twice driving the steel target against the steel lock.

It took the scouts and assistants almost half an hour to settle the crowd.

On their way to the planks, Piapot and Three Killer ran into Dalton and his wife.

"Why did you not put the glove on your hand like Cathy? You taught the nation how to do it!" Three Killer exclaimed.

"I guess I should have but did you hear the excitement from our young people."

"I heard a pack of wild animals!" Three Killer exclaimed. This brought much laughter as they departed.

Dalton and his wife walked to where Cathy was talking with her mother and father. Dalton congratulated Cathy and gave her a shoulder hug.

"We won twenty dollars. What a daughter!" Joseph exclaimed.

"I won five dollars. Let us go to the planks for rancher's steak and roast potatoes" Dalton said.

The two left the women to talk as they walked through the crowd to the planks.

"Grandfather, my friends and me won over four dollars each! Here is your quarter. Do you need some money grandfather?!"

"Yes. I could use maybe two dollars" Piapot said.

Piapot took the two dollars and watched him and his friends run to the store.

"I will give him back his two dollars before I leave" Piapot said.

"That is wise" one of the elders stated

Piapot said to Three Killer "Tonight we will celebrate but tomorrow I wish to meet all of the Chiefs in the Chiefs' room after church and dinner is over."

"This will be done Chief Piapot" Three Killer replied.

Chapter Twelve

Piapot Speaks to the Nation

"When there are days of hunger and darkness and you do not feel there is anything to thank the Creator for – thank him for the air you breathe."

On Monday afternoon, the Chiefs proceeded to the great hall. Piapot explained that he would return to his reserve near the Qu'Appelle Valley in 1882 to establish rights to the land. Piapot explained further that in the spring of 1883 on the calendar, he would, along with other Chiefs, including Big Bear and Poundmaker, try to sign a new treaty and receive land near the Cypress Hills. Piapot told them that if this failed, he would travel east with the elders to take the land which was given under Treaty Four that he signed in 1875 and the village would be informed regarding the nation's location. Also, those who wanted could travel to the new location but he urged everyone, as he said before, to stay in the mountains until the Canadians intentions were clear.

"What about education at the new location?" Beth asked.

"Those who leave the mountains should not leave with children." Piapot continued, "In the east, the children are taken away and forced to be schooled by those who wear the cross."

After a lengthy meeting and many questions, the Chiefs retired to the great hall. Piapot asked Joseph, Wandering Buffalo, Three Killer and Dalton to remain.

Piapot spoke "I will need a family of four, who are fair to ride to Fort Qu'Appelle. They will stay with the McDonalds and wear the white mans' cloth." Piapot continued "Chief Joseph, your wife and daughter Cathy could be part of the family. You will not be far from your family for you will choose fifty killers and ride with us as well. Wandering Buffalo, your son William is also fair. We will meet here tomorrow for a decision. I am asking you to ride as well Chief Dalton."

"These issues will be decided by tomorrow Chief Piapot" Wandering Buffalo continued. "I can tell you now that my son will ride."

"And I will be riding also" Dalton added.

"I will speak with Victoria and Cathy but I think I would have a problem stopping them" Joseph stated.

There was much laughter and Piapot told them to bring the women to the meeting tomorrow at the same time if they were riding.

On Tuesday, Wandering Buffalo, Three Killer, William, Dalton and the girls met Piapot at the great hall and went into the Chief's meeting room.

"Do we have a family of four?" Piapot asked.

"Yes we do" Dalton answered.

Three Killer spoke, "Two scouts have returned from Wood Mountain. Just about all of the Sioux have returned to their reserves. Sitting Bull and the rest will leave soon. Inspector Walsh has been sent to For Qu'Appelle. Also, there is much talk about the Canadian railroad that is coming west from a place called Winnipeg."

"The railroad is what will kill the bargaining." Piapot continued "Walsh told me it was coming and it would make the Canadians strong. He is in Fort Qu'Appelle because he speaks too much Cree and wears too much buckskin."

"When will you know about the nations new location?" Wandering Buffalo asked.

"We will know early in the spring of 1883." Piapot replied.

"When will you need the fifty warriors and the family?" Dalton asked.

"I will need twenty-five warriors when I leave. I do not know the condition of the elders or how much repair is needed in the village so it will be necessary to take pemmican and medicine. Also I have no intentions of spending a winter on the reserve. Be sure to include the two stone breakers for we will build a village in the Qu'Appelle valley."

"The pemmican and medicine will be taken care of by Chief Big Man Walking" Three Killer stated.

"How much money will you need Chief Piapot" Wandering Buffalo asked.

"How much can you give?" Piapot said with a smile.

"How much can you pack?" Wandering Buffalo shouted.

This brought well needed belly laughs from everyone.

"Give each rider ten dollars." Piapot continued "Early in the spring, I will need the family and twenty-five more warriors."

"I will be eighteen by then and living in the second village with the fellas!" Cathy exclaimed.

"Cathy!" Victoria scolded.

"Fellas?" Piapot asked.

"Buck warriors" Joseph answered.

Piapot smiled for he admired the girl's boldness.

"Where will we meet you?" Victoria asked.

"The family will ride to Fort Qu'Appelle and live with the McDonalds. I will send the twenty-five warriors and they will tell them you are coming." Piapot continued "You can wear the buckskins when you ride but when you arrive at the McDonalds' you must always wear the best cloth. The family will be the eyes and ears of the nation."

Wandering Buffalo spoke "The village will provide the finest cloth and the white man's carrying bags."

Dalton added, "We will bring dynamite for it may be needed. When we reach the McDonalds', we will put our weapons and dynamite in each of our carrying bags so everything will be out of sight."

"Yes" Piapot said.

"Am I riding with the last twenty-five warriors?" Joseph asked.

"Yes" Piapot answered. "You and your warriors will ride with the family to Fort Qu'Appelle and meet the other warriors. They will be in the valley with the Muskopeeting and the Saulteaux."

"We will send more money if you need it" Wandering Buffalo stated.

After a few more questions, the meeting ended. Piapot and Three Killer stayed in the great hall for a little wine and biscuits and were joined by several elders.

Early the next morning, Piapot sent for Big Man walking. When he arrived, Piapot told him he wanted two warriors with strong medicine and food sent to the Piapot village.

In the afternoon, Big Man Walking reported to Piapot. "I have seven warriors and five pack horses ready for loading. Two of the warriors have strong medicine and will know the elder's needs."

"You have done this in good time. Send them in the morning." Piapot said.

"This will be done Chief Piapot"

The month of July was passing quickly and it was the last Sunday in July on the calendar.

"I said I would leave on August 1st but I will leave early tomorrow morning" Piapot said.

"I will prepare the twenty-five warriors" Joseph stated as he left for the warriors' lodge.

Just before Church, Beth approached Piapot and asked him if he would speak to the nation after Church. Piapot told her he would be pleased to say a few words.

The village heard that Piapot would speak and everyone who was not in the kitchens were in front of the planks. There were hundreds of people waiting for their Chief to speak. The elders sat cross legged close to the planks, others stood behind the elders and hundreds sat cross legged on the two high places to the west and east. Even the mothers and fathers were sitting with their children on the edge of the pools.

Beth said a very short prayer and asked Piapot to come forward.

"For the two years I have spent in the mountains, each day has brought great enjoyment. The Chief Piapot Days held in my honor I will never forget. I know there was much planning and many people worked very hard." Piapot paused and said with a smile, "But I deserved it!"

There was a roar of laughter. Some fell over, and rolled on the grass. The crowd shouted "Chief Piapot! Chief Piapot!"

When the laughter and chanting subsided, Piapot continued "I have sat many Sundays in the Christian Church and listened to Chief Beth and her assistants read from the black book. Many in the nation have asked me what I think of the gospel of Jesus Christ. Let me tell you this! If you find a trail that leads you to the Creator – take it!"

Beth wept openly and tears streamed down her face.

"In the Assiniboine nation, everyday is Creator day. No matter where you are, there is always a quiet place where you can sit cross legged and thank the Creator for his abundance. When there are days of hunger and darkness and you do not feel there is anything to thank the Creator for - thank him for the air you breath.

Over the years, many of the English and French tongue have joined our nation. Chief Beth and her daughter Anne followed us home because they wanted to go east but they have remained and have given us much. Chief Dalton made men out of six boys when he would not back down from eight Cree renegades. I cannot say enough about the girls who followed my dog warriors home from the east. Girls like Annette and Madeline who have given our nation the gift of music. Raincloud, the Great Sioux warrior, has laid his life on the line for the nation. He brought us his sister and her children, and Victoria and Cathy.

I will tell you this, those among you who are French or English and those of you who are from the Sioux and the Cree nations are Assiniboines and I am proud to be your Chief."

Those who were sitting cross legged rose to their feet and tried to make their way to the planks as the crowd shouted Chief Piapot's name.

Piapot raised his hand and spoke, "Many of the young who I panned for gold with spoke of the forts they visited and the white man's flags. They asked why we did not have a flag for our nation. Today I am going to give the nation a flag.

When I was a small boy of three years, the Sioux captured me and my grandmother. I was sixteen years old when Chief Strong Eagle and the mighty warrior scout Grey Owl rescued us. Grey Owl brought two magnificent buffalo horses and led us through a small hole in a wall of fire that was set to hold back the Sioux. We rode several days to the old village and I was given gifts from the nation."

Three Killer handed Piapot a jacket.

"This jacket is one of the gifts. It was made by the elder women and Three Killer's wife. I have kept this jacket with me almost fifty years. It has two red flames against a black sky with two tiny yellow stars between the flames. It was a gift to remind me that sometimes we must ride through fire and feel the heat in order to find freedom.

The white man is on the plains and in the years to come we must ride through the fire and feel the heat. I give you this jacket for your flag. I am Chief Piapot and I have spoken!"

There was a deafening roar from the crowd and eyes filed with tears as Three Killer tied the jacket to a post.

When the crowd quieted down, Piapot visited his wife Anne. "You and my other two wives are young. The three of you are free to find warriors for I will not be back." There was sadness as she watched him leave.

Piapot found his grandson and spoke with him. "There will be much celebrating today. Here is the two dollars you loaned me."

Piapot watched him run to the store.

As he walked to the great hall, Piapot saw many young people looking at his jacket. Dalton and Three Killer came and walked beside him.

Shortly before noon the next day, Piapot and his eighteen killers left the village. Two stone breakers with dynamite were among the eighteen.

Chapter Thirteen

Piapot Returns to the Plains

"It was the summer of 1881 and Piapot was back on the plains."

It took twelve days to reach the old strong Eagle Village. They rode up the east side of the ravine passing the landings where the old warriors hung in the trees. They raised their repeating rifles in respect each time they rode past a landing.

When they reached the top of the ravine, Piapot stopped to observe the beauty of the plains before him. Piapot turned his buffalo horse and faced the dog warriors. He danced his horse from one side to the other then turned and drove for his village.

It was the summer of 1881 and Pipaot was back on the plains.

They neared the Piapot village in two days and a scout came to greet them.

"We have been expecting you Piapot!" Strong Eagle exclaimed.

"I would have been here yesterday but we stopped to kill the only four buffalo we saw on the plains. I would have left them but wolves were close by and they would have been eaten alive!" Piapot exclaimed.

"It will be good for the village to have a buffalo feast. We have been hunting only small game" Strong Eagle said.

As they rode into the village, Piapot went immediately to speak with the warriors who had strong medicine. They told Piapot that the elders were in good shape except for the usual weaknesses.

Two Horns came forward with several council members and greeted Piapot. "It is good to see you and the dog warriors."

"It was a long ride and it is good to be back on the plains."

Two Horns reported that eight elders passed and were placed in the trees. Also, there was money left as the women traded much cloth to the whites at Fort Walsh. He thanked Piapot for bringing the buffalo meat.

Piapot walked down to the river for a swim with the warriors. While they were in the water, the women brought them the white man's under cloth and doeskin for drying. They gathered up the young warriors cloth for cleaning.

After a good swim, the Piapot party put on clean cloth and walked up the hill to feast.

"You came at a good time, we have new potatoes and corn!" Little Calf exclaimed.

"Fried potatoes and buffalo steak for me" Piapot said.

After the feast, the young riders cleaned their weapons and lit several small fires. The elders gathered in small groups and Piapot visited each group answering their questions which were mostly about the mountains and where they would locate.

"Chief Piapot. Will we be going east?" an elder asked.

"We will know in the spring of 1883 on the calendar" Piapot answered.

"The young warriors have told us much about the mountains. But we would like to see how the dynamite works" Little Calf stated.

"Tomorrow I will ask the stone breakers to show you how the dynamite works."

When clean-up was over, the women walked among the young warriors and listened to their music and singing.

In the morning, the elders took Piapot down to the garden and showed him a very large stone

"This stone we could not move with three horses" an elder said.

"David! Do you think you and Benjamin can get this stone out of here?" Piapot asked.

"Yes! We will blast it into the lake" David replied.

The two stone breakers dug down behind the stone and placed one stick of dynamite with a long fuse underneath the very large stone.

"Move to the top of the banks" David ordered.

Benjamin lit the fuse and the two stone breakers scrambled up the banks. Within seconds, a large blast was heard and the stone was blown apart sending the pieces flying into the lake.

The elders whooped and hollered as they gathered around the stone breakers. The stone breakers told the elders that for war, the enemy could be destroyed from a distance.

"Show us!" the elders shouted.

The stone breakers looked at Piapot, who nodded his head. The stone breakers went to the pack horses and came back with a strong bow and long arrows. Benjamin tied a stick of dynamite to the arrow with sinew. The sinew was tied to both of the ends of the dynamite and fit into two very small nicks in order to secure the dynamite and allow the arrow to pass over the bow without resistance.

The crowd followed the stone breakers along the banks until they came to a very tall dead tree. Benjamin lit the short fuse as David drew back the arrow and let the dynamite fly. The arrow hit the bottom of the tree and the dynamite exploded bringing the tree to the ground with a thud.

Once again the crowd went wild. The elders gave the stone breakers shoulder hugs and even Piapot whooped and hollered for he had not seen it before.

"How did you know how long of a fuse to use?" Piapot asked.

"We have practiced this many times" Bemjamin replied.

After the celebrations, the young warriors left in different directions to bring in wood for winter. Piapot and the elders went to the garden to gather in the vegetables.

"Big Bear was here" an elder stated.

"What did he want/?" Piapot asked.

"He wanted to know where you were and when you would be back." The elder continued, "He said Poundmaker and several Chiefs have returned to their reserves".

"I knew Big Bear would be last to leave" Piapot said.

"He said he would meet with you when the snow melts. We gave him several bags of potatoes left from last year and he was happy to get them" the elder added.

Piapot and his council walked up river to pull nets. They discussed the nations business as they gathered fish to put into the holding pens.

The winter passed with only two elders being put in the trees.

When the snow melted, Piapot sent two scouts to tell Big Bear that he would leave immediately to Fort Walsh and to meet him there. Piapot put on old buckskins and ordered his warriors to leave their weapons in the warriors' lodge before riding. Several warriors remained behind to train the twenty or more two year olds to the saddle as they would soon turn three and old enough to ride.

Big Bear and several Chiefs rose to their feet as Piapot and his warriors approached. They were happy to see each other and after much laughter, they sat cross legged to discuss the much desired confederation of nations.

Piapot said to the Chiefs, "I have travelled half my life in the east where you have not been. The white man is gathered below the big lakes in huge numbers and will soon have a railroad to bring them here and further west. Inspector Walsh told me several years ago to make the best deal I could before the railroad arrived. I should have taken his advice and so should have you"

Big Bear looked to the ground before he raised his head and spoke, "I do not like to hear you speak these things Chief Piapot. There are many things I do not like. I do not like the needless slaughter of the buffalo. I do not like to beg for food. I do not like to be caged and treated as an animal. Most of all, I do not like the way the young recruits look at us like we are people of no value."

"This is to be expected for they did not know us when we asked for nothing" Piapot continued. "I am going to my reserve and will return in 1883 to try one more time for a reserve here in the Cypress Hills." The chiefs agreed to return in the spring of 1883.

"Bring Poundmaker with you. Maybe he can put them to sleep" Piapot said.

The chiefs laughed and left in different directions

Piapot returned to the village and spoke with his council. It was agreed that Piapot should travel west to the reserve near Fort Qu'Appelle and more or less establish occupation.

"I have no intentions of staying on that reserve but I need a place to camp until a village is built in the Qu'Appelle valley." Paipot continued "Joseph and Dalton will be here soon. Tell Joseph to leave two scouts with you in case they are needed. Also, have them bring the two year olds for trade or gifts. Give them anything else you will not use. Do you have enough money?"

"Yes, we have all we need until next year" Two Horns continued. "The women have made much cloth and we will give them what we do not need. Also, there is much wine."

"Send the wine!" Piapot exclaimed.

The next morning, Piapot took four riders east and left the remainder to wait for Dalton and Joseph. The Piapot party reached the reserve in May, 1882 and set up camp. The four warriors hauled poles to make a large teepee with the hides given to them by Two Horns.

When the teepee was finished, Piapot sent the four riders to the nearby reserves to tell the Assiniboine elders to come to their reserve.

Within a week or two, over one hundred fifty elders arrived at the Piapot reserve accompanied by drivers and wagons from the other reserves. The drivers unloaded the poles and hides and stayed to help put up the teepees. They brought with them a good supply of rations and cooking utensils. The hunters from the other reserves delivered fish and small game each day.

Near the end of May, Joseph and Raincloud arrived at the reserve. They were surprised at the size of the camp.

"How many Assiniboines live around here!" Joseph exclaimed.

"These are just the elders" Piapot stated.

The four riders were glad to see Raincloud and Joseph after many laughs and tall tales of the journey east, Joseph gave Piapot a report.

"We are camped west of the fort and the Dalton family is at the McDonalds."

"I have spoken with the police and there will be a ceremony here the next week in June on the calendar." Piapot continued "There is no need for any of you to attend. The police will know who you are soon enough."

"Do you need money?" Joseph asked.

"No! We will have rations soon."

"When should we start the village?" Raincloud asked.

"Let the ceremony take place and the camp get established. Leave me two scouts. They will report to you often."

The ceremony took place in June and in attendance was the agent McDonald, Superintendent Walsh, several member and a few settlers.

After the flag raising, Walsh approached Piapot. "It is good to have an old friend nearby."

"And it is good to see you Superintendent Walsh."

The two spoke for some time mostly about Fort Walsh and towards evening Walsh, McDonald and the members rode to the fort.

Several days passed and the drivers who were to deliver rations did not arrive. Piapot sent his two scouts to meet with Joseph and purchase food.

The two scouts arrived in the valley where the rest of the warriors were camped and gave Piapot's orders to Joseph.

"The Muskapeetings have wagons. We will trade for them" Joseph continued. "Ride to their reserve and ask how many three year olds they will need for two wagons."

The two scouts rode east just less than a mile to the Muskapeeting reserve. They returned in less than an hour and reported to Joseph.

"The Chief said he does not want anything for the wagons. We can use them anytime we want and just bring them back when we are done."

Joseph ordered two of his warriors to bring a three year old as a gift for the Chief and they rode east.

When they arrived at the reserve, Joseph spoke with three Crees who had teams. He paid them to drive their teams and gave the three year old to the Chief as a gift. The Chief was pleased and told Joseph that a great buffalo horse of this value was too much of a gift. Joseph disagreed. He jumped on his horse and the party rode out towards the fort.

The three wagons entered the town followed by the dog warriors and pulled up in front of the post. The riders lined up two deep on either side of the wagon as people gathered on the planks. Some of the riders wore buckskin and some wore cloth and buckskin. Several had on blue yankee tunics bought from the Sioux who defeated Custer at the Little Big Horn.

Each of the dog warriors wore two colts and had automatic Winchesters in cases strapped to western saddles. Ammunition was on their waist and across their shoulders bangles and feathers dangled from their hair and the mains of the magnificent buffalo horses they rode. They wore beaded moccasins and had a knife tied to one leg.

Joseph slid from his horse and motioned four warriors to follow him into the store. As they stepped on the planks the crowd stepped aside to let them pass. Joseph saw the Dalton family and walked by them without speaking as four police constables watched from across the street.

Joseph said to the store owner, "Do you still buy buffalo hides?"

"Yes. As many as you have" the owner replied.

"Here is a list of supplies." Joseph continued "We will bring in the hides when you give me a total".

The owner took the list and began working on a total. Outside on the planks people began to speak.

"Who are they?"

"Are they Sioux?"

"Are they going to attack us?" one of the ladies said to Dalton.

"I do not think so. They have wagons with hides for trade. They will not attack if they get food."

"Good Lord! Give them food!"

The warriors could sense their fear and began to speak to them as they sat on their horses. The crowd was shocked by their perfect English.

Two young ladies began speaking French.

"I wonder where they are from" one of them said.

"They must be from the east" the other stated.

Vincent Sugar, the eldest son of John Sugar, said to one of them in perfect French "Mademoiselle, we are from the west and never before have I seen your beauty."

"Oh my God!" the young French girl exclaimed

This was too much for Dalton. He turned and walked away from the crowd for he was about to laugh out loud. William followed for the same reason.

"That son of a bitch. He has Little Fawn Dancing in the mountains" Cathy whispered in disgust.

"Keep it down" Victoria said.

Joseph came out of the store and had several of the warriors carry in the hides. The owners inspected the hides and gave Joseph eight dollars in dominion money.

"This is the difference I owe. You can start carrying out the supplies" the owner said.

When the warriors were finished loading, Joseph came out of the store and walked by Victoria and Cathy. Once again, he did not speak to them.

The wagons turned west escorted by warriors riding in front and behind. Joseph and several warriors remained on the planks to speak with a settler.

"One of your men told me you might have some three year olds for sale" he stated.

"Yes. They have just turned three" Joseph said.

"Are they as magnificent as the horses you ride? the settler asked.

"Every bit as good and trained for the saddle" Joseph replied.

"How much?"

"Ten dollars a horse" Joseph replied.

"That is a lot of money for a horse but I will pay it." The settler continued, "Bring them to the corrals tomorrow and I will meet you there."

"We are camped two hours west on this side of the river." Joseph continued, "Bring one hundred dollars Canadian before noon and you can pick ten horses. We will help you take them to your corrals if you do not have riders."

The settler smiled "I will see you before noon tomorrow."

Joseph and his warriors caught up with the wagons before the road forked south. At the fork Joseph and six riders followed the wagons south and he sent the rest of the party west to the camp.

"I will return to camp early tomorrow morning" Joseph shouted.

When the wagons reached the hills, two riders roped on to each wagon for the climb. They reached the Piapot camp before sundown and unloaded. The women made something to eat while the men sat cross legged.

"Have you seen Dalton?" Piapot asked.

"Yes we saw them at the Fort when we picked up the supplies" Joseph continued. "He will visit us soon and we will send a rider to give you a report.

"Leave four warriors here for I may have to send them to the Fort or your camp." Piapot continued "I do not think the Canadians will honor the treaty. Have the warriors build a new village in the valley west of the reserves for we will go there no matter what the Canadians say."

Joseph left four warriors with Piapot and the three returned to the camp.

When they returned, Joseph gave the warriors Piapot's orders.

Chapter Fourteen

The Qu'Appelle Valley Village

"Chief Piapot belongs in the valley and I will go down fighting for his right to be here."

Two builders approached Joseph and one of them spoke, "We must find a place where there is water above the new village. We will trench it below the frost line with shut-off valves. The water will not be fit to drink but no one will have to go to the trees. If there is a spring above camp level, we will use the white man's pump to fill a stone reservoir and bring the drinking water into the village in the same way as we bring the slough water."

"It is July sixth. We will find the location and begin immediately" Joseph stated.

Early the next morning, several builders and the two stone breakers rode west to find a location for the village. Joseph sent Vincent Sugar and Raincloud to the Fort to purchase supplies. On the way, they stopped to talk to the settler and several of his friends who were riding to the camp.

"How much further?" the settler asked.

"Less than two miles" Raincloud answered.

They spoke for a while and left in different directions. Raincloud and Vincent stopped at the reserve to pick up a driver and continued to the Fort.

When they reached the Fort, Raincloud and Vincent entered the store and spoke with the owner.

Vincent returned to the planks with a small bag of candies and tobacco. A young lady approached and said to him, "You were here yesterday. My name is Mary and my father is riding to your camp to buy horses".

"My name is Vincent and yes, we passed him on the way" Vincent replied in perfect English.

"Do all your friends speak both English and French?"

"Yes" Joseph continued, "Most of my friends speak both English and French."

"The young French girl you spoke to yesterday told me to say hello if I saw you at the Fort" Mary said with a smile.

Vincent lowered his head and looked at his Yankee boots.

"Do not be embarrassed" Mary continued. "Her name is Louise and she is here teaching school. She is staying with me and my family and we go to Church in Lebret every Sunday."

"Yes, I know of the Church."

"Maybe one Sunday you could come to the Church and say hello. I will tell Louise that I spoke with you."

The owner told Raincloud where he could buy mortar and sold him several shovels, picks and two-man saws. Raincloud returned to the wagon to get Vincent and the driver to help load.

After leaving the store, they purchased the mortar and headed back to the camp.

As they neared the camp they, once again, met the white settler and his friends leading the ten buffalo horses.

Raincloud spoke, "These are magnificent buffalo horses and it is too bad they have to be put to the harness."

"Do not worry. I am buying cattle and they will be used for saddle horses. It is a good thing I took more than one hundred dollars. Joseph sold me saddles and bridles as well" the settler said.

The settler introduced his friends and himself as Sam McKinnon. Raincloud told McKinnon their names and they spoke as friends.

"I met your daughter Mary on the planks" Vincent said.

"Do not tell me – I know! Never before have you seen her beauty."

There was loud laughter from everyone especially from McKinnon and Raincloud.

"She has much beauty" Vincent replied with that winning smile.

It was plain to see that McKinnon liked young Vincent and as they departed, he told the three of them to drop by the ranch whenever they were in the area.

It was just after twelve o'clock when the three reached camp and there was much excitement. Joseph called them over and had one of the stone breakers explain the good news.

"We have found much water. There will be no need of a pump." David continued, "Less than three hours ride west, there is a ravine that has several springs that run all winter."

"How do you know they run all winter?" Vincent asked.

"Because they are very few dead leaves from the plants where the water comes out of the ground" David replied.

"Will there be enough water to drink and for the sewer?" Raincloud asked.

"There will be more than enough water and we will not have to bury the entire line. We will build a stone channel about four feet wide and two feet deep down the ravine. We will build the same size channel from the springs to the main channel. The water in the channel will flow fast downhill which will prevent freezing. The great hall will be located near the ravine on a flat place with only the rear of the hall required to be cut into the bank. It is here where we will channel the water under ground into the great hall which will be located on the same side of the ravine. This will only be a short distance and should take only weeks."

One of the builders spoke. "The great hall will be the same as the great hall in the mountains only much smaller. There are many good size trees and stones are nearby. We have strong horses and they will each work four to six hours a day."

"The settlers on the flats above pay us to haul stones and put them in a pile. We could bring them to the village" the Cree driver explained.

"You bring them and we will pay you as much as the settlers pay you" Joseph replied. The driver left for his reserve to tell his drivers and pickers that they would now be paid twice for the same load.

The builder continued, "We will cut into the bank and build the back of the hall first so the stone breakers can build a huge holding tank for the water and the sewer line. When this is done, twenty stone breakers will build the channel from the springs to the rear of the great hall."

"How long will this take to build?" Joseph asked.

"It is second week in July and the construction should be done by the end of September" the builder explained further. "The inside work will be finished before the end of November."

"Complete with fireplaces and stalls?" Joseph asked.

"Yes."

"Good! I am tired of going to the trees!" Joseph exclaimed.

One of Piapot's scouts rode into the camp and told Joseph that the Dalton family was coming in a few hours for a visit and fish. Joseph told the scout about the plans for the new village and told him to stay in camp.

Joseph spoke, "Tonight we will feast with the Dalton family and drink the wine we brought from the plains. We will begin work tomorrow afternoon."

The camp was buzzing as the warriors went to pull nets, gather wood and get ready to cook.

"Chief Joseph. I am going to the corrals to comb and rub down the horses. Cathy is not pleased with me" Vincent said.

Joseph smiled and gave Vincent a little hit on the shoulder before he left for the corral.

The Dalton family arrived and were greeted by Raincloud and Joseph. Victoria jumped from the wagon and threw her arms around Joseph and Cathy left to talk to the fellas. Two young warriors led the team away to unharness and water them.

"Well Dalton, what is new at the Fort?" Raincloud asked.

"There are a hell of a lot of people coming and going now that the railroad has arrived."

Dalton sat cross legged with Raincloud and a few of the older warriors discussing Chief Piapot's reserve and the building of the new village.

"Chief Piapot belongs in the valley and I will go down fighting for his right to be here" Dalton stated.

"I think everyone feels the same way" one of the warriors stated.

"Chief Raincloud, Chief Piapot wants you to be in charge of six scouts who will travel from the camp to his reserve and to the Fort" Dalton continued. "Only the same two or three scouts should show up at the Fort and the reserve. He is sending his scouts back to the camp. The two or three scouts will ride to the reserve once every week with information and a fish or two."

"Tomorrow, I will choose the six scouts."

"Joseph. Here! Take four hundred of the five hundred dollars Wandering Buffalo gave me before I left the mountains. You will need this money to buy supplies" Dalton said.

After a few laughs and much discussion, the group left to eat and drink a little wine.

Victoria and Joseph returned from the river bank carrying their buffalo blankets as they went to the wagon and carried two boxes of plates to the big fire. "I did not buy mugs for I know you fellas brought your own with you" Victoria said.

Cathy was busy making bannock when she suddenly realized that Vincent was missing.

"Where is Vincent?" Cathy asked.

"He knew you were coming so he went to look after the horses" Joseph answered.

Cathy made a plate of fish, fried potatoes, bannock and with fork in hand, walked to the corral.

"So you found me" Vincent said.

"Someone has to feed you!"

Cathy watched Vincent eat and he did not look up from his plate.

When the food was gone and with no reason to look at his plate anymore, Vincent raised his head and said to Cathy "I had to say something nice. Those people on the planks were about to attack us."

"You mean those little old ladies and unarmed business men?"

"I could have more than one wife. You have more than one fella."

"That is true, but I have never told one of them I would be their wife as you have told Little Fawn Dancing that you would be her husband. The days of more than one wife are over. You are a brave twenty-four year old warrior and you should make up your mind Vincent!"

Cathy picked up the dish and fork and returned to the big fire to cook bannock.

Vincent watched her leave and said to his horse, "My father has three wives you know."

After supper, Dalton, Raincloud and Joseph sat cross legged and discussed the village.

"We will leave to Regina this week" Dalton said.

"How long will you be gone?" Joseph asked.

"We will take the train there and back. We should be gone only a week or two."

"The village will be well along in construction by the time you return" Raincloud said.

"Why are you going to Regina?" Joseph asked.

"Chief Piapot wants the family to learn all there is to know about buying land." Dalton continued, "We are Cathy, Victoria, Bill and James Wilson in case anyone asks".

"The scouts will tell this to Chief Piapot" Raincloud stated.

In the morning, the Dalton family left to the fort as the builders and stone breakers began moving west.

Chapter Fifteen

Piapot Moves to the Village

"I will go to the Qu'Appelle Valley or there will be blood on the snow."

The Dalton family arrived in Regina and Victoria and Dalton went from building to building asking questions about homesteading. They also met several settlers who gave them a great deal of information and advice.

Back at the Fort, the McDonalds and several friends went to the reserve on weekends and broke stones for the new village. Now Pete Gopher and the Cree drivers had wagon loads of stones ready for use.

When the Dalton family returned from Regina to the McDonalds, it was the second week in September and in the new village water was flowing in the stone trench.

"Have you been to the village?" Dalton asked.

"No. I do not think it is wise to associate for it may cause the constables to begin asking questions about you and the family" Richard continued. "On the weekend, I have gone to the reserve to split rocks and I talked the stone breakers into enclosing the trench with rock arches. It will prevent leaves and debris from entering into the system. With the stones we split, it will not take much longer to have the channels enclosed."

"I wish I could help" Dalton said.

"I know it is difficult to stand by and watch good men work but you and the family must keep a distance."

"Why do you help us?"

"Because my family is of mixed blood and we have experienced the discrimination"

"Have you spoken to the scouts?"

"Yes. One of them came to the house a few days ago. The scouts do not carry their weapons in town and they dress like the rest of the natives."

"What did he want?"

"They needed a little advice on the large holding tank that will be built in the rear of the great hall. They will have the great hall finished in less than two weeks."

"This week I will ride out after supper and take a look at things" Dalton stated.

On the reserve, Piapot complained several times to the drivers about the food rations without much success. Finally, in December, an agent from the Fort arrived to speak with Piapot.

"The meat is spoiled and the flour has taken on water" Piapot told him.

The agent inspected the rations and agreed with Piapot.

"The problem we have here is that with the railroad construction in progress, we are having a difficult time to deliver good rations to you and feed thousands of workers at the same time. When the line is completed and the settlers start producing more meat, flour and vegetables, we should be able to deliver decent rations." The agent explained

"I do not think the elders will survive the winter. We will have to go to the valley and find small game and fish."

"I do not blame you for making this suggestion Chief Piapot. Everyone should have a right to find food but the fort constables may try to stop you. If they ask me about this matter, I will tell them about the spoiled meat rations and your right to find food."

"That will help."

The agent left and the women began to prepare the rations that could be eaten.

"Go to the snow pile and bring fish and deer steaks" Piapot ordered.

"We have the best meat on the plains!" one of the elders exclaimed.

There was laughter as Piapot helped the elders bring wood for cooking.

In January of 1883, Dalton and William rode out after supper to meet with Joseph. When they reached the village, they could see two new out buildings. Several dog warriors who were waiting took their horses to the barn for feed and grooming.

"How was the trail?" Joseph asked.

"The snow was almost up to the horses bellies. What is in the two new buildings?"

"One building is for weapons and bending steel and the other one is used for preparing meat to be stored in the great hall" Joseph replied.

"The scouts to the fort have told us that Chief Piapot is ready to move."

"Yes, this is why we have sent for you. Chief Piapot wishes to meet with the two of us and Raincloud."

"Is the building ready?"

"Yes. There is water and stalls everywhere. Even in the outside building" Joseph explained.

"I will meet you and Raincloud at the Chief Piapot camp tomorrow night."

Dalton and William returned to the fort just after midnight. Cathy and Victoria made something to eat and the four stayed up late discussing the Piapot move.

The next day after supper, Dalton rode to the Piapot camp. Raincloud and Joseph were already there when Dalton arrived. There was a vigorous greeting for Dalton from Piapot and the elders.

"Our camp has done good with government-rations and the fresh meat delivered by the scouts but I do not wish to remain on this reserve and neither do the elders. Our heart is in the Qu'Appelle valley and that is where we will go. The scouts have told me that Inspector Walsh is in charge at the fort. What do you know about the white police Chief Dalton?"

"Including everyone, there are about forty-five police stationed at the fort. They are in charge of the surrounding reserves and kept busy patrolling."

"And Inspector Walsh?"

"I have heard the police speak of the Chief Piapot reserve. Walsh has instructed the constables to leave you alone unless you call for them or trouble is reported. Sometimes when I was on the planks, I heard Walsh speaking to his older members of Commissioner Irvine and Prime Minister McDonald with great disgust. Walsh feels he should have been made commissioner for his accomplishments at Fort Walsh and Wood Mountain. He has real hatred for both of them and the police force in general."

"We will leave for the valley this week."

"What supplies are remaining?" an elder asked.

"There are about twenty buffalo hides, all the cloth and a good supply of potatoes, meat and pemmican. We also have the good clothes you sent with us."

"I can hardly wait to take steam and put on my cloth!" an elder exclaimed.

"The constables do not patrol at night" Dalton stated.

Raincloud spoke, "Tomorrow night Pete Gopher will bring five sleighs to help move the elders. Also, most of the dog warriors will come and ride double with those who do not ride in the sleighs. We will return the next evening for the buffalo hides, supplies and the few elders that remain."

The elders nodded their approval. They were pleased that the hides would be taken to put on new teepees. Dalton returned to the fort and Joseph and Raincloud to the village.

The next evening, the Raincloud party along with Pete Gopher and his drivers moved most of the elders to the village. Piapot was not among them.

The elders were amazed with the great hall for they had never been to the mountains to see this kind of building. They bedded down for the evening and had to be told about the stalls and how they operate.

Piapot and the elders spent the next day tearing down the teepees. They put the hides in one pile, the posts in another and they covered the supplies that would be taken to the village.

Shortly after dusk, the Raincloud party arrived at the reserve. They loaded everything that was to be taken and only a few of the elders got on the wagons.

Piapot spoke, "The elders that remain wish to walk with me to the valley. We will leave in the morning and walk past the settlers on our way. I do not wish to hide for we will have to confront the police sooner or later. We have our buffalo blankets and we will not freeze. Send only five scouts to watch from a distance just in case of bloodshed."

"This will be done Chief Piapot" Raincloud stated.

Piapot told the drivers to travel west a short distance before turning north so that the police could not see their tracks.

"Tomorrow we will bring two sleighs near the edge of the valley and wait for Raincloud's orders to advance" Peter Gopher added as he picked up his lines.

Piapot smiled and nodded his head.

In the morning of the first week of February, Piapot and the seventeen elders of good strength set out on foot for the valley. As they neared a settler's farm yard, a rider from the farm rode towards them.

"I have been watching from the house Chief Piapot. Where are you going?"

"To the valley where there is spring water and small game" Piapot answered.

"You are not to leave your reserve and we have been instructed by the police to report any movement in the area."

"Then you should report it" Piapot stated.

"I do not wish to report it but he will." The settler pointed to a house built on a high place.

They watched as a rider left the yard riding north to the fort.

"My name is McKinnon. I did business with Joseph a while back. Come to the barn and warm up before you leave. You will not make it to the valley before the police arrive anyhow."

Piapot looked at the elders and there was a nodding of heads.

The barn was a good size with a large heater to one side. McKinnon stoked up the fire as the Piapot party gathered around. McKinnon went to the house and returned to the barn followed by his wife and two daughters. They carried large steel pots of coffee and baskets of bread. The girls put the coffee pots on the heater and passed around a basket of buns. There was a small table where Mrs. McKinnon put out cups and homemade jam. The Piapot party thanked the girls many times.

"How did you know Joseph was from my reserve?" Piapot asked.

"The first time they came to the fort I was on the planks and watched them arrive. I left the same time they did and I saw the wagons being driven to your reserve" McKinnon answered.

"What do the people at the fort say about my warriors?"

"The merchants like the way they do business as I do but the police are curious."

The Piapot party began to file out the barn door.

"What will happen if they arrest you?" McKinnon asked.

"I will go to the Qu'Appelle valley or there will be blood on the snow" Piapot replied.

Piapot turned his head and pointed his nose in the direction of a distant ridge. McKinnon looked to the ridge and counted five heavily armed warriors.

"I hope it does not come to this" McKinnon stated.

The two shook hands and Piapot joined the elders.

It was just past noon and the Piapot party was close to the valley when two riders appeared on the horizon. They dismounted and waited for the Piapot party to reach them.

"Where are you going?" the old sergeant asked.

"To the valley for fresh water." Piapot continued, "The rations of meat are rotten and we wish to fish and hunt small game."

"Yes, the agent has told us about this" the sergeant said.

The young constable interrupted and pointed to the warriors on the ridge. The sergeant went to his saddle bags and removed his binoculars. He scanned the ridge and could see Raincloud looking back at him with his binoculars.

"They are the most heavily armed people I have ever seen. Chief Piapot, none of your people have arms. I am going to let you continue to the valley for two reasons. First, the agent is disgusted with everyone for the bad rations you have received after travelling so far to reach your reserve. Second, Superintendent Walsh ordered us to avoid confrontation. He said that after reading my report, you will be easy to find if it is necessary."

The two members mounted and the sergeant took one more look at the warriors on the ridge.

"I guess you know that with the railroad now here, we could bring two hundred recruits to the Fort in just a matter of days" the sergeant stated.

"Yes. Tell the two hundred recruits to bring us decent rations!" Piapot exclaimed.

There was great belly laughter especially from the young constable.

When Walsh read the Sergeant's report he almost fell off his chair with laughter.

"Listen to this!" Walsh read the part about Piapot telling the two hundred recruits to bring them decent rations and there was a roar of laughter from the members who were in his quarters.

"He has a sense of humor! I'll give him that!" one of the members shouted.

"We will pay him a visit in the spring" Walsh concluded.

Chapter Sixteen

The Police Pay a Visit

"Take more! I will only throw it out."

When the police left, Raincloud raised his lance and signaled Pete Gopher to advance. The remainder of the Piapot party reached the village before dark. The seventeen elders were amazed with the village but Piapot knew it well.

The next few days were spent getting everyone settled. Almost all the elders wanted teepees. This was agreeable with Joseph for the warriors were sleeping in the great hall as they waited for their outside sleeping quarters to be finished.

Soon after Piapot and the elders were settled, the Dalton family arrived in the evening with many jars of canned berries.

"Where did you get all the berries?" Joseph asked.

"We paid the Crees to pick for us." Victoria continued, "The McDonalds paid half and we helped with the canning. Dalton knew your pemmican was almost gone so we thought it was time to bring you some berries. There are also ten crocks of pickles and five crocks of wine."

Wildfire and several friends took the horses to the barn and carried the jars and crocks to the kitchen storage room.

Piapot was told that the Dalton family had arrived and he walked to the great hall for a visit.

After the Dalton family finished eating, Piapot, Joseph, Raincloud, Dalton and a few elders met in the warriors' room where they sat on benches at a very long table.

"Chief Dalton. What have the police decided?" an elder asked.

"On the planks, the merchants say good things about our people." Dalton smiled as he continued "I sat with two sergeants with two different opinions. One thought we should be forced back to the reserve and the other disagreed. They said Walsh would send a patrol to visit the camp in the spring. Also, Walsh and Steele have spoke to the members about a rebellion north of the big river. Dumont has been to Montana to speak with Riel."

"Dalton! Joseph! How much money is left?" Piapot asked.

"I have just about sixty dollars which will last us into summer" Dalton said.

"I have about two hundred fifty dollars" Joseph added. "This will last us well into summer depending on how much more we build. We are making money by selling fish to the settlers."

"The scouts who ride to the fort will inform the agents that we will pick up our rations at the fort" Raincloud added.

"It is March on the calendar and the police from the fort will visit us soon. Before May, we will know if we remain in the valley or if there will be trouble. If we are not allowed to remain here, there will be blood shed and much of it will be ours. The young warriors should take this into consideration. Anyone who does not wish to die may return to the mountains. I do not think they will try to make us return to the reserve as the merchants, most police and the agent feel we belong in the valley. It is a different world, do not take weapons when they come. When it is clear that we may remain in the valley, those who are still here and wish to return to the mountains should do so."

"Chief Piapot, I have spoken with the warriors and no one is gong anywhere until this issue is settled" Joseph stated.

Piapot nodded and the meeting ended.

The winter passed quickly and one morning in April, a scout rode into the village and reported to Raincloud. "Four police are less than one hour from the village."

"Where are the other two scouts?" Raincloud asked.

"They will backtrack and remain between the fort and the village" Wildfire answered.

Joseph went from building to building and told everyone about the police and to keep doing what they were doing. Piapot and the elders came to the great hall.

The two constables and two sergeants entered the village and stopped at the first building. They looked around at the buildings and were amazed. Before going to the great hall, they stopped at each building and asked to go inside. They were impressed with the forge and also the warriors' quarters which were finished very recently.

"There is water and latrines in every building!" one of the constables exclaimed.

After looking at the last building, Joseph invited them into the great hall to meet Piapot and the elders.

"We will take your horses to the barn for feed and water and rub them down" Wildfire said to one of the sergeants.

"That would be fine. Thank you."

The horses were led away and the four police entered the great hall. They were not prepared for what they saw.

"Jesus! Look at this!" the old sergeant shouted.

Piapot came forward to say hello to the young constable and the old sergeant who met them on the plains. The old sergeant introduced Piapot to the other two.

The four police watched the women preparing food in the kitchen at the back of the hall.

"Chief Raincloud will show you the other rooms and then we will eat." Piapot said.

Raincloud and the stone breakers went from room to room with the police. They especially liked the chiefs meeting room and admired the skins on the walls which had beaded art work.

They went into the warriors' room where several elders were taking steam. This was almost too much for the police to believe.

"Where is all this water coming from? There is water in all the buildings and every room!" the sergeant exclaimed.

Raincloud explained the springs and how they channeled the water with stones. A young constable asked to see the holding tank and how the water was distributed. They walked to the back of the kitchen and looked at the huge holding tank.

"I see" the young constable continued. "The tank is higher which allows the water to flow throughout and into the sewer."

"What is this column of rock work?" the old sergeant asked.

"It is an overflow from the top of the tank to the sewer for when the tank gets too much water" one of the stone breakers answered.

"Amazing!"

When they had seen everything, David led them to Piapot's table in the dining room.

The women brought large wooden platters filled with baked fish, fried potatoes, berries, nuts, cucumbers and soft biscuits.

The Piapot table and the four police filled their plates and ate heartily. When a platter was empty, the women brought more. The fish and berries were the first to disappear.

"Take more! I will only throw it out" Piapot said to the four police.

Everyone laughed. Even the police knew he would not throw it out.

When the meal was over, their horses were brought to the planks. The four police thanked Piapot for dinner and gave many complements. They especially liked the fish.

On the way to the planks, Pipaot told the old Sergeant that an early decision would be desired as there was much construction still to be done.

As they reached the planks, the old sergeant said to Piapot, "Quite frankly, I think Superintendent Walsh is looking for a reason to let you stay. I hope our report will give him that reason."

The police turned and rode east to the fort.

On their return to the fort, the old sergeant submitted a positive report to Walsh and Steele. The other three members gave separate statements stating they were in full agreement with the report.

"With the government's ration situation being the way it is, I think they will get at least a temporary permission to remain in the valley" Steele stated.

"Do you object to giving Chief Piapot a reserve in the valley?" Walsh asked.

"No" Steele replied.

""Here is what I think." Walsh continued, "As you know, the word from Ottawa is that war with the metis under the leadership of Louis Riel and Dumont is imminent. We know Chief Piapot has fifty heavily armed warriors with him in the valley and at least five hundred more between here and the Cypress Hills. We are not quite sure where these five hundred are but he has them. Also, there are many plains Cree who will follow him into battle. Intelligence tells us that Chief Piapot can put a thousand warriors on the battle field. We could probably give Chief Piapot a permanent reservation in the location he has now chosen in the Qu'Appellle valley if he agreed to abstain from directly or indirectly assisting any party that would make war against the government."

"If he signed that kind of an agreement, it would be a mutual gain for all concerned" Steele agreed.

"Prepare a draft agreement to send to Dewdney in Regina" Walsh ordered.

Within hours, Steele and a staff sergeant returned with the draft agreement which was signed by Superintendent Walsh and Steele.

The staff sergeant was given the signed draft and he led a dispatch to Regina.

Chapter Seventeen

Vincent Goes to Church

"In our nation, Chief Piapot allows us to worship the Creator each in our own way."

It was the last Saturday in April when Vincent and the two stone breakers met with Chief Piapot in the Chiefs' room. Piapot and a few elders sat at one side of a long table. The three sat down across from them and looked at one another as though asking each other to speak.

Vincent finally spoke, "Tomorrow is Sunday and we were wondering if we could go to church in Lebret."

Piapot and the elders looked at one another and smiled. "Does anyone here mind if they go to the white man's Creator day?" Piapot asked.

"I think it is a good sign. Many of our young men think only of girls" an elder stated.

Piapot and the elders looked at one another and held back their laughter.

Vincent and the stone breakers looked down at the table.

"Do not look at the table." Piapot added, "When you meet a young woman who has beauty beyond compare, you should at least say hello to her."

The elders and Piapot could no longer hold back their laughter. They gave the three shoulder hugs and wished them luck.

The three of them walked across the great hall to the women's room and had their hair washed and cut to shoulder length.

"Come early in the morning and we will put the tiny braids on each side" one of the women said.

They left for the corral and took their horses to the barn for grooming. They combed the knots out of their mains and tails, trimmed the hair on their hocks, put the small braids in their mains and brushed them until they shone.

Early Sunday morning they returned to the barn to feed and water their horses, give them a quick brush down and put the saddles on them and after that, they returned to the warriors' lodge and washed up and they put on their cloth before going to the women's room to get their hair braided.

Vincent wore black pants, a white shirt buttoned up, a black vest and black Yankee boots. The stone breakers wore the same except their pants and vest were grey. Each wore a beaded doeskin medallion that hung from a black leather lace tied at the back underneath their collars. Vincent's medallion was black on black doeskin and the two stonebreakers medallions were turquoise on black doeskin. Their belts were made of black beads on thick black leather.

When they reached the women's room, the women gave them much praise. There was hugs and kisses on the cheek.

The women put the small braids on each side and put red beads at the end of each braid. The great hall was now full of people who laughed and gave them much praise as they grabbed soft biscuits and headed for the barn.

They arrived just before 10 o'clock as the church began to fill. As they walked down the aisle people in the front turned and watched every move they made as they picked a bench and sat down. The congregation was white and of mixed blood. Sam McKinnon, his wife and two daughters and Louise sat across the aisle from them. Sam caught their eye and gave them a smile and a quick wave. The girls could not help but look at them and whispered back and forth.

The priest gave an interesting sermon and when it was over, McKinnon and his wife went down the aisle to meet the two stone breakers. The girls left the church and waited outside. McKinnon and his wife soon arrived with Vincent and the stone breakers and introduced everyone.

"This is Vincent Sugar, David Stonebreaker and Benjamin Stonebreaker. These are my two daughters. Mary, who you met at the fort Vincent, my youngest daughter Esther and Louise Perrot who teaches school and stays with us at the ranch."

Vincent felt like looking down but he got himself together and said to Louise in English "I think I scared you outside the store."

"You did but you do not scare me anymore."

A crowd was starting to gather around them so McKinnon thought it was time to rescue the meeting.

"My wife and I would like to invite you fellas to the ranch for dinner" McKinnon said.

The three looked at one another and said nothing.

"It is not that far from your camp" Mary added.

"We would like to see your ranch" Vincent said.

"Good! Follow our buggy."

In the buggy, the girls could not stop talking about Vincent and the Stonebreakers.

"They look so handsome."

"I wonder who made their clothes."

"Did you see the bead work?"

"I like their tiny braids with the red beads."

"I have got to get myself together and stop staring at Vincent" Louise said.

"It is because of you that he came" Mary offered.

"I like Benjamin" Esther said.

"He is the older of the two and you are only seventeen" Mary retorted.

"Mom was only sixteen when she got married and dad is seven years older than mom."

"I do not think it matters" Louise said.

When they reached the ranch, McKinnon let the girls off at the house and drove his team to the barn.

"Put each of your horses in a box stall and give them a little feed."

The three unbridled and unsaddled their horses and put them in the box stalls. McKinnon brought the team into the barn and unharnessed them. After hanging up the harness, McKinnon put halters on them and turned them loose in the pasture.

A corral, attached to the barn, held five horses.

"These are five of the ten three year olds we sold you Mr. McKinnon" Vincent said.

"Yes and they are good ones!"

The four stood by the corral talking and laughing until Mary came to the porch to tell them dinner was ready.

After a quick washing of hands, Vincent and the Stonebreakers were seated at a table of food across from the girls and Mrs. McKinnon. McKinnon sat at one end of the table and an elderly hired hand who introduced himself as Mike Miller sat at the other end.

"Maybe one of the fellas would like to offer a blessing" McKinnon said.

Mrs. McKinnon opened her mouth and was about to speak when McKinnon looked at her and quickly moved his head once to the left and back.

Vincent and Benjamin turned and looked at David.

David lowered his head and spoke, "Creator of the plains and all things, we thank you for this food and new friends." Everyone except Vincent and Benjamin raised their heads as David continued. "Creator, we ask that where there is darkness, let there be light, where there is hunger, let there be sharing, where there are lies and hatred, let their be honesty and forgiveness. Creator, we ask that your servants who go forth each day will offer strength where there is weakness, peace where there is war and purity where there is evil. We ask for these things in Jesus' name."

Mrs. McKinnon and the girls could not look up for tears rolled down their faces and under their chins.

"There are not enough buns. I will get more buns" Mrs. McKinnon whispered.

"I will help."

"Me too."

"Me too."

Mrs. McKinnon and the girls quickly got themselves together the best they could and returned with buns and jam.

Sam McKinnon cleared his throat.

"Better get those potatoes going around Mike."

"Have you fellas been raised in the Catholic Church Vincent?" McKinnon asked.

"No sir. In our nation, Chief Piapot allows us to worship the Creator each in our own way. I do not follow the teachings of Jesus Christ as David does" Vincent replied.

After dinner, Vincent and the Stonebreakers went to the planks with Miller and McKinnon. They spoke about the ranch, the horses and much about the chiefs and nearby reserves.

In a short time, the girls came to the planks. McKinnon and Miller went back into the house.

"Well, you asked for a blessing and you got one" Margaret said to her husband.

"Yes, I did. Yes, indeed."

"Who the hell are these kids Sam?" Miller asked.

"I have no idea. None at all."

When it was time to leave, Vincent and the Stonebreakers went into the house to thank the McKinnons for the dinner. The girls stayed on the planks and watched them disappear over a ridge.

"Well, what do those three fellas think they are going to do for a living?" McKinnon asked.

"Vincent will work with numbers, Benjamin wants to be a builder and David said he will be a shaman like Chief Piapot" Mary reported.

"They have much water and will build a pool for swimming. We are invited when it is done" Esther added.

"I should not go but I probably will" Louise whispered.

"I guess I better get going. I got horses to feed."

"I will go with you" McKinnon said.

When they reached the planks, McKinnon asked Mike if he had any whiskey left in his bottle. Mike told him it was just about full and the two of them went to the barn for a drink.

Chapter Eighteen

Piapot signs Peace Agreement

"The fact that this agreement was offered to you by Ottawa, makes you according to their intelligence, the most dangerous Chief on the plains."

The first week in May, the old sergeant along with the same two constables, arrived at the Piapot village. They rode up to the great hall and dismounted.

"I have a message for Chief Piapot" the sergeant said to one of the elders.

"Come into the Chiefs' room and I will send for Chief Piapot."

Chief Piapot soon arrived with Raincloud, Joseph and the remainder of his council.

The sergeant spoke "here is the deal. Dewdney and McDonald have agreed to let you have 53,419 acres in the location you are now on with conditions.

I will not begin to explain every detail but if you read the agreement you will find that Prime Minister McDonald and Dewdney are concerned about your loyalty to the Government. They want you to agree to reasonable trespass by the police until December 31, 1884. Also, you will not knowingly assist the enemy directly or indirectly in a war against the Government of Canada.

They want you to understand what indirectly means and have given examples. Further, the land is yet to be surveyed and provided you adhere to the terms of this agreement, you will officially be given this reserve before December 31, 1884.

If, with the full knowledge of your actions, you break the terms of this agreement, you will be removed by the police and the army if necessary."

The sergeant handed Piapot two agreements signed by Dewdney for Prime Minister John A. McDonald and witnessed by Commissioner Irvine.

"It is also stated that these documents are classified. Their contents are confidential between the two parties. This is a very serious term of the agreement."

Piapot took the two signed agreements and gave one to Joseph and one to Raincloud.

"I will send for David. He will do a better job of reading this" Raincloud said.

In a few minutes, David entered the room and began to read the documents.

"We will go to the great hall. You did not see the ice house the last time you were here" Piapot said.

The four along with Benjamin, left the Chiefs' room and proceeded to the ice house which was located at the back of the kitchen. Piapot opened the door and it was so cold, they could see their breath. Three of the women were cleaning fish and cutting steaks.

"Where did you get the sides of beef?" one of the constables asked.

"We trade fish for beef" Piapot replied.

"How do you keep it so cold in here?"

"The ice house is built into the bank and covered to keep the heat out." Benjamin explained further "in the winter we cut blocks and haul them to the ice house. These blocks of ice you see stacked on each side of the work benches will last all summer."

"I am glad you showed us this. I plan on buying a ranch and I can tell you right now that my ranch will have an ice house!" the sergeant shouted.

There was laughter as they returned to the great hall. Piapot left to the Chiefs' room to speak with his council and two chiefs.

The women came to the table and Benjamin asked the police if they wanted steaks or fish. The three of them asked for fish.

A few elders joined the police and Benjamin left for the warriors' lodge.

After several readings, Joseph and David explained the agreement.

"It is not stated but they fear we will fight for Dumont and Riel. They do not realize that Dalton reports to our council. In my heart, live or die, I wish to fight along side Gabriel but there is no future in it for our nation. The railroad has changed everything. The Canadians can now move an army of thousands in just days. "

Piapot placed a bullet on the table. "It is the same today as it was ten year ago. Without these, a Winchester is just a walking stick and the rebellion will fail." There was silence in the room.

"It would be wise to sign the agreement" a councilor suggested.

Raincloud and Joseph nodded in agreement as did the remainder of the council.

The sergeant and two constables were brought into the Chiefs' room where they signed as witnesses to Piapot's mark of X.

The sergeant gave a signed copy of the agreement to Piapot and placed the other signed copy in his case.

"Superintendent Walsh had a great deal to do with you getting this reserve." The sergeant smiled and added, "The fact that this agreement was offered to you by Ottawa, makes you according to their intelligence, the most dangerous Chief on the plains."

"I am now what the white man calls 'retired'."

The police laughed and thanked Piapot for the meal.

Chapter Nineteen

Walsh pays Piapot a visit

"I have come to you because I know you have killers and it will take killing to steal the money."

Towards evening, May 16th, two scouts sat cross legged on a high place and watched a lone rider advance from the east. Wildfire raised his binoculars "I am not sure but I think it is Superintendent Walsh" Wildfire said.

"You stay here! I will ride to the village!" the other scout exclaimed.

In a few minutes, the scout reached the village and went to Piapot's teepee.

"Superintendent Walsh is approaching the village" he reported.

"Who is with him?"

"He is alone" the scout answered.

"I will go to the planks and wait for him."

Piapot, who no longer took his weapons with him, walked to the planks. He saw Walsh coming and smiled. It was like old times for Walsh was dressed in buckskin.

Walsh dismounted and removed a small bag that was tied to his saddle horn. Two scouts took his horse to the barn.

"Are you here to inspect our village?" Piapot asked.

"I have heard a great deal about your village and I can see why the members will not stop talking about it. I am not here to inspect. I am here to bring you some news."

"Let us go to the great hall and speak in the Chiefs' room" Piapot offered.

"No. This is very private and I would like to sit cross legged in your tent."

Piapot ordered two of the young fellas to bring a small bag of biscuits and nuts to his tent.

They went into the tent and Piapot lit two lanterns and several candles. Walsh sat down cross legged on the skins. The fellas arrived with baskets and Piapot told them to sit a distance from the tent.

"I will not take swigs from your steel bottle."

"And I will not sip from the small bag."

The two laughed as Walsh took a big swig and Piapot took a sip from the small bag.

"I guess you know that McDonald and Irvine had me sent east two years ago."

"Yes. That has been the talk in the reserves."

"For eight years, I did more to keep the peace than those sons a bitches did all put together."

Walsh took another big swig.

"They wanted me out of the way so they could gang up on Chief Sitting Bull. They spoke with other Sioux chiefs like Sitting Bull did not exist. Irvine talked the other Chiefs into leaving with most of Sitting Bull's people."

Walsh was talking louder now so Piapot lifted a basket and Walsh took a biscuit and emptied his flask with a couple of swigs.

"What is done is done" Walsh said with a kind of sadness to his voice.

"Yes. What is done is done. What is the news?"

Walsh looked at Piapot and then from side to side as though making sure no one was listening.

"The railroad has not paid their workers for almost six months. They will soon send three hundred thousand dollars to the detachment at Maple Creek to be distributed between the workers and local suppliers because the workers are threatening to walk off the job and the suppliers cannot be held off much longer.

I will know the exact time they will reach each stop from Winnipeg to McLean. My detachment's assignment is to secure the McLean area where the train will take on water, coal and various supplies.

In case of any mishap, all the detachments from Fort Qu'Appelle and along the main line to Maple Creek will know when the train will arrive at each stop. I will know this schedule soon. I am asking you to help me steal the money."

"I know what a hundred dollars can buy but I have never heard of three hundred thousand dollars. Why have you come to me?"

"I have come to you because I know you have killers and it will take killing to steal the money."

"There are very many people watching between here and Swift Current. The money must be taken between Swift Current and Maple Creek" Piapot stated.

"That is another reason I came to you. You think like a general. So! Are you interested?"

"Where there is money there is always interest."

Walsh took another flask from his bag and offered Piapot a swig. Piapot smiled and took a big swig. "I am not riding. "Tell me Walsh. How much of this money do you offer my nation?"

"Well, I was thinking of half."

Piapot smiled and took a sip.

"Maybe a little less" Walsh said.

Piapot held up three fingers on his left hand and with his right index finger he pointed to Walsh and then to one of the three fingers. Piapot gave Walsh the small bag and he took a big sip.

"I could probably live with that" Walsh said.

Piapot Lifted the skin to his teepee and motioned his two scouts to the tent.

"Have the women cook up two of the settlers steaks. Tell them to burn them on both sides. We will have the soft potatoes and boiled carrots. Tell them to save the steak juice for our potatoes and we will have burned bread with the white man's grease."

"Do you want wine Chief Piapot?" one of the scouts asked.

"Yes. We will have some wine."

The two scouts left for the great hall.

"Jesus! Are you running a hotel!" Walsh exclaimed.

"Several of our men and women work in the evening so there is always women in the kitchen. They like to cook."

After the two talked a little longer, they left on shaky legs for the great hall.

They sat at Piapot's table in the great hall and were joined by Joseph, Raincloud and several builders.

In a few minutes, the steaks were served on large plates along with the bread and mugs of wine. Piapot and Walsh ate everything on the plates.

"That was a meal fit for a king. Far too good for John A. McDonald" Walsh declared.

There was laughter and many salutes to the kitchen.

Walsh and Piapot walked to the planks. "I will come tomorrow evening at the same time" Walsh said.

"Yes and we will meet in the Chiefs room where drinking is not allowed."

Walsh's horse was waiting. It was almost dark when he mounted up and disappeared over the ridge.

"Raincloud! Take a scout and bring the Dalton family to the village."

Piapot added, "Tell them they will stay in the village for maybe two days."

As Raincloud and Wildfire rode east, Raincloud stopped to talk to the scouts.

"Has Walsh passed by?" Raincloud asked.

"Yes" a scout replied.

"How far ahead is he?"

Maybe a half hour" the scout replied.

"Good! We do not have to ride slow."

Raincloud and Wildfire reached the McDonalds in good time and stopped for biscuits and coffee.

It was late when they left for the village but the sky was clear and they made good time. Joseph and the fellas came to meet them as they rode to the planks.

The great hall was busy and several women worked in the kitchen. The only people who knew about the Walsh deal were Joseph, Raincloud, the council and Piapot. Piapot ordered the warriors into the hall to ask them questions if necessary. There was much excitement for the warriors knew something big was happening.

The fellas took the horses to the barn and the Dalton family entered the great hall.

David approached and told Dalton, Joseph and Raincloud they were wanted in the chief's room. Dalton was greeted all around as he took a place at the long table.

"There is a big decision to make tonight" Piapot said.

For Dalton's benefit, Piapot explained the three hundred thousand dollar train robbery and said it would be put to a vote.

Dalton jumped to his feet "Vote! Those rotten land grabbing sons of bitches have it coming! Count me in!"

There was a roar of approval from the table. Piapot sat quiet with a proud smile like when your child does something good. As they settled down, questions and answers went back and forth.

"I do not know if the Canadians would consider this a direct or indirect act of war. They must never know we robbed the train for we must not lose this reserve."

"A robbery should have nothing to do with war but I fear they would find a way to call it indirect war" a councilor stated.

"That is why they must never find out." Piapot went on, "Those who can write will put down questions that must be answered. Everyone else will come with me. I called the warriors together to find out how many of them are known to the police. Those who are known must be at the fort when the robbery takes place. We will answer questions tomorrow after a good sleep."

Piapot and just about all of his counsel left the room to speak with those who were know to the police.

David appeared with pencil and paper to make a list of those who must be visible at the time of the robbery.

After much discussion among them, David read the names.

"Raincloud and the four scouts who were with him when Chief Piapot moved from the reserve to the valley!. Vincent and the two stone breakers who go to Church! Joseph! Those who took the police horses to and from the barn! Those who showed the police the village! Those who went to the Fort only once or twice are not on the list."

When David was finished writing, there were twenty-seven names on the list. Piapot and the councilors returned to the chiefs room and David read the list of names. Joseph and Raincloud were disappointed but they understood.

"I do not think we need any more than twenty-five" Dalton said.

"Yes. You, William and the girls will make twenty-seven" Joseph stated.

"We will talk tomorrow and wait for Walsh" Piapot concluded.

The next day Piapot spoke to those who would rob the train. "I will leave soon for the Cypress Hills to meet with the Chiefs from the big rivers. The two scouts I left at my village I will send to help with the robbery and some of the old warriors will help with the blockade. Let David read the questions. To each question we will find an answer."

David read the questions and after each question was answered, he made a note of the decision. These notes would be read and posted in the chiefs room at the end of each meeting for those who could read. The first meeting was just before noon. When the meeting was over, David read the following questions and decisions and posted them in the chiefs room.

Question: "Where will the Dalton family be?"

Decision: They will be on the train. They will ride to Regina to catch the train. We will wait for Walsh before we make any more decisions about the Dalton family. We must know how many coaches and their description.

Question: Who will deal with the dynamite?

Decision: Benjamin and David will train two stone breakers for the bows and two more for blasting a bridge, ties or telegraph poles.

Question: How do we attack the train?

Decision: The train will be divided in a place where there is a down grade. The coaches will follow until the train reaches an upgrade. These two places must be close together. The coaches we are interested in will be slowly left behind. This is where we rob the train.

Question: Will the engineer not notice that some of his train is missing?

Decision: No. The train will be divided where train swings right to miss a slough. The engineer will see only a blockade in front of him and his problem will be about stopping the train.

Question: Who will die.

Decision: Everyone on the train.

Question: How long will it take to rob the train?

Decision: No more than twenty minutes.

After listening to David, everyone left to eat and David posted the question and decisions for those to read.

In the afternoon, most of questions were decided and the Dalton family moved to their tent west of the village.

"Let us know when Walsh has left" Cathy said to Wildfire.

Walsh arrived before dark and proceeded to the chiefs room. He was greeted by Piapot and those concerned.

"On the table is our plan to rob the train" Piapot said to Walsh.

Walsh read the question and decision sheet and had praise for the plan.

"So! We have a one third – two third deal?" Walsh asked.

"Yes" Piapot replied.

"What do you need from me?"

Joseph spoke, "We need you to draw squares representing the coaches. We must know what coach has the money so we do not blow it apart. Also we must know what day and time of day the train will leave Swift Current - give or take an hour or two."

"Blow it apart? You have dynamite?"

"Yes" Joseph replied.

"I will get you the information several days before the train leaves Winnipeg."

Walsh and Piapot walked to the planks.

"Your hate for the police runs deep. I have disliked many people in my years but I have only killed for the nation. There must be more."

"Yes. There is more. A few weeks ago, the Commissioner came to me with a deal. If I resigned, they would not Court martial me for fathering a child with a Sioux maiden. I will resign before the end of June."

"Did you have a child with her?"

"I do not know but I was with her many times."

Piapot spoke "I will leave for the Cypress Hills before you come again. A warrior will bring me the information I need. You will deal with Chief Joseph and he will tell you where and when your money will be delivered."

"Why are you going to the Cypress Hills?"

"I will stop the train!"

Piapot went to the forge. He asked to have wire cutters and a spike puller made to cut the telegraph lines and pull spikes.

"We will make them immediately. The spike puller we will make in three pieces so that it will be easy to carry."

Piapot nodded and told them to make sure the horses going west were shod. The next day, May 1st, Piapot, Joseph, Dalton and Raincloud met in the chiefs room.

"How do we get the money to Walsh" Piapot asked.

No one spoke. After a few minutes, Dalton offered two solutions. "We can take his money to the mountains and meet him at Lethbridge or take his share to the Qu'Appelle Valley and meet him at Brandon."

"I think his money should come to the Qu'Appelle Valley. To the mountains and then to Lethbridge would take too long." a councilor concluded.

"I agree with the decision" Dalton stated.

Piapot spoke "Send the money west with two scouts who know where the McKays are camped. They can stay there until we send for them. The McKays do not have to know we have the money. Have them bury it close by.

The Dalton family will kill everyone in the forward coaches. When the train is divided, the warriors will fight whoever is guarding the money."

"How will I know when to start dividing the train?" Dalton asked.

"The elders are not far from where the trains go by. I will move several tents to a high place near the tracks and fly the Canadian's flag. When you see this small camp, clear the coaches and divide the train" Piapot stated.

"How far from Swift Current will the camp be?" Dalton asked.

"About half way. When you see it there will be time for you to get your weapons and change into riding clothes" Piapot answered.

"When Walsh tells us what day the train is in Swift Current, I will send a scout west" Raincloud offered.

Piapot nodded and the meeting broke up. The next morning, Piapot rode west with twenty warriors and left one behind to bring word from Walsh. They left for the Cypress Hills leading the Dalton Family's horses.

Chapter Twenty

Piapot returns to the Cypress Hills

"For one hundred thousand dollars, he better speak good words about me."

On May 22, 1883, the Piapot party reached a place north of the railroad less than a days ride south to the Piapot village. Piapot told Painted Horse to send out scouts in different directions to find a place where Dalton would divide the train..

"I will ride to my village and then to Fort Walsh to meet the chiefs. I do not have any more to say but I told them I would come." Piapot continued, "This coulee is well hidden and has water. Let the horses graze for they will soon travel day and night. I will return to this place when the scout from the fort arrives at the village."

Piapot returned to the village and met with the elders and the two scouts.

"The two scouts will come with me to Fort Walsh and we will return soon. We have built a good village in the Qu'Appelle Valley and that is where we are going."

Piapot went on to tell them about the Qu'Appelle Valley reserve, the reserve agreement and the train robbery.

"Maybe it is too big of a chance to take" an elder kind of asked and stated at the same time.

"It is the last chance to put wealth into our nation. Dalton and those of mixed blood will purchase land every ten or fifteen miles apart south of the railroad near the Yankee territory, east to Regina. Those who leave or go to the mountains will have a friendly place to stop."

After a quick meal, Piapot and the two scouts left for Fort Walsh.

The chiefs were gathered as Piapot approached the fort. Poundmaker and Big Bear gave strong argument for the right to have an Indian confederation near the Cypress Hills.

The police command listened to the arguments but in the end, they simply told everyone that Fort Walsh would be torn down within weeks and the lumber used to build a detachment near Maple Creek which was closer to the railroad. There would be no more rations or treaty money until everyone returned to their reserves. The solution was simple. Return to the reserves or starve to death.

Poundmaker was one of the first to leave.

Big Bear and Spotting Horse stayed on to continue their argument but in the end, they too left for their reserves. Piapot pleaded poverty and was granted concessions for the trip east. He would be accompanied by a small police escort and would be supplied with wagons, food and medicine. Piapot agreed to meet with the police escort at his village in a few weeks.

"Why will you not take the train?" a sergeant asked.

"The elders will not ride on the beast that has helped destroy our nation."

It was May 26th on the calendar when Piapot and the two scouts returned to the village. Joseph's messenger was waiting for them.

There were shoulder hugs and laughter as the three young warriors exchanged tall tales.

Piapot spoke, "Tell me about the train Thunderchild."

Thunderchild showed Piapot a piece of paper with boxes that made up the train.

"The train starts here! Engine, coal and water, a kitchen coach to feed the wealthy, a coach with whiskey, chairs and long chairs that seat four or five, a coach with dining room tables and chairs, two sleeping room coaches, a long coach where twenty to thirty soldiers will sit , the mail coach where the money is and on the end, a box car with saddle horses owned by the land buyers and soldiers.

"Soldiers?" an elder asked.

"Yes! Soldiers! Walsh said they are police recruits but trained as soldiers to kill and not to keep the peace!" Thunderchild continued, "The train will leave Regina tomorrow early in the morning and arrive here tomorrow, late in the afternoon. It will make stops in Moose Jaw and Swift Current to drop a long coach of settlers and box cars of horses and buggies. These settlers have already purchased land south of these places."

"The sleeping cars and coaches are for the wealthy."

"Who are these people?" Piapot asked.

"They are the Dalton family, land buyers who buy towns, one army officer, two constables and two army cooks who are called chefs. Everyone will be armed. The chefs will have their weapons in the kitchen!

Also, there is a Yankee marshal on the train. He was given permission to travel west."

"How many cars will be left behind?" Piapot asked.

"The train will be divided between the first and second sleeping coach. The Dalton family will use the last sleeping coach to shoot from. They will stop the soldiers from escaping from the back of their coach."

"And Walsh? How will he get paid?"

"Walsh has already made arrangements for lodging in Winnipeg and his family is already there. Raincloud and Joseph told him a white man and his wife, dressed in a blue dress and a white hat, would meet him train time from the west on the 15th day of July, on the railroad planks in Brandon. Walsh will bring a buggy to take the couple to a place where there will be two buffalo horses saddled and ready to ride. Also, there will be automatic Winchesters, binoculars and ammunition. Walsh said he was not worried about getting paid. He speaks good words about you Chief Piapot."

"For one hundred thousand dollars, he better speak good words about me!"

This brought much belly laughter.

"We must move immediately! Do we have five or six pack horses?" Piapot asked.

"Yes!" an elder stated.

"How many riding horses are there?"

"We broke eleven colts to the saddle" one of the scouts replied.

"Good! Early in the morning we will take two tents to a high place near the tracks. Three or four elders and three or four women will ride with us. We will take food for cooking!"

In the morning, two tents were taken down and the party rode north to the railroad tracks.

It was well before noon when the Piapot party reached the tracks.

"Wait here! I will ride and bring the warriors."

Piapot returned with the warriors before noon. He spoke to the elders, "The scouts have found a place to divide the train. You will ride two hours east and put up the tents along with this flag at a high place near the tracks. We are going to ride west to where we will stop the train. When the train passes, leave the tent posts on the ground, and put everything else on the pack horses and return to the village.

An elder looked at his pocket watch and took his party east.

The Piapot party rode west with great speed and reached a place where the tracks had a slight rise as it turned north west along a cut bank to miss a slough. The tracks leveled out and the Piapot party stopped.

Piapot looked around and spoke to his warriors, "You have found a good spot. I will stop the train here. Now remember, everyone rides south west to the mountains except the two who will take Walsh's money east. Do not stop at the old village for the police may have already found it. Go further south! It will be dark before the police come from Maple Creek or Swift Current. Travel at night and you will be in the trees before the sun rises. If you run into police or ranchers along the way – slaughter them. You two who will ride west – are your pack horses ready?"

"Yes" one of them said.

"Put scouts out to watch the train divide. The coaches should roll back to you. Use dynamite. If you can,, let the horses out after it quiets down and run them south east on the plains. For those who wish to return to the Qu'Appelle Valley, do not return for several weeks and no more than two at a time. I am Chief Piapot and I have spoken."

Piapot took two of the warriors and they rode a little west and stopped.

"We will take the spikes out of this rail on the south side. If the train makes it to here, it will roll to the south and into the slough."

When the spikes were removed, Piapot spoke to the scouts, "Take my horse and ride to a high place. So long as I am alive, do not kill anyone. If I am killed, slaughter everyone who survives."

Chapter Twenty-One

The Dalton Family Boards the Train

"I have over twenty Canadian killers back there who wake up every morning just waiting to kill Indians."

The Dalton family, who now travelled by the name McCord, boarded the train in Regina and proceeded to their sleeping cars. Dalton and William carried a small trunk which held their pistols, ammunition, dynamite and Winchesters placed diagonally. Victoria and Cathy each had a small bag containing their riding clothes, pistols and ammunition.

The train stopped at Moose Jaw and arrived in Swift Current shortly after noon. The Dalton family proceeded to the dining room and counted the soldiers as they went to and from the station.

A chef came to their table and waited as the Daltons agreed on dinner. After the chef left, a robust army officer approached the table and introduced himself and two young constables. Dalton introduced his family as the McCords.

"So! Are you headed west to settle or buy a town?" the officer asked Dalton.

"Maybe a little of both. We have relatives meeting us at Maple Creek. We will decide after we see the surveyors certificates and the land."

"Come to the lounge when you are finished eating and join us for a drink."

"Actually my family does not drink alcohol but we will drop in to say hello."

When dinner was over, the Dalton family proceeded to the lounge and seated themselves on a chesterfield overlooking the room. The buyers were already drunk as they enjoyed themselves talking about their journey west. The marshal sat at a small bar and was not drinking.

"I understand you and your relatives may settle west of Maple Creek" a buyer stated.

"Yes, that is correct."

"Well Officer Stanfield here says they have all the Indians out of the way and just about starving to death."

"That's right!" Stanfield continued, "The treaty money they get is like gold and if they do not like the rations, they can eat gophers."

There was laughter from everyone except the US marshal.

"What is the problem marshal? You people killed a lot of Indians south of the border. Selling Indian scalps was big business in Texas."

"Maybe that is why I rode north to Missouri."

The US marshal narrowed his eyes when he spoke to Stanfield and he reminded Dalton of someone.

"I have over twenty Canadian killers back there who wake up every morning just waiting to kill Indians. They are the new police force trained by the British army and will be part of the force that goes north to kill those half breeds and their Indian friends. Those horse riding do gooders in Maple Creek who call themselves police will be trained to do the same when I am done with them."

"I sure feel a lot safer now" the marshal said sarcastically.

"Do you not like our company marshal?"

"As a matter of fact, I think I'll ride up front with the engineers if that's alright with you."

"Yes, you can join the two constables who are there guarding the engineers."

The marshal put his rifle over his shoulder and walked to the locomotive.

Cathy and Victoria could not stand laughing anymore and told Dalton they would retire to their sleeping car. William went with them and they forced a smile before leaving the lounge.

As the train pulled out, Dalton moved over to the small bar and ordered a round for the lounge.

"I thought you didn't drink" a buyer said.

"Well, I like a shot or two when the family is not around." Dalton continued, "That marshal is a strange one! Who is he looking for?"

"A guy by the name of Dalton. Seems like he shot a sheriff down south in a place called Missouri. The marshal says the sheriff of a small town shot his young Indian girl friend in the back because she was off the reserve and ran from him. I guess this Dalton was just a kid and put two bullets into the sheriff quicker than a wink."

"I wonder why they wouldn't send a bounty hunter. Is there a bounty?"

"Yes. One thousand dollars."

"Is that all! Maybe that's why they sent a marshal."

"According to the marshal, they want him back alive to stand trial and clear his name. I guess they want it over and off the books so to speak. If the marshal doesn't find him, he will be given up for dead."

Dalton laughed, "That will get him off the books!"

"Well, if that Indian lovin' son of a bitch comes around here he is going to be dead alright" another buyer hollered.

Dalton bought another round and left the lounge. He stopped and told the girls to come to his sleeper when they were changed and no one was looking. William already had his pistols on and his rifle beside him as Dalton entered the sleeping car and put on his pistols and belts of rifle ammunition that hung crossways from each shoulder. The girls soon arrived with the same fire power.

Dalton gave each one of them two sticks of dynamite and the white man's matches. He put the remainder of the dynamite in the pockets on the inside of this suit coat. He took out four cigars for them to light the dynamite with when it was needed.

Dalton looked at his pocket watch and spoke to Cathy, "Are you ready Cathy?"

"I am more than ready!"

"Good! I counted six buyers, two army chefs, two constables and an army officer. William and I will leave our rifles here and pick them up on the way back. We will proceed very quickly through the dining room to the lounge. I will turn left and William will turn right at the lounge. The shooting will start immediately. Victoria, when you and Cathy are finished in the dining room, use your rifle to kill anybody in the centre of the lounge and Cathy, you move back to the sleeping cars and protect our back. This should only take minutes. When we are finished I will uncouple the two sleeping coaches and drop a long fuse stick of dynamite to blow the track. We will stop the recruits from escaping to the sleeping car."

"We should be there soon. Watch for the tent" Victoria said.

"I put this glass of whiskey on the ledge. Do you see how the whiskey is getting higher on the left?"

"Yes, the train is slowly coming out of the down grade" Cathy concluded.

"I see the tent and the flag!" Victoria exclaimed.

"Let's move!"

Dalton and William moved with speed through the dining room and did not stop to look at the four or five who sat at two tables. The shooting started in both coaches almost at the same time as the train rattled and shook on the narrow rails.

Victoria took aim at two buyers eating and drinking wine. She blew out the side of one buyer's head and shot the other one in the chest. Cathy shot two buyers in the chest driving them off their chairs as Stanfield rose and reached for his pistol. Cathy drew her leg pistol and fanned three shots into his head before he hit the ground. Victoria fired into the lounge as Cathy put bullets into the heads of the three buyers who were hit in the chest.

As Cathy moved to the sleeping cars, a buyer came into the aisle. She raised her rifle shooting him once in the chest and once in the head. No one else came out as she kept moving to the second sleeping car.

Dalton, Victoria and William ran to meet Cathy. Dalton moved to the second car and told the three to reload.

When they were reloaded, they advanced to the second sleeping car as Dalton uncoupled the coaches and lit a cigar. When their coach stopped and started to roll back, Dalton lit a stick of dynamite and threw it on the tracks.

In a few minutes, the dynamite exploded sending a rail down the cut bank and into the slough. They all moved to the back of the sleeping car and heard the sound of breaking glass as the warriors began to attack the train.

Chapter Twenty-Two

Piapot Stops the Train

"Unless you have five dollars to give me for trespassing through my land, you must back up the train."

Up track, the two scouts on the hill watched as Piapot walked east on the soft shoulder of the track. He was unarmed and wore beaded buckskins. His long silver hair had small beaded braids on both sides. When Piapot walked thirty paces or more, he stopped and sat down in the middle of the tracks.

"What is happening?" one of the scouts asked.

"I do not know but it is out of our hands."

"I thought he was going to walk west from the loose rail and just observe the train crash."

"So did I."

Piapot saw the engine coming down the track winding around the slough.

"Creator! This is the beast you showed me many years ago. Today, you want more from me than a rail without spikes. A peaceful protest is what you ask of me and this is what I will give to you. There will be a witness to this peaceful protest and nothing can stop the testimony. "

Inside the engine room, the engineer spotted Piapot on the tracks.

"Jesus, what the hell is he doing? There is an Indian sitting in the middle of the track. I have to stop this train!"

"Do not stop this train!" a constable shouted.

"I did not sign on to kill people!"

"You just do as you are told!"

"Stop the train or I will stop it for you!" the US marshal ordered.

The private turned and went for his revolver. The US marshal lowered his Winchester and put a bullet into the private's head. The private hit the steel superstructure and dropped to the steel floor. The back of his head was blown out.

The other constable fired his rifle and hit the US marshal in the shoulder. The US marshal's Winchester fell to the floor as he drew his colt and blasted two shots into the other constable. One hit him in the stomach and the other shot grazed his head.

"Now stop the train!"

"Yes sir marshal."

The marshal watched as the train began to slow as it approached Piapot.

"I do not think I can stop this train in time."

"Can you spin the wheels backwards?"

"I will try."

The engineer put the engine into reverse and the steel wheels began to howl and smoke. The engine shook as the train came to a stop.

The two engineers and the US marshal stood and looked out from the engine room.

"I do not see him! Jesus! Is he under the train!" the engineer shouted.

"I will take a look" the US marshal said.

The two engineers followed the marshal to the front of the train. As they reached the front of the train they saw Piapot sitting cross legged just spitting distance in front of the steel catcher.

"My God man! Another ten feet and you would be dead! Who the hell are you?" the US marshal asked.

"It does not matter who I am. This is the place where I am supposed to be! I have seen the future and before this day ends you will see a white light which very few people will ever see."

A shot rang out hitting the young engineer in the head killing him instantly. Another shot hit the US marshal in the stomach as he drew and turned. The US marshal unloaded both pistols into the constable who had crawled to the front of the train. The US marshal dropped to his knees and he coughed blood. He struggled to his feet and walked along the train hitting the side of coaches as he went.

Piapot remained sitting and ordered the engineer to put the constable and dead engineer inside the engine room. When he was done, the engineer returned to where Piapot was still sitting.

"You did well to stop the train. A few more paces and the train would have run off the track."

The engineer was astonished as Piapot showed the engineer a bag of spikes.

"Unless you have five dollars to give me for trespassing through my land, you must back up the train, for not only are you trespassing but you are also missing half of your train."

The engineer went to a high spot and put his hands over his head.

"My God! I will back up the train!"

"Be careful of the tracks."

As the engineer backed up the train, the two scouts came down the slope and brought Piapot his horse.

"We watched from the top of the hill and we cannot believe your courage Chief Piapot" one of the scouts said.

"My courage comes from another place. It is a place you should get to know."

"We will try Chief Piapot."

After putting the rail in place and driving in the spikes, the two scouts rode west to the train robbery. Piapot covered up the footprints and rode south to his village.

Chapter Twenty-Three

The Train Robbery

*"The great Canadian killers ran away and did not even
bother to take their rifles!"*

Dalton looked out the window of a compartment and
saw an arrow with a stick of dynamite fly through the air.

"Get into a compartment!" Dalton hollered.

Everyone jumped into a compartment just before the
dynamite exploded. The blast blew apart the back part of
their coach sending debris down the aisle.

"Is anybody hurt?" Dalton yelled.

William and the girls came out of the compartment
into the aisle.

"We are okay" Victoria yelled back.

They heard the Canadian killers screaming as their
coach caught fire.

"Follow me out the back! We are going to dynamite what is left of this coach."

They ran to the back of the coach and before jumping to the ground, Cathy light a stick of dynamite and threw it to the centre of the coach.

They ran as fast as they could and jumped into the ditch near the slough. The dynamite blew the coach into the air in all directions.

"Look! The Canadian killers are crawling away from the train!" William exclaimed.

The four opened fire killing the recruits as they crawled. Some got to their feet and were cut down as they raised their hands to surrender.

The warriors started to surround the train and proceeded to kill what was left of the recruits.

"The great Canadian killers ran away and did not even bother to take their rifles!" Cathy said.

"Let us find the money!" Dalton said.

Dalton and his party walked to the mail car which was not damaged. As they walked, Thunderchild approached the Dalton party.

"What would you like us to do Chief Dalton?"

"Take several warriors and let the horse out on the slough side and drive them south east across the small stream. When they clear the stream, fire an arrow of dynamite behind them. They will run for miles and the white police will follow them. Stay in the water and wait for us. When we are finished, we will meet you and ride the stream south west."

"I will do this immediately Chief Dalton."

The Dalton party walked to the mail car. Victoria and Dalton climbed to the back of the mail car one on each side of the door. William and Cathy stayed on the tracks and leveled their rifles on the door. Dalton reached over and banged on the door with the butt of his rifle. Two shots rang out blowing holes in the door.

"Shoot the lock!" Dalton ordered.

Cathy and William leveled their rifles and blew the lock apart. Dalton reached over and banged his rifle against the door. The door opened as Cathy and William emptied their Winchesters into the mail car. Victoria and Dalton immediately entered the mail car without any fire being returned. A civilian and a constable cowered in a corner of the mail car and begged for their lives.

"I am a civilian."

"We have put our weapons down."

"That is what you should have done before you tried to kill us!" Dalton shouted.

Victoria and Dalton shot them in the head and began looking for the money. They found three canvass bags of money under a bench.

"We only have to count one bag to see if contains one hundred thousand dollars." Victoria continued, "That will be the bag we send west."

"There is a safe" Cathy pointed out.

"We will deal with that last. You and William go through these compartments and see if there is anything else worth taking."

Victoria and Dalton counted one hundred thousand dollars which included coins.

"What do the coins total?"

"The coins total ten thousand dollars" Victoria said.

"We will take the coins and put ten thousand dollars of paper into the Walsh bag."

Cathy and William did not find anything of value. The warriors broke a side of the mail car with axes and pushed the safe out of the mail car. A stone breaker lit a small charge of dynamite and blew the safe door. Inside the safe was found jewelry, money and documents. These were put in a separate bag for the mountains.

The two scouts who would ride west were loaded and told to ride in the small stream until dark.

Thunderchild reported from the water that the horses were driven west.

"When we exploded the dynamite behind them, they almost flew across the plains! They will be in Winnipeg soon!"

The sound of Dalton's laughter brought more laughter from everyone.

"Look!" Cathy shouted. "The train is coming back."

They watched as the train slowly travelled towards them. Thunderchild took his binoculars from his saddle bag and observed the train.

"There is a white man sitting on the coach steps. I think he is wounded."

"Yes! It is the US marshal. He was shot in the stomach. Him and the engineer are the only ones alive" one of the Piapot scouts stated.

The train hit the damaged track and piled up. The engine rolled slowly into the slough, pulling the coaches over on their sides and the US marshal was thrown to the soft shoulder before the coach rolled. Dalton jumped on his horse and viewed the crash with his binoculars.

"It is the US marshal!" Dalton shouted.

Dalton ordered his party to mount up.

"Did we lose any warriors?" Dalton asked.

"Yes! We lost four and there are several wounded. The medicine men are working on them and they will ride."

"Wait here!"

The Dalton party reached the US marshal and slid from their horses. Victoria knelt on one knee to look at the wound. Dalton wiped some blood with the hanky the US marshal wore around his neck.

"The blood is dark - from this kind of wound you do not recover." Dalton said.

The US marshal could hardly speak.

"I thought I killed both the constables but …but one of them I only grazed."

"Why did you kill the constables?"

"Because …because they would not let …..would not let the engineer …. stop the train. There was an old …. an old Indian sitting …. sitting ….sitting in the middle ….of the tracks."

The Dalton party looked at one another.

"You four …. and …. and the old Indian …. robbed the train."

"Yes we did."

"Good for ….good for you."

"You will not live much longer. What is your name?"

"James …. James Masterson."

"My name is Chief Joseph P. Dalton."

"Son of ….son of a bitch."

The US marshal opened his eyes wide and with a last bit of strength stretched his arms and stared with awe at the sky.

The Dalton party looked to the sky but saw nothing. The US marshal dropped his arms and fell backwards.

There was a slight smile on his face. The US marshal was dead.

They hung the dead marshal over Cathy's horse and Cathy jumped up behind Dalton.

"Victoria! We will take the marshal to be buried with our four warriors. You and William burn what is left of this train!"

"What about the engineer?" Victoria asked.

"Leave him where he is. Dead or alive, this is a game that only Chief Piapot understands."

Dalton and Cathy returned to the mail car and had the four dead warriors and marshal Masterson put inside the coach.

"Remove anything from our warriors that will not burn. I have already taken the US marshal's badge, colts and gold chain. Did you inspect the coach for bodies?" Dalton asked.

"Yes! There are no bodies on the coach!"

"Good! I do not want our warriors and this US marshal to burn in the same coach as those other bastards! When they are inside, burn the coaches and cut the telegraph line."

After the coaches were lit on fire, a stone breaker let go an arrow of dynamite and blew the telegraph pole in half. The line and pole almost hit the ground as a warrior rode forward and cut the line.

Cathy and William returned to the mail car. Everyone all met in the shallow stream and drove to the south west. Assiniboine war cries could be heard above the sound of the horses hooves pounding the shallow water and their long hair blew in the wind. It was the spring of 1883 and there was money on the plains.

Chapter Twenty-Four

The Aftermath

"Bring everyone here. They know what you know, which is very little."

With Fort Walsh being torn down, the force was in disarray as the detachment near Maple Creek was still under construction. When the telegraph system ceased to function and the train was an hour late, it was obvious that something was very wrong. The commander of the detachment decided to sent out a telegraph repair team to repair the line and locate the train.

"How far east should we go?" the sergeant asked.

"We know the train left Swift Current so you should not have to travel very far. Do not take civilians". The constable in charge left with several recruits and a wagon load of equipment to repair the line.

Just before six o'clock, the sergeant and his repair crew came within two miles of the train wreck and could smell the smoke as it drifted towards them. In minutes they reached what was left of the train. The derailed coaches were still smoldering and the engine was half submerged in the slough. The only thing left on the coaches were charred bodies and the lower steel frame with the wheels attached.

The second part of the train was still on the track and more charred bodies smoldered in the debris. The recruits were speechless.

"You two ride back to Maple Creek and report what you have seen. We need a locomotive from the construction site to bring ties, spikes and four rails. The telegraph line will be repaired before you get to the detachment. Tell them to stop all civilian west bound trains coming out of Swift Current."

In the distance, a locomotive could be seen coming west.

"You two! Stop that train!" the sergeant ordered. "Do not let any civilians approach the site. This is a massacre!"

The sergeant and the remaining recruit rode to the half submerged engine. The sergeant crawled to the engine door and looked inside. He saw a dead body floating and a hand hanging on to a steel pipe. The engineers face was above water and he was alive.

"Constable Wilson! Give me a hand! /The engineer is still alive!"

Wilson crawled on the engine and the sergeant could feel it move.

"Stop! This bloody engine is just about ready to roll! Find me a rope and stay off the engine!"

The constable rode back to the wagon just as the train from the east pulled up. Police members ran towards Wilson.

"The train is full of members. They were sent for the same reason as we were. There are no civilians aboard."

"We have a dying engineer in the engine room. The sergeant needs a rope!"

Several of the recruits ran to the engine while the remainder stayed to assess the massacre.

Wilson threw the sergeant a rope. The sergeant knotted one end and passed it down towards the engineer. The engineer grabbed the rope with one hand and then with the other as he let go of the steel pipe. The recruits pulled him forward enough for the sergeant to grab his arm.

"Give me the other end of the rope!"

The sergeant made a kind of lasso and slipped it over the head of the engineer. He told the engineer to let go of the rope as he placed the lasso over his shoulders and under his arms.

"All right! Steady now!"

The recruits pulled slowly on the rope as the sergeant hauled the engineer out the door.

"Is there anyone medical here?"

"Yes there is!"

"Then come forward!"

A young officer came forward from the group and approached the sergeant.

"Sorry sir. I did not see the gold braid."

"Do not give it a second thought. You just continue with what you have to do."

"Yes sir!"

The young officer sent a member for his bag and ordered the two members to make a soft flat bed of dirt.

"Unsaddle four horses! We will need three or four saddle blankets to put on the dirt."

When this was done, the engineer was place on the blankets and the young officer began his examination.

The sergeant left two constables with the young officer and took the remainder with him to repair the telegraph line.

"Go to the ravine and bring back two tall poles."

In less than an hour, they returned with two poles that were being dragged by horses. The poles were put in place and the linemen tied in the line.

"Is it working?" the sergeant asked.

"Yes! The test indicates it is working" a lineman replied.

"It will be dark soon. We will take as many of the bodies as we can find and put them on the flat cars to be hauled to Swift Current.

The sergeant ordered several members to take the wagon and bring back all the bodies from the wreckage up track. Most of the bodies and parts of bodies were on the second half of the train. Getting the bodies from the up track wreckage did not take long and with the help of lights from the locomotive, all the bodies and parts of bodies were recovered before dark.

The doctor and two constables arrived with the engineer hung sideways over a horse.

"He had internal injuries which caused him to bleed and suffocate. Put him with the rest of the bodies."

"Is the telegraph working?"

"Yes sir."

"Fine. I will return to Swift Current and leave all the members here to help out. I am leaving you in charge sergeant."

"Yes sir!"

It was dark as the train backed up for Swift Current. The members lit fires and ate what rations that were in the wagon. After the horses were turned loose to graze, the sergeant motioned Wilson to his fire.

"Did the engineer speak."

"Yes – a few words. It is classified."

The sergeant smiled and stared at Wilson.

"When the doctor asked him what he saw, he said an Indian sat in the middle of the tracks."

"Did he say who killed the two constables in the engine room?"

"Yes – the U.S. marshal."

"What did the Indian look like?"

"The engineer said he looked like an Indian."

"Piapot! Who else would sit in the middle of the tracks and stop a train!"

"Was there anything else?"

"No! The engineer refused to speak further and he died."

Before dawn, a construction train arrived from the west. It had a bunk house, two dining coaches and several cooks. The coaches carried over fifty members. No civilians were present.

An officer approached the sergeant and was given an appraisal of the situation.

"The doctor left you in charge and I am doing the same. Early in the morning, I will send ten members and track the killers. You and your men should go to the dining cars and get a good hot breakfast."

"Yes sir!"

In the morning, a constable reported that they found the tracks of many shod horses headed south east. The officer ordered twenty of them to follow the tracks. He took two constables with him to pay Chief Piapot a visit.

When they arrived at the Piapot village, the women told them Piapot and the elders were fishing. The officer and the two constables rode to a high place and watched Piapot and the elders bring in the nets.

Piapot saw them and walked to where they were.

He spoke to them in French but they did not understand so he spoke to the elder constable in Cree.

"What brings you to my village?" Piapot asked in Cree.

"There has been a slaughter to the north. The train was robbed and everyone on the train is dead."

"What brings you to my village?" Piapot asked in English.

The three looked at one another.

"Let the officer answer in English" Piapot said.

"Jesus! Why did you not tell us you spoke English?" the officer yelled.

"You did not ask."

"My God man, we are at your village because an engineer saw you sitting on the tracks!"

"You have no proof of that. The engineer is dead!"

"How do you know that?"

"I know because your constable told me. He said everyone on the train is dead."

"Do not try to confuse me Chief Piapot. He said he saw an Indian sitting in the middle of the tracks."

"Am I the only Indian on the Plains?"

"Everyone knows you are a killer!"

"Bring everyone here. They know what you know, which is very little."

The officer rose quickly and mounted his horse.

"We will be back!"

"Yes I know. You are going to help me take my people to our reserve!"

Piapot smiled as they rode away. He could hear their voices in the wind.

"That old son of a bitch sat on the tracks!"

"He spoke three languages."

"He is a cold blooded killer!"

"They say he speaks six languages."

"The old bastard robbed the train!"

"But you have no proof."

"Shut up and ride!"

Before night fall, the tracks were repaired and what could be used was put on the flat cars. The horses were loaded and the construction train moved back to Maple Creek.

The members who chased the robbers south east showed up in Swift Current two days later and reported that the horses they chased belonged to the recruits.

The officers at Maple Creek and Swift Current gave up the chase and notified the Wood Mountain detachment to be on the lookout.

Three days had already passed as the warriors reached the mountains. They were all talking about the hot pools and "Piapot Days."

Chapter Twenty-Five

The Government Blinks

"Chief Piapot denied being there and reminded the officer that he had no evidence as everyone on the train was dead."

It was early in the morning of May 31, 1883, the fourth day after the robbery, when Lieutenant Governor Dewdney left his quarters and walked down the hall to preside over an emergency meeting regarding the train robbery.

"There has been a great deal of innuendo implicating Chief Piapot in the train robbery of May 27, 1883. And two days ago I asked for evidence. The Prime Minister has asked me to find this evidence to verify the accusations. Now! Superintendent Steele, what evidence, if any, have you acquired from the Fort Qu'Appelle detachment?"

"Sir!"

"Let us dispose of sir, Her Majesty and any other irrelevancy at this meeting!"

Superintendent Steele continued. "The detachment in Fort Qu'Appelle has no evidence of Chief Piapot's involvement. To the contrary, there is evidence that he was not involved. The day before the robbery, two young constables, by invitation, attended the Piapot Village to celebrate the completion of a Church. A significant number of white families were in attendance as were all of the Piapot warriors known to the detachment and those who were not known."

The Government lawyers nodded and took notes.

"Commissioner Irvine!"

"It is true that Chief Piapot was in the area during the time of the robbery. However, he had a reason for being there. He met with several Chiefs at Fort Walsh to acquire several reserves near the Cypress Hills in order to establish an Indian confederacy of nations."

"After the robbery, did anyone attend Chief Piapot's village to question him?" a lawyer asked.

"Yes."

"What did you learn?"

"Chief Piapot denied being there and reminded the officer that he had no evidence as everyone on the train was dead."

"How did he know that?"

"A constable made the mistake of telling him."

There was silence and then controlled laughter from the lawyers. Even Lieutenant Governor Dewdney found it somewhat amusing.

"Did anyone from your command try to track and pursue the robbers?"

"Yes. Our members tracked many shod horses headed south east and chased them for two days."

"Did you find the robbers?"

"No! The horses were our horses that were turned loose from the train before it burned."

This time there was uncontrolled laughter from everyone. Commissioner Irvine turned red.

"Doctor!"

"I arrived on the train from Swift Current in time to examine the engineer, the only survivor on the train. He died from internal wounds shortly after I examined him."

"How do you know he was the only survivor?" a lawyer asked.

"The body count coincided with the manifest."

"Did you question him?"

"Yes."

"What did he have to say?"

"He was near death but managed to report that an Indian sat in the middle of the tracks and the soldiers would not let him stop the train. The U.S. marshal killed a soldier and wounded the other one. He stopped the train and the wounded soldier killed an engineer and shot the U.S. marshal who unloaded his pistols into the constable. I asked him what the Indian looked like but he did not know. He died before I could ask any more questions."

"Well it sounds like Chief Piapot is not much of a killer or he would have shot the engineer" a lawyer concluded.

"He is a cold blooded killer!" Irvine shouted.

The senior lawyer rose to his feet and spoke, "It has been documented that you consider Chief Piapot a trouble maker and a killer. So tell me Commissioner

Irvine, do you know of anyone alive today who can testify that they have seen Chief Piapot commit a murder?"

"No!"

"Thank you Commissioner."

Lieutenant Governor Dewdney dismissed everyone except the lawyers.

"Mr. McGregor! I would like you and your associates to meet me here at one o'clock."

At one o'clock, the team of lawyers returned to the board room with their report for Dewdney.

"You may proceed Mr. McGregor."

"Well! Let me see what we have here. The legal analysis of the situation regarding Chief Piapot is this: to begin with, the Government does not have a witness that places Chief Piapot at the scene of the massacre. You have the word of a dying and now dead engineer who stated that he saw an unarmed and unidentified Indian sitting in the middle of the railroad tracks. Even if Chief Piapot stood up in the Court room and confessed that he sat in the middle of the tracks and stopped the train, the most you could charge him with would be some kind of mischief or obstruction. The fact that he sat in the middle of the tracks and stopped the train does not implicate him in the massacre of forty-one people and the robbery of three hundred thousand dollars. Quite frankly, I do not feel the Government could even get a conviction of mischief or obstruction. Chief Piapot would be seen as having carried out an unparalleled peaceful demonstration. There is very little law on the books that prohibit a peaceful demonstration.

Further, your members at the Fort confirm that the known Piapot warriors located in the Fort Qu'Appelle area could not possibly have participated in the massacre and robbery.

Also, the hundreds of tracks on and around the crime scene were those of boots and shod horses. It has also been confirmed that dynamite was used extensively.

Therefore, any lawyer would argue that this robbery was carried out by white men and probably from south of the border.

To conclude, the Government has absolutely no case against Chief Piapot and his associates."

"What is going to happen to the railroad? They are now bankrupt!"

"The railroad will survive. The majority shareholders have allowed the railroad to issue three hundred thousand dollars worth of shares to the Government. It will deplete the value of their shares but like they say in the business world, ten percent of something is better than one hundred percent of nothing."

"When is the money coming?"

"It has already left from the east under heavy military guard. The money will arrive in Regina early tomorrow morning."

"Why was I not advised?"

"There are leaks in the telegraph system. I was told to advise you."

"My associates will leave immediately to Ottawa with a copy of this report. I will remain until tomorrow to tie up any loose ends."

"And my report?"

"You are not to send a telegram unless you think it is necessary."

"Our local intelligence indicates a certain amount of civilian conversation about the massacre, robbery and the involvement of Chief Piapot. What does the Government suggest we do about this?"

"Civilian conversation is the Government's most paramount concern. You must tighten up enlisted security. The Government has already solicited the proper newspaper people who will reduce Chief Piapot's involvement to an unrelated construction incident. The robbery and massacre did not occur. The train simply derailed killing several people and the payroll was burned in the wreckage. There will be letters sent to the next of kin with condolences and compensation.

The railway will be completed within two years. By this time, the army will have been established in the west and the land settled. After these eventualities, civilian conversation will be of little consequence. I am also to convey that the Prime Minister desires fairness for the Indians."

"I knew from the beginning that a trial would be counter productive" Dewdney stated.

"I am pleased you agree with my assessment."

"Let me pour you a drink Bill."

"That would be splendid."

"Now you have stated a strong case for Chief Piapot but do you know why I really do not want a trial?"

"Why?"

"I do not want anyone to know that we chased our own horses for two days!"

Once again there was uncontrolled laughter. Dewdney, known to be stodgy, wiped the tears from his eyes.

"Well, that God damn old fox sat in the middle of the tracks and stopped the train" Dewdney conceded.

"And made it back up" McGregor concluded.

The two clinked glasses, threw back their whiskey and departed from the board room.

A few days later, at the Fort Qu'Appelle detachment, Walsh was cleaning out his desk when someone knocked at his door.

"Come on in!"

The old sergeant who visited the Piapot village entered Walsh's quarters.

"Well sir, I know you are leaving tomorrow and seeing as how you have not been made aware of what has been happening in the last few days, I thought I might tell you about Chief Piapot."

The sergeant went on to tell Walsh about the robbery and massacre. He told Walsh that Chief Piapot sat in the middle of the tracks and stopped the train.

"He did what?"

"He sat unarmed in the middle of the tracks and stopped the train."

Walsh was truly surprised.

"I just thought you might like to know and I wanted to wish you good luck sir."

Walsh walked with the old sergeant to the door.

"I also wish you the very best sergeant."

Walsh picked up his flask and took a big swig.

"Son of a bitch! He stopped the train."

THE END

Epilogue

On the fifteenth day of July, 1883, a young well dressed couple stepped off the east bound train in Brandon. The wife was wearing a blue dress and white hat and her husband carried two black suitcases.

When they reached Walsh, he met them with hugs and handshakes which is what a relative does when relatives come to visit. Walsh showed them to a fashionable buggy where they embarked and headed west until they reached a humble farm cabin.

"I bought this quarter section just for this occasion."

"Allow me to introduce my wife Mary. I am Samuel J. Dalton, the second oldest son of Joseph P. Dalton."

Walsh and Samuel counted the money while Mary left to change into her riding clothes. The money was correct and Mary returned ready to ride.

"The horses are saddled and everything you asked for is in order."

"Thank you Superintendent Walsh. David from the Qu'Appelle village has determined a shortfall of almost one thousand dollars in money spent. Chief Piapot says you do not have to pay the one thousand dollars, but it would go a long ways in helping build the library."

Walsh smiled and removed two stacks of money from the black suitcase. "This is for the shortfall and this is my personal donation to the construction of the library."

"Two thousand dollars will more than build the library!" Mary exclaimed. "We will use what is left for books! Thank you ever so much!"

Walsh watched them ride north west for as long as he could see them.

Shortly after selling the quarter section, Walsh disappeared from the plains and became very wealthy supplying coal to the Canadian Pacific Railway.

Several years later, it was reported to Chief Piapot that Walsh turned up at Fort Benton. He was seen leaving for the east with a fine Sioux woman and her daughter who was fair.

In the summer of 1883, Chief Piapot and his people, under police escort, left the Cypress Hills for their reserve near Indian Head. It was a thirty-four day march with much hardship and several deaths.

Chief Piapot was not allowed to take his people directly to the Qu'Appelle Valley village. The police explained that Dewdney ordered a more or less administrative process before going to the village in the valley. Piapot expected rough treatment and was not surprised.

In the fall of 1883, a young well dressed rider knocked on the door of a very humble Masterson ranch house.

"Are you here to accuse my husband of a train robbery?"

"No, I am here to deliver a package from an old friend."

The rider handed her the package and left.

When she opened the package she found a U.S. marshal's badge, two matching colts, a gold chain with a locket that held her picture and two thousand dollars in U.S. funds. Tears filled her eyes as she ran to thank the young rider but he was gone.

In the winter of 1884, and after forty or more deaths, Piapot moved his people to the reserve in the Qu'Appelle valley. No one tried to stop him but Dewdney got his pound of flesh.

In the spring of 1884, Dumont gathered an army north of the big river and war was imminent. The Canadian Government sent high ranking officials to meet with Piapot. The Government knew Piapot could put hundreds of warriors on the battlefield and they demanded his loyalty. Piapot demanded official status, without conditions, for his reserve in the Qu'Appelle Valley.

In the summer of 1884, the Stone Breakers married the McKinnon sisters and Vincent Sugar married Louise. In the same year, Thunderchild married Cathy and they moved to Calgary to open a gun shop.

In September of 1884, Piapot was given his reserve in the Qu'Appelle Valley. The war between the Canadians and the metis began in 1885 and Piapot did not get involved.

Chief Piapot fought for Indian rights until his death in 1908 and the Chief Piapot Indian Reserve exists today.

In 1885, Dumont and a friend were spotted near the old village headed for Montana and they were taken to the fourth camp. Chief Three Killer was informed and sent horses, food and Yankee money.

In the mountains, many of mixed blood, under Dalton's instruction, left to the plains and homesteaded north east along the Yankee border. Some of the money from the train robbery was used to establish businesses on both sides of the border and some was invested. Money, when needed, was sent to the Qu'Appelle Valley.

In 1889, Three Killer died and Dalton was made Chief of Chiefs. Dalton, Victoria, Joseph and many more of the dog warriors and their children refused to leave the mountains and were never seen again on the plains.